SANCTUARY LINE

JANE URQUHART

MACLEHOSE PRESS
QUERCUS · LONDON

First published by McClelland & Stewart, Canada, 2010
First published in Great Britain in 2012 by MacLehose Press
This paperback edition published in 2013 by

MacLehose Press
an imprint of Quercus
55 Baker Street
7th Floor, South Block
London W1U 8EW

A CIP catalogue record for this book is available
from the British Library

ISBN (MMP) 978 0 85738 639 7
ISBN (Ebook) 978 0 85738 640 3

10 9 8 7 6 5 4 3 2 1

Designed and typeset in Cycles by Libanus Press, Marlborough
Printed and bound in Great Britain by Clays Ltd, St Ives plc

For the fallen

Slowly and beautifully the land loomed out of the sea. The wind came again. It had veered from the northeast to the southeast. Finally, a new sound struck the ears of the men in the boat. It was the low thunder of the surf on the shore. "We'll never be able to make the lighthouse now," said the captain. "Swing her head a little more north, Billie," said he.

The Open Boat
STEPHEN CRANE

Look out the window.

The cultivated landscape of this farm has decayed so completely now, it is difficult to believe that the fields and orchards ever existed outside of my own memories, my own imagination. Even by the time I was in my early twenties, the terrain had already altered – almost beyond recognition – what with the bunkhouses deteriorating and the trees left unpruned and therefore bearing scant fruit. But that was during the period when my aunt was beginning to sever parts of the property so that it could be sold to developers; a step, I believed then, in the march toward some kind of future, or at least a financial future for her, and for my mother, who had just begun to live here as well. Now my aunt is dead and my mother lives at a place called the Golden Field, an ironic moniker if there ever was one, especially in relation to the one remaining field at this location, its greyness in the fading light.

It's true, certain vestiges of the past remained for a while: the rail fences built by one of the old great-greats and the odd cairn of stones the great-greats had hauled out of the fields. "The first harvest every year is boulders", was the news they passed down to us, their lazy descendants. My uncle repeated this statement often, though there was little enough ploughing in his life. In the end, he told us, many of the fieldstones had gone into the building of this capacious farmhouse that has stood in place, firm and strong, since the middle of the prosperous nineteenth century, when it was built.

What's more, according to my uncle, the *very* first harvest would have been the slaughter of acres of forest in order that a field, any field, boulder-filled or golden, could be seeded at all. I seem to recall that during my childhood there was a trace of the shallow foundation of the original log house in which those pioneer tree-choppers must have lived. Evidence was so faint, however, that only someone like my uncle could find it, point to it, and insist that you look at it. I remember him showing the few scattered stones to Teo, who stood at his side gazing obediently at the ground, then turning to me with a quizzical glance, trying, I suppose, to fit me, a spoiled girl from the city, into the rough stories my uncle was telling him about the spot. Dead babies, young men lost in blizzards, horses stumbling through storms. Teo listened politely, his brown eyes coming to rest on my uncle's handsome face, but during the moist heat of those summers of the 1980s, when the farm was a flourishing business, those tales must have been almost impossible for a child like him to believe.

Sometimes in the evening, after I have washed my few dishes, I find myself examining the splendid furniture of this old house, a collection of cold artefacts. In spite of my intimacy with each table, every chair, and the knowledge that the hands that either purchased or constructed them – and the bodies that touched them – made me what I am, they seem to come from a culture so brief and fragile that no one can name its properties, never mind care about its persistence. These solid shapes, so esteemed by my uncle and his wife, so carefully maintained, so talked about in the development of family tales, now stand in one corner or another as dead as the grandfather or great-aunt or distant relation who gave them a story and a meaning. Now there are nights when I wonder who I am keeping the clocks wound for, or why I continue to remove dust from the pictures and mirrors. Like someone of uncertain lineage in an undiscovered tomb, I have all the furnishings and comforts I will need for the afterlife carefully arranged around me. Except I am alive and forty years old. And, unlike you, I do not believe in any kind of afterlife.

Another thing. Because my aunt was fond of glass and, by extension, indoor light, this house is filled with reflections. Images of the great lake, therefore, swing into sight where you least expect them. North windows that face south windows reproduce and scramble marine views, mirrors refract lake light, and now and then poplars from the lakeside flicker on the old painted landscapes framed under glass and hanging on the parlour wall. Glass doors open to rooms where shutters are flung wide to a view of water. The stone walls that once surrounded my aunt's rose garden are mirrored in the round looking-glass over her dressing table. At certain times of the day, if you pull open one of the glass doors leading from her room to the patio, the view of those garden walls will be overlaid by a series of waves chasing one another toward an unseen shore.

In August the monarchs rise against blue lake water on the glass of a storm door, and surf often feathers the face of the wall clock. I never noticed these reflections when I was in my teens and the house was merely a place one entered unwillingly after the action of the day was finished. But all this confusion, this uncertain, changing imagery, is mine now. There is no one else who needs it.

———

As you know so well, it is one year after Mandy's burial, a full year since those of us who remain went to the air base to attend the repatriation ceremony, then drove in the slow cortège down the highway renamed to honour the heroes of the current war. It felt like a lengthy journey, though Toronto, where the military autopsy was performed, is only ninety miles west of the air base. As we moved toward that city, we passed beneath dozens of overpasses filled with onlookers respectfully holding flags and yellow ribbons. I had read that crowds always lined the route when a soldier was brought home. Still my mother and I, and the boys too, were surprised and moved by the sheer size of the turnout. "Poor Mandy," my mother kept saying each time we approached an over-pass. "Who would have thought it?" At the air base she had said, "Poor little Amanda . . . she always called me auntie, even when she was a senior officer." Then she had begun to weep, and I could feel my own eyes filling as I put my arm around her. The words *improvised explosive device* kept repeating in my mind, the sound of them coming out of the mouth of the official who had delivered this impossible news a few days before. There was something too surprising and playful about that phrase – a jack-in-the-box, fireworks – and if I couldn't erase it altogether, I wanted to reshape it, slow it down, give it more dignity.

The whole town of Kingsville came out to meet us two days later, once we arrived here in the deep south of this northern province: all of Mandy's high-school friends, the women who had helped my mother look after my aunt during her last illness, the mayor and council, and the people who had known my uncle when he was still in the vicinity.

Various attempts had been made to find him on this terrible occasion. Don was on the Internet day and night, and Shane contacted Interpol; messages were sent off to embassies – all to no avail. He has been gone, after all, for well over twenty years. He must be dead, Don said, during one of our booze-soaked evenings that week or the week after, or he would have come home for this. He may very well be dead, I thought, but I wondered if he would come back even if he were alive and in any condition to travel. Neither Don nor Shane had been caught in the drama the night their father disappeared. And Mandy hadn't either, thankfully, though they all were witnesses to the coda of that drama.

But I had been there, right on the spot, at the wrong time.

What would there have been for him to return to anyway, even if he'd been able to do so? All his older relatives were gone, his wife as well, his dead daughter so changed by military glory even his memories of her would have felt unreliable. His sister, my mother, is still nearby, but after all this time she does not really resemble the woman he knew. And then there is me. And the farm, well, it barely exists.

Except for this house, now inhabited by me.

During the course of that long-ago summer when there were still many of us and the days walked slowly across the calendar, more or less in the way they always had, my uncle's farm felt as certain and as established as a time-honoured empire – he, the famous Lake Erie orchardist, the agricultural king of the oldest part of southwestern Ontario, his territory and its lore delivered to us on a regular basis at dinner tables or beside campfires on the beach. Even now, when I wake on summer mornings and look out over the two remaining meadows filled with stumps, dead branches, and milkweed, I am startled by the disarray of the orchards, briefly surprised that there are neither ancestors nor Mexicans busy in the fields and trees – although, as I said, everything has been gone now for a considerable period of time.

I know something about orchards in a way that I never did before. Being the summer cousin, I wasn't born to it, as Mandy was. By the time she was ten years old she could sort a basket of produce blindfolded: the ripest fruit on top, the too-soon harvested lining the bottom. I would watch her as she did this, a faint wrinkle of preoccupation on her smooth forehead, her busy hands assessing the firmness or softness of each fruit. Later, I would think she looked something like a blackjack professional dealing cards when she was sorting apples or pears. But when we were children, these quick, confident movements were to my mind a magical skill, made more magical by my uncle's nod of approval when she had completed the job. She could also climb trees and shake cherries into the lap of the waiting apron of a tarpaulin, while my role was to stay earthbound and collect the few pieces of fruit that had rolled into the grass. Not that either of us had an official job as children, as Teo did. Teo, the picker. He could give Mandy a run for her money, his small brown hands darting along the ground of the fields or moving in the trees of the orchards, his eyes on the task.

Strawberries, cherries, peaches, pears, tomatoes, apples: that was the rhythm of ripening, put in motion by my great-great-grandfather on what was still a mixed farm, then improved by my great-grandfather, and perfected by my grandfather, who became the fruit specialist, obsessed by orchards, dismissing the animals and crops as if they had been mere incidentals and not what had come between his ancestors and certain starvation.

Oh those ancestors with their long shadows and their long stories. By the time we were teenagers, Mandy and I would exchange ironic glances whenever my uncle began what we called "the sagas", tales in which he often called the head of each ancestral household "Old Great-great" rather than having to work his way mathematically back through the generations. It was as if all previous Butler males were the same Butler male anyway: obdurate, intractable, given to prodigious feats of labour in impossible conditions, one reign after another. Possessors of impressive strength, they were achievers of glorious successes and victims of spectacular failures. In the old photos, the full white beards and stern expressions of the great-greats resembled the frightening Old Testament figures – perhaps even Yahweh himself – illustrated in the family bible. You see, religion *did* play a role in the family once, but it was an unforgiving religion, one that became less essential to us as the generations progressed, while those things it was unwilling to forgive gained in importance.

Mandy and I were at our closest in our early teens, could communicate through eye contact, and were prone to shared fits of uncontrollable laughter at moments not entirely appropriate for laughter. Often these bouts of hilarity were at my uncle's expense, though I am fairly confident that he never knew. This was in spite of our love for him. We were trying, I suppose, to separate a little from his power and his presence, which had dominated us since our earliest childhood. Or perhaps we were attempting to step away from the genetic inheritance that he enforced almost on a daily basis, though we certainly wouldn't have known that at the time. We were part of the family. It never occurred to us that we wouldn't be part of the family. Had we been asked, we probably would have insisted that our forebears had created the ground we walked on each day because without them there would have been no orchards, and without the orchards there would have been no sustaining livelihood.

Yes, having watched them wither and decay, I know something about orchards. I am intimate with the shortness of their lives. Sixteen years, tops, my uncle told us, or anyone else who would listen. The good fruit is borne between the third and the twelfth year, after which the yield begins to thin out. At the end of each season the "old" trees were cut and dismembered by the few Mexicans who stayed to complete the task. Teo, who had by then always returned with his mother to his home and presumably to school, was never among them. But that last summer I'd heard that he'd come back in April in time to burn the tangled brush of the previous years' discards. I wasn't at the farm until late June, but he told me about the burning when I arrived from the city with my mother.

When a job at the Sanctuary Research Centre brought me here and I took over the house, a few trees were still producing in what remained of one peach and one apple orchard. The cherry orchards along the lake had been sold almost immediately to developers and the wood harvested by specialty craftsmen. The tomato field behind the house gradually filled with wildflowers and, happily for me and for the butterflies, milkweed. I tried to keep a half-dozen apple trees going without the help of the sprays that I had come to detest because of what they had done to the butterflies, but the trees stopped producing. And then, of course, other life forms took up residence in their flesh, and the orchards began to die.

As for the monarchs, in those early summers we didn't even know where they went or where they came from, depending on your point of view. We simply accepted them as something summer always brought to us, like our own fruit, or like strawberries or corn at roadside markets, or, for that matter, like the Mexicans. It would be years before the sanctuary on the Point began to tag the butterflies in order to follow the course of their migration, and several years more before the place where the specimens from our region "wintered over" would come to my attention.

Still, each summer we were stunned anew by what we came to

call the butterfly tree. In the intervening months with winter upon us, preoccupied with school and other pursuits, we would have forgotten this spectacle, so its discovery was a surprising gift at the end of the season: an autumn tree that is a burning bush, an ordinary cedar alight with wings. Glancing down the lane, we would presume that while the surrounding foliage had retained its summer green, the leaves on that one tree had turned orange overnight. Then, before the phenomenon had fully registered in our minds, we would recall the previous occasions.

Not that the butterflies hadn't been around all summer: one or two could be seen each day bouncing through the air in the vicinity of flowers and feeding on nectar. But, until the butterfly tree, they would never have gathered in such stupendous numbers. This multitude, this embarrassment of wings, covered every available inch of leaf and bark, or sailed nearby, looking for a place to light. We would take the image of that tree with us as we turned toward the day, not remarking on it again until the shock of it had dissipated and the tree and its inhabitants had become a statement of fact. *The butterflies are back on the tree.* That announcement, more than anything else, was the beacon that lit the close of the season, the code that told us the games of summer were over.

Oddly, in those days we asked no questions about such an occurrence. Not one of us had ever witnessed the moment of the monarchs' departure, which I imagined – not incorrectly – as an enormous orange veil lifting from the tree, then floating out over the great lake, heading for Ohio. They had surprised us and were no longer among us. We were blessedly young. We had no time for reflection.

Old enough to require explanations now, suspicious of unpredictability and impressions, I complete my fieldwork and my labwork with a meticulousness I couldn't have even imagined in the thrall of those summers. These days it is all pinned specimens, tagged wings, and permanent records.

When I was in graduate school and was first told about the tagging of the monarchs, I considered the whole notion of fixing adhesive to something as fragile as a butterfly's wing to be barbarous. But now I myself am a tagger, a labeller, one who is driven to track down the last mysterious fact until there is no mystery left. Yet I cannot explain how something as real and as settled as my uncle's world – which was also our world – could shatter in one night. And while I might partly understand why he vanished, it is not possible for me to determine where he has gone. I picture him sometimes, standing on a mountain in Mexico surrounded by exhausted, tattered butterflies. Mating accomplished. Journey's end. The temperature too cold for flight. Everything grounded. Not a single monarch ever returns, incidentally. The ones who come back to us may look exactly the same as those who departed, but it is their great-grandchildren who make the return flight, the two previous generations having mated and died at six-week intervals in springtime Texas and Illinois. The third generation we welcome in June mates and dies six weeks later in our very own Ontario fields, engendering the hardy fourth Methuselah generation, which amazes us on trees like the one at the end of the lane and lives an astonishing nine months in order to be able to make the long journey back. All that travel and change, all that death and birth and transformation takes place in the course of a single year.

And yet the pieces of furniture that surround me now, the mirrors that reflected our family's dramas – even those we should never have been witness to – remain firmly in place, unmoved, unchanged. The mystery of Mandy: her march toward order and regimen, passion and death, remains in place as well, unsolved. I cannot explain the perfect symmetry of a boy's eyebrows or the exact design of a butterfly's wing. And then there is the mystery of that Mexican boy himself, and what did and did not pass between us.

Once, late in the season of that distant summer, when the days were getting shorter and the nights cooler, when the last of the tomatoes were harvested and the apples were beginning to be picked, I observed my uncle watching my aunt. She was wearing dark pants and a fuchsia cardigan over a white blouse. Her blonde hair was pulled back from her sculpted face, on which there was just a trace of makeup: eyeshadow and lipstick, blue and red. The delicate gold band of a small watch surrounded her left wrist and moved slightly when she lifted her arm. Each gesture, as she bent to clear plates or turned to speak to her sons or her daughter, was a study in grace. Her poise, her demeanour, was perfect.

I had given little consideration at that time to how one mature person might respond, in an unspoken, inner way, to another. The whole adult personality was to my sixteen-year-old mind so fixed, so certain – even my uncle's volatility had its own predictable patterns – that the idea of one citizen of that community causing a hidden reaction in another, especially within my own family, was unthinkable. I had my own secret moods by then, and believed that the journey I had found myself taking into privacy and preoccupation was something uniquely mine, perhaps because I was not old enough to shake it. For the previous month while I had talked and laughed with my cousins, or played soccer after supper in the yard, or swum, or dried the dishes, there was something beyond my control growing in my mind: a variety of longing, though I wouldn't have called it that at the time.

My uncle looked at his wife, and for the first time I was able to read his thoughts, dark fish swimming behind the solemnity of his blue eyes. He needs her, I thought, and he admires her, but he is not at ease with either his need or his admiration. Her beauty and her strength diminished him somehow. At least that is what I remember thinking, though admittedly these may have been observations nurtured in hindsight being, I now see, far too complicated for the girl I was then. Still, regardless of how I might have interpreted that look, I noted it and was startled and vaguely frightened by what it might hold, by all that remained unexpressed between that couple and would remain, I knew, unavailable to me.

What can I do now with all that ambiguity and doubt? There is no information I can bring to it, no light I can shine on it to make it any clearer. Despite the evidence of subsequent events, each theory I have developed lies discarded somewhere in the shadows. I have even attempted to examine the opposite of what I intuited and later observed, believing that if I could at least disprove *that*, I might strengthen one hypothesis or another. But it is impossible to follow this line of reasoning to its logical conclusion. There is no scientific method by which to establish that the look I apprehended was not one of uncomplicated adoration without even the rumour of approaching contempt to interfere with its clarity. She was beautiful and talented and intelligent in ways that he admired, and he loved her. End of story.

But it is not the end of the story. The story ended in the sorriest of ways out on Sanctuary Line, the road I drive each day to the research station at the Point. Or perhaps it ended before that while we romped through the summer days and clung to the furniture of the past. Yes, perhaps even then it had ended. The minute that boy put his hand in my hair and his face next to mine, for example, I could feel something change and close up behind me, I could feel something ending. But perhaps that was only the beginning of the end; perhaps the true finish was the military pomp, the ceremony that marched poor, exquisite Mandy from a country whose name we barely knew as children to the old graveyard where her mostly forgotten ancestors awaited her arrival.

After two full decades of life experience it still astonishes me to admit that I brought no more insight to what happened to Mandy while she was over there than I brought to the night everything fell apart all those years ago. In spite of the lengthy phone calls placed in the early hours of the Afghan morning, phone calls during which Mandy, a brilliant officer and ambitious military strategist, barely mentioned the war, her passion and obsession having eclipsed even that ongoing catastrophe. In spite of the times when she was home on leave and making every effort to pay attention to each of her old friends while her mind was thinking, thinking, thinking about one man. In spite of the way she returned to this house and collapsed into an orgy of confession with me as her unlikely priest, I couldn't really hear what she was saying. Except, when one is set apart by passion and goes into the world of that secret, there seems no reason to take heed of anything beyond those gestures that protect the secret. If I believed in destiny, I would be compelled to call it destiny. There seemed to be no tools with which to examine it, you see, and no weapons with which to blow it up. I could only assume that hidden, unknowable forces were at work. But I am a scientist. I am supposed to believe that what appears to be unknowable is merely that which has not yet been thoroughly examined.

The thing about scientific system taxonomy – *Life, Domain, Kingdom, Phylum, Class, Order, Family, Genus* – is that while it pretends to inject predictability and comfort into our world, it can't really cause either of these states to come into being. I've been taught that we can define every life form in this manner, by simply moving in a deliberate way down the list. Everything, that is, except for extinction, which carries out its own scientific duties in an opposite manner. Working its way slowly up through the divisions, it is creation in reverse. First a species disappears, then a genus, then a family, an order, a class. Extinction is relentless, and it is flourishing. I believe it will win in the end.

I spend my time now moving back and forth between the field and the lab, between the quick and the dead. Everything is at risk, not just the orange and black *Danaus p. plexippus* of the Lepidoptera family, but everything. The old barns – those that have not burned or been taken down – sag and collapse. The small white churches are almost empty on Sundays, if they haven't already been sold and turned into cafés or antiques stores. All of my ancestors and their houses sleep in closed and unexamined albums. Neither my much-loved cousin nor my enigmatic, haunted uncle is ever coming back.

My uncle was a dynamic man, an experimenter, a risk-taker, always pulling the new into a traditional world, wanting to be the first to grow an exotic crop, use innovative equipment, employ the science of chemical farming, build new structures. Perhaps having been born, as I now believe he was, into the full flowering of previous men's pioneer labour, he knew that to cling to tradition – no matter how much one loved that tradition – was only to encourage eventual loss. He, who came of age in this county when the second growth of trees was entering its lush maturity, and the pastures, fields, flocks, and herds were fed and cared for, and the children educated and inoculated, might have spent his days watching everything he admired grow old and irrelevant around him had his vibrancy not caused him to lean toward change. He was the first farmer in this part of Ontario to cause a strawberry crop to ripen twice in one season, and one of the first to employ foreign workers. He invented a method of staggering the development of plants, and the growth of trees, so that he was able to use his workers to the maximum, with five or six significant harvests a summer. He had the bunkhouses built and the Mexicans flown to the cargo terminal at the Toronto airport and the governments of both countries convinced before anyone could question his purpose. And, in spite of the low wages he paid, he was kind without being patronizing to his employees. Or so we were told, perhaps by him. And it seemed, at the time, to be so. The same men came willingly back year after year, the same men and a couple of women returned and worked steadily from dawn until dusk; all this happening on one of the oldest farms in Essex County, in the fields and orchards that surround this marvellous fieldstone house. It was built long ago, as I've told you, by the second Canadian Butler in the middle of the nineteenth century, and built, I would imagine, without a thought given to Mexican labourers or chemically encouraged farming. Built at a time when the success of each tree in the orchard and the fattening of each animal in the barn seemed to be a gift provided by the relatively moderate climate near the great lake, the hardwood lumber, and the wonderful rich soil of what in those days was called "the front." Various fruit trees on the farm were named at that time for the men of the family who planted them, so that there was Eber's tree or Oran's tree or once, inexplicably, even Matilda's tree, though no one ever told us who Matilda was. Varieties of apples were identified by the Old World locations they'd come from or, now and then, the New World spots where they were first grown: St. Lawrence, Northern Spy, Hubbardston Nonesuch, King of Tompkins County, or the famous Butler Light, named for the lighthouse-keeping side of our own family. Or so our uncle Stan Butler told us. There was not a single exotic apple tree on the farm by the time my cousins and I were born – only the reliable

McIntosh remained – so we had neither seen the blossoms nor tasted the fruit of those legendary, vanished trees.

What can I say about my Uncle Stanley? That he was the father I never really had, the man who would guide my way into adulthood? No, he was the father I never *could* have had, the performing father, full of jokes and hijinks and important-sounding, often conflicting – but always oddly believable, at least to us – pronouncements concerning politics, history, animal husbandry, grafting, and pruning. There were the spontaneous summer adventures: trips in pickup trucks to ghostly old mills and abandoned cheese factories situated in parts of the back townships that only he seemed to know about. "I'm going exploring!" he would announce, springing up from a chair on a Sunday afternoon. As children, even as young teenagers, we would call after him, running to keep up, begging to be included, and he would relent with an air of feigned resignation, as if he hadn't intended us to join him all along. All that celebration and enthusiasm! And then there were the dark moods, also significant and admirable simply because they were his.

We all adored him, of course, and madly courted his favour, which was not always visibly present, no matter how we tried to please. Seldom unkind, he was nonetheless seized by bouts of vague withdrawal, sometimes by downright absenteeism in our midst, as if a grey veil had been woven between him and us. I now see that as we tried harder, he withdrew further. Then, abruptly, some small thing that not one of us had thought of would bring him back, and almost always this would be an external phenomenon, something that really had nothing directly to do with him.

Once it was my cousin Shane, who at the age of about eleven had begun to whittle farm animals from pieces of driftwood he had found at the edge of the lake. My uncle would be interested, you see, not so much in the carvings themselves but in Shane's absorption in the carving – a window, perhaps, that he hadn't noticed before into his son's character. Then, without warning, he would lunge into the whole idea of carving animals, scouring libraries for books on the subject, finding just the right piece of driftwood on the shore, insisting we all become involved until Shane himself would be completely overwhelmed by his father's enthusiasm. In this way, I now understand, my uncle was a variety of appropriator, a hijacker or robber, having to make everything his, having to own the lion's share of any experience. Were he here now, he would undoubtedly follow me to the lab, keep records of the fall and spring migrations, and in no time know more about the monarchs than I do, I who have been studying for so long.

But during those summers it would be the sailboat that Don was trying to build or Mandy's fossil collection that might seize his attention. The fossils were a hobby she had been working on for years, one that her father had never, to our knowledge, even noticed, until he *did* notice and became a connoisseur. Soon he had found a quantity of fossils among the pebbles of the beach, each one rarer, more unlikely than the one before. A week later he was using words such as *trilobite* or *protozoa* in many of his sentences and reciting long lists of Latin names for prehistoric life forms at dinner. Then, while Mandy reddened and looked at her plate, he would make ridiculous demands, insisting that she tell him the life story of a brachiopod or suggesting that the two of them leave the table immediately to see who would be the first to find a graptolite on the pebbled beach. I don't believe there was malice or even competitiveness in these actions; perhaps he was only teasing. He sensed, I think, a calmness, a steadiness around the tasks that other people loved, a reliable contentment, and in his own unhappiness – if he *was* unhappy – wished to enter the zone where that contentment came into being. He may simply have been seeking some sort of refuge.

It was essential that some of the members of my family or, more accurately, my mother's family, live near water – the men in particular. Exhausted by making both nourishing pastureland and decent crops flourish in wilderness landscape, they seemed to need to sleep somewhere in the vicinity of an unruly element they could see but knew they were not expected to control. If we were to believe my uncle, it had always been that way; every single Butler farmer had ploughed a field or driven his animals through a pasture that had a shoreline for a shoulder.

In the middle of the eighteenth century, however, the family had bifurcated, one half continuing to pursue – fruitlessly, no doubt, judging from the southwest part of Ireland where they pursued it – the agricultural life, the other half entering a profession, that of lighthouse-keepers.

The keepers would have been eventually taken into the world of the elegantly named Commissioners of Irish Lights and would have been considered fortunate indeed by their brothers in that they would have been given a recognizable job, a house, monogrammed silverware, and solid ironstone crockery with the motto *In Salutem Omnium* etched on its surface. They would have been given lamps to light, storms to contend with, lives to save, and an elevated vantage point. Their brothers, on the other hand, while they were still in Ireland, dealt with drenched, unmanageable land, large, cold houses, sickly livestock, depressed wives, and poverty-stricken and eventually starving tenants. The North Americans of my uncle's generation healed the bifurcation by coming solidly back to the land. By the time I was born, there hadn't been a keeper among us for half a century, though the lighthouse my great-great-uncle had manned was still visible to us and shone, and still shines, completely mechanized now, from the end of nearby Sanctuary Point.

Today is the kind of day that would have been a lighthouse-keeper's dream: bright sun and a steady breeze strong enough to make cumbersome sailing vessels dart like insects around nautical hazards, but not so strong that those vessels would be smashed to pieces on the shore. Everything is either shining or sparkling: the waves are picturesquely topped by white foam, but the swell is not large enough to cause danger. The onshore wind moves the branches of trees, making an interesting play of light and shade on the grass, but it is not stiff enough to ground the butterflies, many of whom are undoubtedly making use of its updraughts to travel easily from blossom to blossom.

Occasionally, I can hear the drone of one of the old aircraft they use for training purposes across the lake at the Ohio air base solemnly circling above the water. Just before Mandy enrolled in the Royal Military College, during her Great Lakes search-and-rescue phase, she trained for a while in a Canadian military plane, sailing right over Lake Erie, her old farm, her old life. Eyes fixed on the instrument panel and the sky, and then the few scattered patches of forested terrain, she never once looked down at the remains of the orchards. Or so she claimed later, when I asked her.

Year after year in my childhood, my mother and I left the city of Toronto in June and drove west for three hours to this farm, our summer clothes in the back seat of the Buick, the windows open for air. We lived for most of the year in the brick house my father bought before he died, long enough ago that I barely remembered him or living anywhere else, long enough ago that my mother, and I, had fallen easily back into her family, its generations of agricultur-alists, its Irish origins, its identification with the Ontario land it had adopted and has now abandoned. The city house was a conveni-ence; it sheltered us when I went to school and my mother went to work as a secretary in the same school. But it had none of the allure, the glamour of the farm on the lake, the place where she had been born and her father and her father's father before that. There, each summer to greet us, were the trees planted in the yard and the fences built in the fields by dim ancestors whose stories were reinvented for us by my uncle. And there, also, was the man I always thought of as my other uncle – my mother's other brother – who lived in the town of Kingsville with his wife and children, whom I thought of as my other cousins. There were views of the lake and sessions of play with Mandy, Don, and Shane and the other cousins, who did not sleep at the farm but who burst out of their parents' cars on weekends and ran with us, as if by instinct, toward the lake.

Mandy was almost two years younger than me, but it had never really seemed that way. This may have been because, when she wasn't cavorting around the farm with the rest of us, she was reading, increasing her knowledge of experiences outside of the world of this place and its ancestral narratives. She consumed all of Dickens, I remember, and could speak about orphanages and evil step-parents with authority. By the time she was twelve, Walter Scott had grabbed her imagination and with him came wars and love affairs. This addiction to books was something she came by honestly, an inheritance from several of the great-greats, but I'll tell you more about this later. Robert Louis Stevenson was her introduction to poetry, which had happened at a very early age. I have begun to read Mandy's books now, and the other night I let *A Child's Garden of Verses* fall open in my hands. How could I not think of those summers when I read the following stanza:

> To house and garden, field and lawn,
> The meadow-gates we swang upon,
> To pump and stable, tree and swing,
> Goodbye, goodbye, to everything!

My mother was the sibling in her generation who had, through marriage, taken the first tentative step into the domain of business, professions, and cities. The next generation – all those cousins – would follow her with enthusiasm. There is no one, no one left. I live in a landscape where absence confronts me daily. But my uncle's disappearance – his departure to nowhere – was the most dramatic, and the most deliberate: the most final abdication of them all.

———

Moving around the house, I often pass by the roll-top desk, which was my uncle's and his father's before him, and his grandfather's before that, and I know that the accounts he tried to keep during that last summer still lie, untouched, in the drawers. I have not opened the files, not wanting to go anywhere near this evidence of my uncle's last, sad attempts to maintain some kind of order. The list of Mexican workers is hidden in there, I suppose, and if I were to examine the paper it is written on, I would likely discover the boy's last name, which, incredibly, I had no notion of at the time. And all the preparations for buses, and the pickup from and delivery to the airport cargo terminal, are in there as well, I expect, yellowing in darkness. Quite likely there are some earlier, ancestral documents pertaining to this farm in one of the desk folders. In the top left-hand drawer, no doubt reeking of mould, lies the Essex County phonebook from 1986, the tradespeople named in its pages perhaps retired or dead now, and a listing of small businesses that

36

have likely vanished into air. There is also a harmonica my uncle sometimes played and a timetable for trains that no longer stop at the abandoned station and probably a schedule of Saturday events for the Sanctuary Point Summer Dance Pavilion, which closed and then was burned by vandals at least fifteen years ago.

I once tried to find the cargo terminal at the city airport in an effort to understand what it must have been like for Teo to arrive and depart from there, being human and not, therefore, technically cargo; what it would be like to be picked up and delivered like office supplies, or mufflers for cars, or, I suppose, more accurately, farm equipment, then transported from the shipper to the receiver. But that airport is so large now, and the cargo terminals so numerous, it was impossible to tell one industrial building from another. That's the way it is: terminals, orchards, and dance halls, all gone now, or lost, or just indistinguishable among the clutter of everything that follows. "I wanted to stop it," my uncle said the following morning, his voice hoarse, almost a whisper, "but what could I do?" Was he talking to himself or to me? Should I have answered? Could I have dug even the briefest of responses out of my teenaged heart? We turned from each other then, my uncle and I, both of us disappearing in our own private way into the abrupt end of the summer. No more apples on the bough, no more swimming in the lake.

Goodbye, goodbye, to everything.

Every few days I visit my mother at the seniors' residence in the nearby town. This is, in part, so that we can talk about the past, or at least those aspects of the past she is willing to discuss, and in part because I am at least as lonely as she is. I miss Mandy, though her leaves had been sporadic and our time together often fractured by her need to please everyone. I miss the long, trans-oceanic phone conversations we had in the middle of her night or mine, even though she often placed the calls because she could no longer bear the suffering brought to her by the man she was involved with, and sometimes, I admit, I resented her inability to stray from that subject. Now that I am living in this place, I miss the children we all used to be before everything broke apart, and I miss the children who should have replaced us but haven't.

The Golden Field is not really objectionable as these places go, and I am not as put off as I thought I might be when I park my car in the lot, pass through the entrance, and walk down the hall to the door with my mother's name, *Beth Crane*, printed on a small card and thumbtacked into the wood. I was baptized Elizabeth in honour of my mother, but she was always called Beth and I was always simply Liz. Crane, of course, was my father's name, which separated both of us just a little from my mother's family, the Butlers, but not so much that that family would not always be home to us. This was not entirely because of my father's death, though I'm sure it would have had a certain amount to do with it. There was a saying among us: "You can marry into the Butler family, but you can never marry out of it." In the case of my uncle's wife, Aunt Sadie, a Butler herself and second cousin to her husband, the problem would never have come up. She, by the way, also lived at the Golden Field for a few years before her impending death made my mother want to bring her back to this house. But she was in a different wing, one that is not so pleasant to visit.

Odd to think of those two women alone, and then together, only on and off. My aunt remained alone in the house after her sons left for university and Mandy went to the military college, until my mother retired from her city job and joined her. Then they were together here, until my aunt's dementia became unmanageable and Mandy and the boys found a place for her in the wing I just mentioned. After my aunt died, my mother stayed for a while in this house, and could still be here if she wanted to be.

I often think of my aunt, and when I do, I think of the striking woman she was during those early summers and not of the woman she became – the sad, confused woman in that wing. Fiercely intelligent and very American, she brought a combination of practicality and panache into a modestly eccentric Canadian world when she left northern Ohio and crossed the lake in order to marry my uncle. She brought other things as well to a family that had been content to muddle along in the fieldstone farmhouse their ancestors had built two generations before. She brought ambition. And she brought taste.

There was almost nothing she couldn't do with the interior or exterior of a house, or with the gardens surrounding that house. According to my mother, my aunt painstakingly restored the "important" architectural features installed by their colonial fore-bears – she had respect, after all, and a sense of history – and ruthlessly disposed of those features she considered to be unimportant. She removed all the flowered wallpaper and painted the rooms pale yellow with white trim. She ripped up the linoleum and had the wide pine floors beneath sanded and varnished. She dug out all of my grandmother's spirea and forsythia bushes and planted roses, lilies, delphinium, and other gorgeous flowers and shrubs whose names only she knew. She took the quilts off the beds, hung the best ones on the walls, and threw those that were too worn into the trash. She had the old lane graded and filled in with white gravel. She had the lawns rolled.

Hers was not a conventional beauty. She was tall, almost rangy, and her face was slightly angular, but part of my mother's admiration for her was attached to what she did with what she had been given: even at her most casual she exhibited a variety of style no one in rural Ontario had been able to muster. My mother admired my aunt's mind, as well. All those years on the farm she had kept the books, and began, right after she took up residence, to "knock some sense", as my mother would have it, into my uncle's head. The one thing that she couldn't do was make tomatoes and strawberry plants bear fruit twice in one season. It took my uncle's lust for risk, and his scientific mind – a mind you could say I have inherited – to do that. But would this have even happened without his wife? My mother thinks not. Sadie was the daughter of the more successful American branch of the family, she once told me, implying that, as such, she brought all the expectations of their flourishing fruit empire with her across the lake.

About two years ago my mother announced that it was time for her to move to the Golden Field. When I asked her why – she was only seventy-three and in good health, so I was genuinely shocked – she looked surprised, then simply said, "There are people there." I was a bit hurt by this; we both knew that I would begin to work at the sanctuary a month or so later and had no intention of living anywhere else. I was close to tears when we were packing up the few things she took with her, though I said nothing. My mother, however, did say something as she was making her last exit out the door leading to the porch. "Now you'll have your own life," she remarked. I sense that my mother wanted me to lean more toward crowds, or to become part of a community. Perhaps she was worried about me leaving the university faculty where, for ten years, I had participated in the easily accessible, though in my case not particularly intimate, social world that existed there. Looking out the back bedroom window that rainy day, though, when I had returned from settling my mother into her three small rooms, I found the flat, opaque wash covering the seemingly empty distant townships mildly comforting, as if it were a painting of my own character. I am a solitary, I thought. I cannot attend fringe festivals, protest marches, council meetings, or engage in any kind of team sport without feeling herded, trapped, and forced to perform. This was where I belonged.

My mother's corner apartment is on the ground level and has sliding doors that one can open in the warmer months for a breeze and gain access to a private patio. I fill her bird feeders and watch the sparrows come and go. The window on the opposite side looks out to the kind of semi-urban sprawl common now to country locations, and sometimes, as she talks, I gaze out at pizza parlours and laundromats rather than shrubbery and birds. An odd combination: these memories of her life at the farm, those birds in winter sunlight, this place named for an acre of farmland in deference to the agricultural "seniors" it was built to house. And then a convenience store, a car wash, office supplies.

About six months ago I asked her outright if she remembered Teo. She had been speaking about Mandy, whose death had greatly disturbed her. "Such a lovely girl," she was saying, "and so clever, so competent. Her father would have been proud."

Proud of what? I wondered. Her ability to survive him, at least temporarily? "Do you remember the Mexican boy?" I asked.

To my amazement my mother shook her head. "I don't think so," she said, and turned to watch a couple of birds at the feeder. "I think that may be a thrush of some kind or another." She reached for the binoculars she always kept on the windowsill, but by the time she had them in her hand, whatever it was had vanished.

"Of course you remember," I said, almost angrily, though the words came out sounding more patronizing than angry. "He came with the Mexican workers."

"So many Mexicans," she said, "every summer. Sometimes the same ones, but often they were different. Didn't your Uncle Stanley use school portables for their sleeping quarters? Yes, I think he did – at least at first, when he hadn't yet decided whether to keep them."

I myself had not known this. The first Mexicans had arrived at the farm two years before I was born so I recalled only permanent bunkhouses and one or two trailers.

"Teo," I said. "His name was Teo."

"Stanley had a dog named Tim," my mother said. "Smartest animal ever born. He could play soccer and did so, I remember, with you and your cousins." She laughed. "He could bounce the ball right off the top of his head, that dog. Mandy was very cut up when he had to be put down. The boys too. Even your Aunt Sadie admitted that —"

"I remember Tim," I interrupted, "but Teo is who I am referring to. Teo played with the dog, he played with us. He came with his mother, every summer." There was no response. "His mother's name was Dolores," I said. "She was a foreman, remember?"

"Apples," my mother said. "I often wondered what the world did with all those apples. Your grandmother still hung them on strings to dry them, to preserve them. I don't suppose anyone does that anymore." A faint visual memory of the wooden sills of my grandmother's bedroom windows came into my mind. And an audio memory of cluster flies buzzing there, the summer after she had died and the room was no longer in use. I had known her only in my early childhood.

"Please remember Teo," I said quietly. "Please say that you remember Teo."

My mother got up slowly from her chair and walked into her tiny kitchen, returning with a damp cloth in her hand. The sun had revealed a tea stain on one of her end tables, and she began to work away at that now, her back toward me, her thin arm moving rapidly back and forth.

"Please," I repeated, aware of a child in me, whining. "Just say it."

She turned toward me then, her look cheerful, kind, her hair backlit by the winter sun. "What was that, dear?" she said.

"God, Mom." I looked at her hand on the cloth. The veins under the skin were like mauve sinews. "Think about it. Think about Teo." I was aware that my voice was rising.

"Oh that." She folded the cloth twice. "No, dear, I don't think so."

The whining child in me was turning into a teenager, and I could feel myself wanting to storm out the door, car keys in my fist, the desire to burn rubber in the parking lot hot in my blood. I suppressed all this, however, and let her have her way, allowing her once again to tell me about the preservation of apples, the making of applesauce, and the trip taken each autumn to the cider factory with a wagon filled with windfalls. I permitted her to ask again about the house, whether I had had the eavestroughs cleaned, the storm windows installed, the lawn furniture put safely away for winter storage. But finally the teenager won, and I reached for my coat.

As I was about to leave, my mother asked about the monarchs. "How are your butterflies, Liz?"

"Gone," I said, yanking on my gloves. "It's winter now. Or have you forgotten that as well?"

"Oh Liz . . ." There was sadness in her voice and a distant expression on her face, and I could tell she felt that after all this time I should accept her discretion and develop some of my own. But I was having none of it. I wanted to punch right through her reticence and lay the whole story out on the coffee table near her knees. I wanted her to confirm, not deny, my resentment.

The boy called Teo became one of us, quite unexpectedly, one summer when we were still children but no longer so young that we were required to stay close to the house. Mandy would have been eight and I would have been almost ten, the boys a few years older. Our cousins from the town – Kath, a year younger than Mandy, and Kath's two brothers, Peter and Paul, contemporaries of my uncle's boys, Don and Shane – were big enough to bicycle down to the farm almost daily in order to swim, build forts in the wood lot and pastures, and take roles in increasingly complicated fantasies based on our collective devouring of the Hardy Boys mysteries and precocious Mandy's reading of *Oliver Twist*. Their own father, my other uncle, Harold, had once attempted to make a living as a tobacco farmer, but the enterprise had proved so costly and eventually so risky that he sold his farm and kilns and went into an auction business. He was the bifurcating one, my Uncle Stan told us, would have been a keeper had everything not gone to the dogs, meaning had the lighthouses not been automated. Still, in spite of his otherness, I dutifully called him Uncle Harold and felt some pride when I watched him perform on the block, the gift of Irish oratory strong in him, selling off item by item, I now see, the detritus of the very world that had produced him. Cast-iron pots, wooden shovels, hutch cupboards, quilts, coal-oil lamps, spool bedsteads, wall clocks, sometimes even cutters and carriages. On and on, weekend after weekend, these now redundant former essentials were gathered together and then scattered like seeds in a strong wind, moving sometimes out of the county but always out of context as they were replaced by plastic, plywood, stainless steel. I remember oxen yokes, sleigh bells, strange dark oil paintings, ladder-back chairs, and infinite varieties of china plates, cups, and saucers. All are dispersed now, gone to God knows where.

Sometimes my aunt (taking Mandy and me with her) would attend these events, having heard that "a particularly good piece" was going to be on the block. She would return with a pressed-glass tumbler or goblet for the collection she was amassing. The glass was displayed on specially built shelves in the house, and admired but never used. We children learned some of the patterns, by osmosis, I expect, not being all that interested in the objects themselves: Nova Scotia Grape, Butterfly and Fan, Diamond and Sunburst, Apple Blossom. My uncle, who couldn't leave the family's history out of anything, told us stories about the Canadian glass houses or glass works of the nineteenth century, claiming that one of the more obscure old great-greats was a blower in the Mallorytown Manufactory. Every Labour Day, he said, there were magnificent parades in that town, during which the glass-blowers would march in battalions, row after row, wearing glass hats and carrying glass walking sticks, sometimes even glass rolling pins and glass hatchets. I came to doubt that tale in my adulthood, along with many others my uncle told, and was therefore startled when leafing through a book on the history of glass one evening a few months ago to find that it was indeed true! The Glass Bottle Blowers' Association of the United States and Canada was both powerful and proud and enjoyed showing off even the most whimsical of its wares. My aunt would collect only Canadian glass, which was surprising in that she was American by birth and by sensibility. Perhaps it was her way of claiming some of the heritage of the country where she had chosen to live her adult life.

Teo, as I've said, came to my attention during a summer when we were all between the ages of eight and twelve and our games had become more elaborate and geographically scattered. During the warm, bright hours of those seasons, the rest of our lives utterly disappeared as we children closed ranks, became almost tribal, our imaginations looping around one another's. My auctioneer uncle would sometimes arrive with what he called "failed job lots" from one auction or another, wooden orange crates filled with cracked dishes and rusty tableware that Mandy and I – and Kath when she was there – were given full access to in the assumption that we would want to play house. Because she was reading *The Children's Treasury of Poetry*, Mandy once recited two verses of a poem she had found in those pages, the lines causing us to pause while we sorted china and wonder how the poet knew about our secret:

> This is the key to the playhouse
> In the woods by the pebbly shore,

It's winter now, I wonder if
There's snow about the door?

I wonder if the flower-sprigged cups
And plates sit on their shelf,
And if my little painted chair
Is rocking by itself?

We had only just become aware enough of the differences of gender to want to segregate ourselves and stake out territories: the boys had their tree houses, the girls had their forts. The orange crates became the furniture of leafy, green rooms, the dented pots and colourful plates were argued over and often stolen during raids on one fort, or tree house, or another. A turquoise plate, I remember, was much coveted, and once, when it was firmly in my possession and therefore on its way to the girls' fort, the boy, who by then I knew was called Teo, pointed to it and said, "From my country, from Mexico." I think it must have been the first time that I had heard him speak, certainly the first time that I remember hearing his voice. Before that, he was simply a rather odd and not altogether successful adjunct to the boys, often running just behind them, as if struggling to keep up, but really slowing his gait in deference to their knowledge of his differences, and his suspicion, well founded, that they really wanted little to do with him. It was my uncle who had taken him out of the bunkhouse and placed him in our midst. There were no explanations. "This is Teo," he had said. "He is learning English. Play with him."

This was so like my uncle. There was an educator fighting strong within him, born partly, I suspect, during the time just after his high-school graduation when my grandparents were alive and in full control of the farm. Needing winter work, he had taught for a season or two in one of the sparsely populated and ill-equipped one-room schools that still stood at the time on thin-grassed one-acre lots here and there in the county. He was sentimental about that small episode of his life and once that very summer took us, Teo included, on an expedition ten miles to the north. I expect he wanted to drive out there alone; maybe he was hoping for a moment of private communion with the past. But we had tagged after him as he strode toward the truck, whining and arguing our case until he relented. He told Mandy and me to get in the cab, and the boys to hop in the back, and we drove out to a mostly abandoned place called Red Cloud, where an empty, weathered schoolhouse creaked in the wind. When we were all inside, my uncle walked up and down in front of the broken blackboard like a ghost, not speaking and tossing the one stub of chalk that had remained on the narrow wooden ledge. Teo watched him, I remember, with frank curiosity in his brown eyes, and for the first time I wondered what school was like where Mexicans lived. Were there large brick buildings, with two classrooms for each grade level, in every Mexican neighbourhood, or did this boy have to take a yellow bus each day to the kind of smaller rural schools my cousins attended? Maybe his school would be like the bunkhouses on the farm, roughly painted, with thin walls, rickety windows, and no playground. Once it had occurred to me that there might not be a playground, I decided not to ask the question that had been forming in my mind. Teo continued to regard my uncle, his gaze following the rise and fall of the chalk.

My cousins were busily removing glass inkwells from the wooden desks that had wrought-iron sides and looked like my grandmother's treadle sewing machine. Shane was even examining the bottoms of the inkwells for the *D* surrounded by a triangle, which would indicate that they were made at the Dominion Glass Works and were truly Canadian. I imagine he wanted to take a few home to please his mother. "Put them back," my uncle finally said. "Someday someone will see how wrong they have been to close these schools and they'll need everything to be in place." Even at nine years old I knew this was ridiculous, the building hadn't been occupied for decades, but my uncle often appeared to authentically believe in such resurrections, his modernity and interest in progress notwithstanding.

He walked to the few shelves of the school library after that and began leafing through the mouldy books, Teo following and hovering, the rest of us lifting the lids of wooden desks, then letting them bang down again, reading the initials and names carved into the varnished oak.

Through the west windows, far off, you could see Red Cloud Graveyard, the odd flash of an upright stone, white among a scant gathering of poplars, practically invisible unless you knew it was there. "Cholera," my uncle said, explaining the presence of the graveyard in the small woods at a distance from what would have been the village, when a village still existed. "An epidemic," he added. The boys could not be kept from it then, this information making it so much more interesting than the other graveyards we had known. They ran out the door, leaving Mandy, Kath, and me with my uncle. Teo hesitated, looked out one of the windows until, anxious, I suppose, to conform, he went outside to be with the boy cousins, who had been momentarily distracted by the discovery of a cow skull in the long grass not far from the open door.

I could see Teo bend over the bone, feigning interest, wanting to be part of the group, while the other boys did their best to ignore him, forming a circle that was difficult for him to penetrate. He took a few tentative steps back toward the building and that one moment of retreat unleashed something in Don, who was the eldest. *Te-oh*, Don began to sing, mimicking the Harry Belafonte song that had been popular some years back, and that my uncle sometimes sang at parties, *Te-e-e-oh, Daylight come and I wanna go ho-ome*. In no time the others joined in. *Te-oh*, they chanted, *Te-e-e-oh*.

I could feel a subtle panic rising in me and looked toward my uncle for some kind of intervention or at least a reaction. But he had a geography book in his hands, and the unusual lopsided squint his expression sometimes took when he was absorbed and gone from us, and I knew he was paying no attention at all to the boys in the yard. Teo himself slowly climbed the three decaying steps that led back into the schoolroom, then discreetly moved to the other side of the open door, where he knew they couldn't see him. He looked at me, probably because I was watching him. "Not my country," he said, "the song."

That was the second thing I remember him saying aloud.

My uncle glanced up at that moment and walked toward the boy, the book still in his hands. "This is your country," he said, pointing out the map of Mexico he had been studying. Then he led the boy to a globe that stood on a scarred table on the other side of the room. "It is here as well," he said, "and this is where you are right now." I couldn't see the globe clearly from where I was standing but knew they would be looking at the chain of Great Lakes and the fist of James Bay punching down from the north. If Teo had been acquainted with maps in the past he made no indication of this, appeared instead to be interested and pleased to be shown something by my uncle, happy to stand in the warmth of his attention. He twirled the globe, which wobbled on its old stand. He, too, it seemed, longed for my uncle's approval.

I should say something about the globe that Teo twirled with his small brown fingers. Not too long ago, cleaning out a corner cupboard in this old house, I came across the teachers' log from Red Cloud School and began, before my evening meal, to read it. I don't remember my uncle taking anything home with him that day so he must have gone back to retrieve it once he realized that the little building was doomed, that no one was ever coming back. The log was begun by a teacher, a Mr. Quinn, in about 1900. The man himself was a bit of a historian and provided a litany of the school's adventures since the 1840s: the raising of money for the schoolhouse construction, the volunteer labour, the first trustees, and original teachers and pupils. But when writing about his own tenure, the central drama focused on the decision to purchase and then the eventual arrival of the globe. "The children," he stated, "were given a holiday because of the excitement and because they could not be kept from the object of their attention. I sent them outside to play and then allowed them, one by one, to enter the school that they might be allowed five minutes each to look at the new wonder. It was," he wrote, "as if this one object was bringing the world to them."

Outside the window were the fields and meadows of what I thought of then as my ancestral countryside, though, as I have since learned, it was the ancestral countryside of a more legitimate tribe, one that had been gone for a long time, leaving in its wake two words, *Red Cloud*: a name stolen and then anglicized by those who came later and pushed that tribe out. Recently, there has been a lot of talk in the biological community about species that have invaded the Great Lakes area, zebra mussels, for example, and a particular kind of Mexican "ladybug", that, according to the experts, "doesn't belong here and is upsetting what remains of the ecosystem". What does belong here? I wonder at such times. Do we?

"Here." My uncle snapped the book shut and passed it to the boy. "Keep it, take it home with you." It was unclear to me, and perhaps to Teo, whether he meant to the bunkhouses or to Mexico, though by then the bunkhouses and Mexican schools had amalgamated in my imagination and I wondered if perhaps my uncle was making a donation to what might very well be classrooms that contained no books at all.

I looked out the window into the mid-August afternoon. The boys were running through a grassy area in which grew brown-eyed Susan, Queen Anne's lace, bachelor's buttons, and other wildflowers named by colonists. They were cantering through long grass toward the distant graveyard and the horizon, which is always such a dominant feature in this flat county. How odd that I can see that scene so clearly now, the various flowers, the boys' striped T-shirts. Often that whole epoch seems so far from me that I cannot conjure it at all. Sometimes my only connection to it is the map made by the fine lines on a monarch's wing. Still, in those days, I would never have examined such a wing carefully enough to know it resembled a map.

"But everything stay," said Teo slowly, reminding my uncle, the English difficult in his mouth.

"Everything *should* stay," said my uncle, emphasizing the conditional. "But it doesn't."

As I've said, now that she is gone, I've begun to read the books Mandy left behind in this house. I wish I had done this earlier; I would have known her and understood her better if I had. I might have become acquainted with the hesitancy, the frailty of spirit that attends certain kinds of love, as well as the baffling tenacity of a passion as difficult as Mandy's appeared to be. If I had read just one book of love poetry, her relationship could possibly have come into focus for me, and maybe I would have seen that certain lovers need to commemorate the knotted feelings, the emotional confusion. And yet, her longing to examine the relationship, to give some kind of voice to it, rode side by side with her desire to protect the secret at the centre of the intimacy. There was, you see, always this sense that naming her lover would be a kind of betrayal, regardless of circumstances. "The loved one is rarely identified in poetry," she once told me, "and it is that discretion that gives the reader permission to be moved, to own the sentiment." Sadly, it's only now, late at night, with these new thoughts and phrases speaking to me, that I have begun to comprehend what she meant.

They have been here for a long, long time, these volumes, ever since Mandy graduated from the military college and went out into a world so transient it was impossible to cart books with her from posting to posting. There are the usual classics, some of which even I was forced to read in the one English course required for my undergraduate degree in biochemistry. *The Mill on the Floss, Jane Eyre, The Mayor of Casterbridge*. But there is a good deal of poetry as well, a world I have ignored until now, though I admit that Mandy tried now and then to make me enter it. I began by reading Robert Frost, as she said I should, because as she pointed out he is both profound and easy to understand, especially for those of us who know farms or who come from farming stock. Most of Mandy's poetry books are paperbacks, but those written by Frost are hardcover editions, complete with dust jackets, and I was surprised to discover my uncle's name, rather than Mandy's, on the flyleaf of each collection. But then I remembered how often literature surfaced in the tales of the great-greats, as if some of them had been afflicted by it in one way or another. One of them was known as "the ex-reader", for example. The other night, a line or two from Frost's "After Apple-Picking" struck me as being the perfect epitaph to inscribe on my uncle's grave, if he had a grave. Something like:

> For I have had too much
> Of apple-picking: I am overtired
> Of the great harvest I myself desired.

Once during that long-forgotten summer, or a summer just like it, when Teo was suddenly one of us, my uncle took it into his head that one of the many ways the boy could learn English was to participate – albeit informally – in square dancing. None of us children, and certainly not one other adult, could come close to matching my uncle's enthusiasm for such bizarre activities. But because we loved him, we all dutifully gathered near the portable record player he had first hauled out into the yard and then attached by a series of extension cords to the power in the house. Teo and I were required to be partners, which meant holding hands and embarrassed us both, while Kath was paired with Shane, Mandy with Peter, and Paul with Don, which, in turn, embarrassed them.

Because it was the close of the afternoon, the mothers, as we called them, were sitting on the porch facing the lake, smoking cigarettes and drinking gin and tonics. My uncle rarely instigated an act for which he did not want an audience, and this was to be no exception. I remember him calling his wife, urging her to leave the veranda. "C'mon, Sadie," he was shouting, and then again when there was no response from her. "C'mon, Sadie. And you too, Beth, get over here." His unacknowledged voice began to sound a bit tired, some of the eagerness fading from it as the women continued to ignore him.

Teo's mother and the man we knew was her brother were standing at the edge of one of the orchards, on the other side of the fence, watching. Though they were still wearing their green cotton over-alls and brown sunhats, work was over for the day. She must have come to collect her child for the evening meal, only to be presented with this odd partnering and the sound, coming from the record player, of a man's voice chanting nonsense over music. She just stood there beside her brother, the trees and ladders behind her, a tentative smile on her face. Teo looked in her direction but likely felt unable to leave the weird ritual into which he had been introduced. At that moment my own mother rounded the corner of the house and moved to the fence where the woman and her brother stood, greeting them quietly with a nod, from the opposite side. The brother disappeared back into the orchard. A bang of a screen door announced my aunt's withdrawal indoors. No one spoke. The sound of the waves on the beach stones mixed in a strange way with the artificial sounds coming from the scratchy record, and I remember thinking, while Teo and I stood very still, that recorded music played outdoors brought something tinny and almost unpleasant with it into a space where it had never before been heard.

All of this presents itself as a tableau in my mind, but one that eventually breaks apart into slow action moving toward full chaos. My uncle followed Teo's gaze and settled on the Mexican woman who was Teo's mother. "Dolores!" he shouted. "Come and join the dance!" She hesitated, then did as she was told, climbing awkwardly over the fence near which my mother stood, seemingly impassive, not looking at us or the Mexican woman entering our territory. Teo made an involuntary movement, one that travelled up my own arm, and I could tell that his instinct was to run to his mother and that he was holding that instinct back.

What, I now wonder, made my uncle believe that hearing lines such as *star through*, *pass through*, *circle round the track*, *drive through*, *pull through, box the gnat* would help to teach a child English? But perhaps he knew more about this boy than I did at the time. Perhaps he felt that language married to music and gesture might nudge the child toward speech.

What resulted was a kind of pandemonium. Dolores was the only one among us who could master a dance step – my uncle was either pulling notes out of his pocket or sending her into one whirling pirouette after another, while the old record player skipped and repeated. My cousin Shane began to break-dance in a clownish way. My mother bent over in laughter. Mandy broke away from Peter and began to fight with Shane, rolling in a tangle on the grass. Teo and I stood entirely still, dutifully holding hands, quiet in the midst of this, looking at each other, then shyly looking away, as children will.

My aunt burst into this peculiar miracle play like a cop breaking into an after-hours club, her face flushed with sun and gin. All she had to do was walk toward the fracas, her arms folded across her silk blouse, for the momentum of the group to falter and stall. We children, knowing we were not permitted to make noise before her morning alarm went off at eight o'clock, and that she had on occasion been able, at seven o'clock, to hear us roll over in our beds three rooms away, were particularly sensitive to her approach. As were all the Mexican workers. Teo immediately dropped my hand, and he and his mother walked quickly toward the field, hastily climbing the fence, sensing their exemption from exclusion was over. My mother unfolded from her clench of laughter. My uncle, however, more fervently involved than the rest of us, was chanting along with the calls on the recording: *Swing your partner round and round, turn your corner upside-down.* Then he stopped, looked up from his notes. "Where'd she go?" He laughed. "What happened to my partner?"

My aunt removed the needle from the record, scraping it noisily across the vinyl as she did so. A dull stillness entered the late afternoon. Then, when she was certain she had our attention, she smiled brightly. My other uncle was conducting a twilight auction that evening in one of the back townships, and his wife, my other aunt, had gone with him for company on the trip, so my other cousins were staying for dinner. "Who wants spaghetti?" my Aunt Sadie called cheerfully as she turned back toward the house.

It occurs to me now that monarchs show every appearance of being cheerful creatures. Their beauty, the fact that they dance across our summer gaze, stunningly adorned and always in the vicinity of brilliantly coloured flowers, their poise, and the apparent effortlessness of their movements give us every reason to believe they are in a state of grace. But, in fact, few insects have such a fraught existence. First, right after conception, there is a series of vigorous and possibly painful transformations: from the splitting open and shedding of larval skin to accommodate the growth of the caterpillar, to the making of the cocoon to house the pupa. This is followed two weeks later by the butterfly itself struggling in the most critical way to free itself from the prison of the chrysalis. Then there is that brief, lovely season of riding the breeze and feeding on nectar in preparation for the most lengthy and exhausting migration, and a collapse, afterwards, into a period of winter dormancy.

All of this inconceivable exertion and unpredictable exposure to danger leads in the end to mating, and not too much later to death.

My uncle stood out on the lawn for what seemed to me to be a very long time, tilting the record my aunt had scratched back and forth in the light to see how much it was damaged. I watched him through the window while I was putting knives and forks on the table. Something about the way his head was lowered as he examined the disc made it possible for me to see that during his most recent trip to the barber the back of his neck had been shaved. The thought of him sitting in the chair with his chin resting on his chest, utterly submissive and covered like a child in a large white bib, coupled with the way he carefully slid that vinyl record back into its sleeve and slowly closed the lid of the record player, made me heartsick, though I couldn't have explained, at the time, why I might feel that way.

I have been wondering these days about charisma, about what goes into its makeup. Is it a sensual experience? Does visual or auditory extraordinariness, for example, determine its properties? Is it learned, or acquired, or is it present in the configuration of an organism from the beginning? And what about butterflies? Mysterious and graceful, abundantly colourful, no one can deny that they are charismatic. But is this also true when they are larvae or pupae? In the mid-nineteenth century, a theory flourished among entomologists: if one were to possess a microscope powerful enough, one would be able to see all of the exquisite features of the butterfly trapped within the organism, even at the larval stage, but this was subsequently disproved. And other life forms, drawn to the charismatic, do they come as predators or worshippers? Perhaps prey is always worshipped to a certain extent, or maybe there is always an unconscious desire to destroy attached to all that is worshipped. We should speak about the spiritual, I suppose, and about worship. It would be interesting to talk about what form your prayers take and why I have no prayers at all.

Because cardenolide, a poisonous chemical contained in the

milkweed upon which they feed, moves through them and is broadcast to the world through their colour and markings, monarchs have few predators. It is not uncommon, therefore, to see a monarch and a starling lounging on the same branch. This gift of toxicity is so powerful that the viceroy butterfly has evolved over centuries to both look and to smell like a monarch in order to increase its own chances of survival. But all viceroys – and even a handful of monarchs – are born lacking the chemical and, though they appear to be no different than their brothers, as beautiful and charismatic and immune to harm, jays, grackles, and cardinals instinctively sense their weakness and know that they are killable and consumable.

My uncle was like one of those few vulnerable monarchs, or perhaps more specifically like its mimic, the viceroy. Most of us sailing in his midst saw only his colour and his grace, and we assumed, therefore, his indestructibility. His enemies, if he had any, would have been impressed by his persona and respectful of his colourful territory and his accomplishments. Only someone very, very close to him would have been able to sense his defencelessness, his helplessness in the face of attack. Only someone who had slept beside him for thousands of nights could have picked up the scent of his weaknesses. There may very well have been – part of me still wants to believe this – no latent poison in him. There may have been nothing manipulative associated with his charm.

But he *was* charismatic. We all followed him, we all worshipped him. Everywhere he went we ran after him, sensing an adventure, wanting to be in his company. And yet I think the charm that emanated from him was a force that evolved as he matured, rather than something that was with him from birth. It was the bright shield he used to draw others into his orbit, to keep them in his line of vision, and to protect himself from the destruction he could always imagine. But evolution, once it is set in motion, is a natural phenomenon rather than one that is willed. As time passed, his magnetism may have become a burden to him, one he was unable to discard, even when he was absent, even when he had disappeared behind the grey veil I mentioned earlier and was not available to anyone at all.

The first time I went to the Golden Field to visit my mother, she told me what my uncle was like as a child, his timidity and silences, and how he broke out of the vagueness and reticence of that and into something more splendid and precise, how that glittering shield was forged.

I was looking at his picture on the table, his picture and the photos of the others she had chosen to display. Lovely Mandy in her dress uniform – with its red worsted material, white braid, black cuffs, and gold buttons, her white gloved hands resting on the hilt of a splendid sword – put my own graduation photo and those of her brothers in the shade. She was ablaze with purpose, with confidence, or so it seems. The photo of my uncle was not as large, and he himself appeared to be smaller and thinner than my memory of him.

"He was such a shy boy, so timid." My mother said this without naming him, as if waiting to see if I would ask her to stop. When I didn't, she leaned back into the cushions she had arranged in her armchair and added, "As you know, every summer we went across the lake to Sadie's farm."

I did know this. At the end of the summers of her childhood, just before the beginning of the apple harvest, when the first crops of summer fruit had been picked and the apples were almost mature, my grandfather would leave the farm for a week in the care of hired hands. Along with my grandparents, my mother and her older brothers were expected to visit their American relatives across the lake in Erie County, Ohio. This was an attempt to maintain their connection with one of the bifurcating though solidly landloving arms of the family.

"Great-uncle John's farm," I corrected, naming the true owner of the place. Sadie, as she was during that long-gone time, was to my mind just a child, passing through, really, on her way to becoming the adult woman I knew – my aunt – firmly planted on our side of the lake.

I knew the history of this particular bifurcation as well: my uncle had, of course, been the deliverer of all that information. It concerned two very different yet equally significant reactions to the American War of Independence. In 1786, one Butler brother, Amos by name, had found after ten years of prayer and meditation that he must remain loyal to the same British monarchy that had established the Butlers – all those years ago – in Ireland. (Butler's Court, by the way, the family seat, was much referred to by my uncle in his tales and was a place that, after much research, I discovered to be entirely fictional.) So Amos assembled his family of six and set out for the British colony of Upper Canada, which, fortunately for him, was only a two-day journey by horse and wagon and a short boat ride across Lake Erie. He had been granted land in the vicinity of Leamington in Essex County, where, after removing an unimaginable amount of hardwood forest, he planted the same variety of apple tree – the Kaziah Red, named for his wife – that had so flourished on his father's farm in northern Ohio. Samuel, brother of Amos, after much meditating and praying (they were fierce Methodists) felt that he must be true to the New Republic of the United States of America as he, and his father, had favoured Irish emancipation from the British in spite of the fact that it was men just like him, living in houses very similar to the fictional Butler's Court, who were making that emancipation so difficult. The American Revolution looked to him like a similar but more successful attempt at the same kind of much-desired liberation.

After this second migration, the first being from Ireland, the sons of Amos Butler began to move west along the north shore of Lake Erie, my own great-great-grandfather establishing the famous orchards our uncle spoke about, which were all cut down and burned and turned into McIntosh plantings just before my cousins and I were born. At the turn of the twentieth century, a member of the third Butler line, a bachelor lighthouse-keeper, emigrated from Ireland to America and eventually established himself as keeper of the light at the Point where I now work and over which I watch the sun rise almost every morning of my life.

The Point was a very different spit of land by the time I was born. The lighthouse was mechanized, and a provincial bird sanctuary was established there. The pier was closed down and the name of old Point Road was changed to Sanctuary Line.

"As far as I'm concerned, Sanctuary Line is still the old Point Road," my mother said, as if following my thoughts. "When I and my brothers were driven along it and then along the Talbot Highway, five miles to Kingsville, there was never any thought that a road could have its name changed to something else. The car was ferried from there, from Kingsville – I remember all those wonderful old elm trees – first to Pelee Island, then across the lake to Sandusky, Ohio. I admire the Americans, but I greatly disapprove of their politics," she told me, not for the first time. "But," she added vaguely, "I suppose I wouldn't have been thinking of that at the time. Was it during the war?" she asked herself.

"Yes," I answered, "but not the war you disapprove of."

"We," she said, meaning the family, "escaped the war at that time. Partly because everyone was either too young or had taken the agricultural exemption." She was quiet for a moment. "Dear Mandy," she said, as if thinking that fate had decided on her death based on an exemption chosen by the previous generation in a completely different war. I looked at my uncle's photo again. In it he, too, was dressed in a kind of uniform, but a uniform designed for no war at all. He was a young man at the time, just a boy, really, and almost anyone would think that the harness he was wearing was one that had recently been or was about to be attached to a parachute. But I knew that it was a picker's harness, and that there were two clasps at the front, to which a basket that would soon be filled with cherries or peaches would be attached. I say peaches or

68

cherries because I can see phlox (*P. divaricata* species of the Polemoniaceae family) growing at the edge of the wood lot in the picture, and it would have stopped blooming by the time the apple harvest was underway.

"I remember looking at the American shoreline from the ferry; how everything there got larger and larger as we got nearer," my mother said. "It's the kind of thing you notice as a child."

How serene that slow, cadenced voyage must have been: the old Loyalist houses sliding by car windows that were rolled down for the breeze, the ferry at Kingsville, the picnic on Pelee Island, the second journey by ferry, the view from which would have included orchards and barns that were a mirror image of the orchards and barns on and around the family's own farm. Yet I think that small family might have moved with unconscious caution through this geographical double, sensing a strangeness on that side of the looking-glass: something to do with one extra degree of orderliness, tidiness, prosperity; your own world improved so subtly that you could feel the change without being able to identify it. The waves approaching that shoreline would be moving in a direction opposite to the direction chosen by their own waves. The same moon would rise in a different part of the sky. And, somehow, though one would hardly dare admit it, almost everything would have seemed to be more certain, confident, independent, and, as my uncle always said, with irony in his voice, "The biggest and the best." It is true, of course, that we are never entirely comfortable in the midst of places or people we admire too much.

There were three children in that other, opposite place, second cousins of approximately the same age as the three children arriving from the northern side of the lake. Tom was paired by age and gender with the boy who would become my Uncle Stanley; Rupert, who was a year older, spent his time with Harry. And then there was the already self-possessed Sadie, who someday would become my aunt but who for now took my mother, Beth, for her companion.

There was also a butterfly tree on that farm so that some summers my mother and her brothers saw that burning bush on the north side of the lake and other summers witnessed the same miracle to the south. My mother told me that until she was about fourteen she believed that every farm had such a tree and experienced such an event.

"One summer," my mother said, "when we pulled up the American farm lane we could hardly believe what we were seeing." They had driven, you understand, into the immediate aftermath of misfortune. When they stepped out of the car the air still held the taste and smell of ash, and charred timbers latticed the stone foundation of what had, just days before, held up the barn. Tom, normally a clumsily energetic boy, did not run out of the house as he had each summer to greet them. Playing with matches, two days earlier, he had accidentally set the barn on fire and it had burned out of control for twelve hours.

Farming being what it was, and childhood being what it is, this would have been considered to be a spectacular tragedy, though being primarily an orchard farm, the animals, only five – two cows, a pony, and two workhorses – had been saved. The pony belonged to Tom, and his father had made a heroic effort to release it from the burning barn and was relieved, he said, to have been able to do so because he was concerned about Tom, about the guilt, perhaps even the anguish, the boy might feel about the accident. The concern was real; the guilt was as well.

But as the days went by, a theatrical element entered the way that Tom was attended to, or at least this is what I've gathered from what my mother told me, and how I like to imagine it now. There would have been a kind of celebrity attached to the event and to the boy who had unintentionally caused it to happen.

"Tom was treated with great tenderness by his parents," my mother said, "almost as if he were an invalid." The other children were not permitted to be rough with him or to taunt him in any way, even if the taunts had nothing at all to do with the barn. His father encouraged Tom to come along with him if he had errands in town, something that would likely never have occurred to the man in the past, and his mother would stop talking or working as the boy walked by, brush the hair back from his forehead, and ask him what he would like to do with the morning, the afternoon, or if there was anything special he wanted for supper. He became, in essence, a sacred child. There would have been a peculiar radiance about him; he was completely unlike the boisterous boy my mother remembered from previous summer visits. He had evolved into a miniature adult, wanted less to run with his sister and his cousins than to work in the fields with his father or help him mend a fence or paint a door.

They were harrowing during that period, breaking up a fallow field because my American great-uncle had decided that he wanted to begin to grow strawberries as well as apples the following year. Tom was encouraged to participate, was even permitted to drive the team that pulled the heavy rack of iron teeth across the earth, and Stanley, my future uncle, would have desperately wanted to be included. "But, in all likelihood, he was not asked," my mother said. "And he would have not dared to make the suggestion. Children – in those times – did not initiate anything, really, did only what they were told to do."

And yet, there was his American cousin, his mirror image, his doppelgänger, welcomed into what until that time would have looked to him like an impenetrable adult world, and welcomed, furthermore, as a blessed recruit whose frailties and hesitancies were pandered to rather than scoffed at.

The fond pandering would not have been lost on the child my future uncle was then for, if I am to believe my mother, people like their own father, my grandfather, and my grandmother too to a certain degree, were not comfortable with a show of feelings. And yet surprisingly my grandparents were able to engage in long, earnest discussions concerning Tom's predicament, discussions during which they allowed that the boy's suffering had to be taken into account. This kind of focus on the boy's feelings must have been quite foreign to them, and would have been absolutely absent from their own Methodist upbringing, which insisted, above all, on not calling attention to oneself or one's own troubles. Stanley, over-hearing some of these conversations, would have felt the sweetness of how the talk circled, in a gentle way, around and around one particular boy's inner life, and how that boy himself was the instigator of something magnificent: a night of heat and colour, an occurrence impossible to ignore, and then, in its wake, a whole season of solicitousness and care.

My mother and Sadie spent those two weeks making clothes for their dolls from scraps Sadie's mother gave them. Then, with the help of Rupert and Harry's carpentry skills, they devised an elaborate dollhouse out of wooden crates they'd found in the barn. The only interaction with her brother Stanley took place during the daily swim. And even then all the children effectively overlooked him, my mother and Sadie being intimately involved in shared imaginary worlds the way girl children sometimes are, and Harry and Rupert being enough older that they swam in deeper waters and dove from more alarmingly high rocks. So mostly Stan, the child my uncle was then, was at loose ends, watching from a respectful distance as Tom talked with a clutch of adult men loitering at the edge of an orchard about the development and subtleties of varieties of apples. It must have seemed to Stanley as if the burning of the barn had been an adolescent rite of passage for Tom, after which he'd been invited, without hesitation, to join in the mysteries and ceremonies of adulthood.

Both my mother and her brother were frightened of their own taciturn father, though they always tried to please him because they loved him and courted his good opinion. There were various chores, for example, that Stanley in particular would be required to perform, and my mother said that he would throw himself into any task with enthusiasm, only to be told by his father that there were worms in the bushel of apples he had picked or that the wood he

73

had stacked made an uneven and therefore dangerous pile. With the exception of reading and composition, he did not excel in school (though my mother did) and this, too, rankled. At harvest time, he tired quickly and often froze on the upper rungs of a ladder. My mother remembered him clutching a branch and weeping while their father baited him, in full earshot of the workers, from his own safe position on the ground. "You're twelve years old," he would shout, "and you're behaving like a six-year-old girl." My grandfather would turn away then, in feigned disgust, leaving Stanley with apples and leaves and in full terror of what my mother claimed was hardly a life-threatening distance between him and the earth. It was she who crept out to the orchard at dusk after the other pickers had left in order to coax him down, rung by rung. There was always something in her that made her want to protect her brother, to actively defend him if necessary. She would continue to coax him down from dangerous heights many years later when he had begun to embrace rather than avoid the fear, the vertigo.

My mother recalled her brother's quietness on the journey back to Canada, how he turned his face toward the car window and the passing farms beyond it or the way he stood at the rail on the ferry and looked down at the frothing water. She remembered his expression as being almost adult in its preoccupation, a look she had seen on their father's face when he had been worried about weather or the price of a bushel of apples, or even (because he was essentially a kind man) when he had been concerned about a neighbour who was sick or who had a problem that needed solving. Now this absorption was visible on her brother's face and in his posture, and she was puzzled by this.

Two nights later, back on the north side of the lake and sleeping in her own familiar bed, she said she was awakened by the sound of men shouting. On her ceiling, a wash of orange and yellow was shifting and intensifying, draining down the wall. When she ran to kneel in front of the low window of her room, she could see cars and trucks, lit by an amber glow, already parked in the yard or coming up the lane, and although the barn was not visible from her room, she knew what had happened and who had made it happen. "And I also knew," she told me, "why he had made it happen."

The following morning, after the barn was gone and the fire was no longer dangerous enough to need constant attention, my grandfather took off his belt and whipped poor Stanley, who had been hoping, my mother knew, for the balm of consolation. Afterwards the boy had gone silently, without tears, to his room, had stayed there all day and night. The next day, he had departed silently for school. She followed him, giving him the distance she sensed his pride might need, and wincing when he stiffened with pain. Neither the boy nor his father ever spoke about the incident, even when the burnt rubble that had once been the barn was being dragged away, but something had altered forever in their relationship. As if the punishment had distanced him enough to provide a clear view of the older man's character, Stanley was able to see a flaw in his father – "A crack in the cup," my mother said – and that flaw made his parent more human and, strangely, easier to love. Stanley's grades improved and he lost his fear of his father. "It vanished completely," my mother said. "Gone, as if it had never been there. And he could do anything he wanted after that, just stared my father down in the face of objections. There was this purposefulness about him, and I could see he was changing, becoming someone else."

Years later, my mother's American cousin, Sadie, now married to my Uncle Stan, would create a flourishing rose garden inside the remaining walls of the burned barn's fieldstone foundations. Eventually, because it would not be needed for either storage or workhorses and was deemed to be unsuitable for conversion into housing for the labourers, the new barn, which had been built in the wake of the fire, was pulled down. Aunt Sadie announced that she was pleased because to her mind the proportions of that building were all wrong and did nothing for the property. But what my mother remembered was how confident her brother had been on the ladder in the weeks following the fire when he and his father were working on the construction of that barn, without, as she said, a hint of tension between them.

Was this the moment then when my uncle's charisma was born and began to grow? A quiet child, inclined to be plump, he became, as my mother described him, a handsome charmer in young adult-hood. Every woman from five to fifty was drawn to him, and there were moments when he was seeing half a dozen girls at one time. Teachers sometimes boarded at the farm, and there was one, I believe, with whom he became physically involved, though the exact details of all that were never clear to my mother, who was most of the time a bit put off by the females who mooned around her favourite brother. Then came the summer when the beautiful and distant Sadie was sent from the other side of the lake in order to remove her from the influence of some undesirable whom she had taken a fancy to.

At first she was sulky and withdrawn, my mother recalled, barely leaving the room that Mandy and I would sleep in during our summers and that she, Sadie, shared with the girl who would later become my mother. If she noticed Stanley or his brother, Harold, or any of their friends, she showed no signs of this. And perhaps it was this very indifference that caused my uncle to react to her so power-fully. When she had been at the farm barely a week, he stopped going to the dance pavilion on the weekends, and by the time two weeks had passed, it was difficult to persuade him to leave the farm for any reason, even if he was offered unlimited use of the car. As if Sadie's presence in the house had brought back to him everything that had made him so uncertain and timid in his childhood, his former silence returned. Occasionally, however, he would break out of this into what my mother called "downright silliness", joking and throwing his weight around until one parent or the other would tell him to stop. At mealtimes he either stared at Sadie or looked resolutely at his plate, his expression pained, angry.

My mother admitted that she had been jealous of Sadie at the time. Her American store-bought clothes, her perfect skin and hair, the movie magazines that were hers and that anyone had to ask permission to look at. She was envious as well of the effect she had on both of the brothers because Harold, too, was not immune to Sadie's charms, though not as disturbed by them as Stanley. It would be Harold who would successfully tease their American cousin out of her sullenness, cause her to participate, usually by baiting her in a cheerful sort of way. "'Went out last night to take a little round,'" he would sing. "'I met my little Sadie and I blowed her down.'" Or he would call her Sadie Hawkins in reference to the spinster who chased bachelors in the *L'il Abner* comic strip. "Well, Sadie Hawkins," he would say at breakfast, "I can tell by the look of you that you're after chasing me today. I'd better start running."

This had a certain effect on my mother's cousin, at least caused her to make eye contact, though in a truculent sort of way. It wasn't until Harold threw a pailful of cold water through an open window while she was quietly doing the dinner dishes – "my parents expected her to help with various household chores," said my mother – a splash of water meant to wake her up – that she fully responded, flinging the damp cloth against the screen and racketing out the door to chase him as he had predicted she would. Stan, who was coming out of the field with the family's few remaining cows, witnessed the end of the chase, his brother and Sadie rolling together on the lawn. Her tanned legs kicking, her blonde hair tangled, his brother laughing as she beat her small wet fists against his chest.

Two days later Stanley enlisted, walking the thirty miles to the Canadian Forces Base at Windsor. He spoke to no one, told no one where he was going. "Just disappeared in the night," was the way my mother put it. It was the early 1960s, there was no war, at least not one that involved our country, so there was nothing romantic or heroic about this gesture and, when they were finally informed, his parents saw his sudden departure as a practical employment decision rather than an act of desperation. Sadie, on the other hand, having paid next to no attention to Stanley when he was present, became almost immediately obsessed by his absence. This, after all, took place at a time when young men in her own country were departing in significant numbers for the war in Vietnam. He was subsequently posted to Maritime Command in Halifax on Canada's East Coast, training, he suggested, as some kind of engineer. He would be there for four years.

As soon as she had an address Sadie began to write letters to him, an activity she continued until the end of his service. These letters remain in the house, and I confess that I have read some of them. Being a chronicle of how her high schooling was unfolding and later of the design courses she was taking at the college of interior decoration, there was nothing in them that could be confused with romance. But it would have been the fact of those letters, arriving punctually, first at Windsor Army Base in Ontario, and then later at CFB Halifax, Nova Scotia, that would have made a man with Stanley's imagination invent the affection that, as far as I could tell, was not really in them. Later he would inform my mother that he had slept with those letters under his pillow and had kept one or two close to his heart when he worked on the ships that I was later to learn he never sailed on. Those letters signed *Love, your cousin Sadie*. Those prosaic letters, and a glimpse of her rolling on the lawn with his prosaic brother, her connection to the ordinary, reinstated his confidence. When he strutted home again, miraculously mature and ready to take over the farm, it was her to whom he was returning, and he began, almost immediately, to make frequent trips to the other side of the lake. They were married three months later.

"He still in uniform, she in a perfectly designed white satin dress," my mother told me as she fumbled in a drawer searching for the wedding photo. "I know it is here somewhere," she said, moving her hand through letters and cards and some old snapshots of me as a child. I allowed her to do this even though I knew the picture was still in this house and not in her room at the Golden Field. My uncle's marriage had collapsed. No use looking for it anywhere.

When I tell you this story now, it does nothing but confirm my belief in the arbitrariness and frailty of the way human families are engendered; how pivotal, for example, the forgotten "undesirable" young American boy or a pailful of water thrown through the window are to the establishment of the seemingly stable world that I myself walked into each summer as a child. What, I often wonder, would have taken place if my uncle had not decided to join the armed forces? Even though his enlistment, looked at in the cold light of day, was mundane, and the activities attached to it – he was, it turns out, a riveter – boring and endlessly repetitive, it determined almost everything that would later happen in the family. It was just a simple departure: there was no glorious cause to espouse, no sacrifice to make. But perhaps you feel differently than I do about causes and sacrifice, being so fully involved at this time in a cause more mysterious and deadly than anything I have ever encountered.

Mandy, to my knowledge, never thought much about her father's stint in the peacetime military, though of course she knew it had taken place. There was that wedding photo, after all: a man in uniform marrying a woman who could not pay any attention to him until he disappeared.

What we are drawn to and what we turn away from are equal, I think, in their power over our bodies and our minds and seem, to me at least, to be equally determining of what becomes of us. A farm boy evolving into a soldier causes a girl to turn the light of her attention from one brother to another. He moves away from her, then she moves toward him, and the whole summer world as I would come to know it is seeded in those shifts of mood and location. A young Mexican in a foreign country panics in the face of violence butting up against adult fear, and he and passion are removed forever from my life. Thrown off course by a sudden shift of the wind, a butterfly will never reach its intended destination. It will die in flight, without mating, and the exquisite possibilities it carries in its cells and in the thrall of its migration will simply never come to pass.

A few nights ago the Coast Guard's airborne search-and-rescue team was conducting training exercises about a mile offshore. Large cadmium-orange discs, designed to illuminate a sizeable expanse of open water, floated slowly down toward the lake, causing parallel gold paths to appear on the lake's skin as if there were a series of autumn moons reflecting there. Were it not for the slowness of their descent, these ovals would seem almost celebratory: a variant of fireworks. *Feu d'artifice*, as the French would say. Artificial fire.

Fire has always been a part of our family's story – there was that barn my uncle burned, of course – but it was a significant factor in the settlement of this flat, prairie-like landscape, here in the southern part of the province as well. My uncle said that the earliest settlers, our own great-greats among them, were so overwhelmed by the sheer number of hardwood trees, and the tremendous size of those trees, that rather than continue to cut them down themselves, or hire choppers, they set acres of forest on fire. As far away as the then small settlement of Chicago across the lake, people apparently saw the glow in the northern sky and knew it was the burning of

Essex County. My mother often talks about seeing an orange stain in the night sky in the 1960s and being told that Detroit had been set on fire in the midst of civil unrest. And Mandy, poor Mandy, would never fully recover from the "friendly fire" that had dropped from an American war plane on a platoon of recently arrived Canadian troops in Afghanistan, killing six of her colleagues.

Certainly, the nighttime exercises I witnessed the other evening were not as charged with meaning as those I have just mentioned, and yet how sad and stately the orbs of light seemed. Their appearance was like a rehearsal of tragedy with just a hint of possible redemption trembling at the edge. They have nothing to do with migration, of course, but I couldn't help but think of the weaker monarchs that, exhausted by the effort of crossing the lake, are drawn down from the sky and into the waves. And I couldn't help but think of Mandy either, Mandy and her father.

Not long after things fell apart, Mandy decided she wanted to become a search-and-rescue specialist and enrolled in night classes at a nearby college while she was still in high school. The courses she took had names like Managing the Lost Person or Lost Person Behaviour, and young though I was, I was not unaware, all things considered, of the significance of this. I was fighting with my own loss at the time and had turned inward, having neither the maturity nor the confidence to do anything else with my grief. Back in the city, my mother and I carried on with the routine of our lives, and now and then Mandy and her mother and brothers visited. Most of the time the boys slouched morosely near a television set with some kind of game scrabbling across its screen until it was time for bed, while Mandy and I withdrew to the room, my city bedroom, which we were to share for the night.

It was during one of those visits that Mandy told me what she intended to do in the future. "A peacekeeper," she said, adding that it was difficult to get into military college, though more possible now for girls because of affirmative action. She looked downwards as she spoke, thinking aloud, only now and then glancing in my direction, as if she had just remembered I was there. This sort of introspection, even when she spoke, had been a part of her ever since that summer night. Mandy, the girl who in the past was so certain in her gestures, her stance, now talked quietly – if at all – and rarely made eye contact. Her posture had changed as well: she kept her head down, almost slunk through a room, and she had begun to wear large, ungainly garments that hid her hips and breasts without extinguishing either the extraordinary beauty that was her birthright or the physical strength she had acquired by swimming all summer in the lake and all winter in her high-school pool. It seems to me now that she was in the chrysalis phase, hiding behind the subtle anger that was evident in her attitude and posture and wrapped up in those clothes.

I asked about this "affirmative action" I had never heard of, and she said it had something to do with enabling girls and women to do the things they had never been encouraged to do before. The search-and-rescue courses were just the beginning, she told me. They would look good on her application, though her academic marks would have to be very high as well. Her mother was in favour of this notion probably, Mandy conjectured, because entrance to

84

the officer training program would place her in the midst of the well-bred, good-looking, and intelligent young men who had always filled the halls of that historic institution. But Mandy was having none of that. According to her, she intended to outrun, outmarch, and outmanoeuvre these boys at every pass. She would study harder and train longer. She reminded me that she had read more books than they could even imagine and then rolled up her sleeve to show me the small, tight muscle on her upper arm. She was surprised, she said, that I had not started to think about my own future and a bit shocked that I wasn't familiar with the term *affirmative action*. You're the city girl, she said, looking fully into my face for the first time. I thought, I still think, she was suggesting that that fact alone should give me some connection to a more vital and therefore more comforting life. I looked around my room. It was the place where I spent most of my time now. The city had become a distant hum, the soft noise of the world going on without me.

All the time Mandy was talking I envisioned her in a long line of volunteers, walking through the fields of her farm, beating back thick grass, searching for and eventually rescuing her father. Then I imagined her making peace between her father and mother, though exactly how she would achieve the latter, or the former for that matter, never came fully into focus. But then her future role in the military never came into focus either, at least for me. Beyond the echo of my uncle's own short-lived experience at Maritime Command in Halifax, there was nothing solidly military anywhere near me – or near her.

What about the poetry? I asked her. She had always kept secret notebooks in which, she had once confessed, she tried to write poetry. And then there were all those books. A volume by a man called William Carlos Williams was on the night table on her side of the bed. I remember thinking it was odd that the name Carlos, which felt Mexican to me, would be bracketed by those two Williams.

Search-and-rescue is perfect for poetry, she said with what I now see as a surprising amount of insight. Think of it as a metaphor.

I mean, at the military college I thought you wanted to do an English degree. I simply could not imagine her fully absorbed by what I believed to be the banal world of army manoeuvres. But you could do anything, everything there, she told me. The college granted arts degrees, just like any other kind of university. She would be able to study the poets while she sought-and-rescued and kept the peace.

I was sitting on the chair in front of my desk with my back to my homework. I was about to enter dangerous territory.

"Do you really think you're going to find your father?" It was a brutal thing to ask, but I had been carrying brutality with me for the last six months and I needed to ask it.

She was silent for some time, her face closed and her eyes averted. "No," she eventually said. "A lost person must in some way or another choose rescue." This phrase, potent under the circumstances, was one she was no doubt quoting from some course or another, but it sounded to me like my own limited idea of poetry.

"He doesn't want us to find him," she said bitterly. "I just know it. He doesn't even want us to look for him." She was on the very edge of tears, but I knew she wouldn't allow herself that comfort. She straightened her spine instead, lifted her head, and looked out my window at the grey city street. "I never want to see him again," she said.

She was my cousin, practically my sister. She was the only person whom I had ever shared a room with. I knew her sleeping patterns, how she held a book in her hands, the order in which she put on her clothes: her socks, then underwear, a T-shirt, jeans. I had been there for her first period, her first bra. And I had been there earlier when we were both losing our baby teeth. I knew how she wriggled into a swimsuit. I had been in and out of the lake a thousand times with her, and I knew what she looked like when she had been in the lake too long, her lips blue and her shoulders quivering. I knew her moods, her romantic and poetic side, and something else in her that was a combination of pride and stubbornness, a recipe that would later evolve into what I saw as ambition.

"Mom hates him," she added, and then after a pause, "I do too."

I got up from the chair and walked toward the door, having neither the nerve nor the heart to carry the conversation any further. I knew her very, very well. And I knew that she was lying. But at the time, when I told her I hated him too, I still honestly believed that I was telling myself the truth.

About a month ago, driving over to the sanctuary, I saw two farmers standing like phantoms in a lane beside a pickup truck that was parked near a large, badly maintained barn. With their heads bent, their caps pulled down over their foreheads, they seemed to be absorbed in a matter of great importance to them. Perhaps they were cementing an agreement regarding an animal or a delivery of hay. Or maybe they were discussing the barn itself, arranging for its demolition, because I suddenly saw the structure for what it was: a colossal sagging monument from another era, as ancient and shaggy as an extinct beast. It was so out of place in the midst of what was developing around it – a gravel pit on one side of the road, the beginnings of a subdivision on the other – it could have been a Roman granary, a stage set based on a medieval drawing, or some kind of huge wooden freighter from earlier times that had found itself inexplicably moored near the twenty-first-century asphalt of a secondary highway.

Our family had had problems with barns long before my uncle set fire to the one whose foundations would contain the remnants of my aunt's rose garden. As my uncle would have it, that barn, which he never admitted to burning, was merely a replacement for a more splendid, more capacious, and more beautiful barn destroyed in the nineteenth century as a result, he said, of covetousness. The first Canadian Butler had built a log barn for his animals, quite early in the game, after migrating from the American side of the lake, even before he constructed the log house. What else could he do? my uncle used to say. The place was rotten with wilderness, trees and vines, and undergrowth. Mostly swamp, he said, animals up to their fetlocks in muskeg. Had to get something up fast or nobody, animal or human, would have survived the winter. Loyalty to the Crown so far had brought him nothing but heartache and labour and dead children. He didn't want to lose the animals as well.

Time passed, a reasonably spacious log house had been built, and the barn made of logs began to seem too small. By then my great-great-grandfather had four strong sons to help him clear trees and plant essential crops. He also had a wagon and a horse so that he could take his grain to be ground at the nearest grist mill some ten miles away. A terrible journey, my uncle claimed, the tracks nothing but mud and boulders. A sledge on the frozen roads of winter would have made the voyage much easier, but in winter, of course, there was no grain to be ground, so the mud and boulders of the warmer seasons had to be conquered. Many things were shipped by water on the great lake so close to my ancestor's door, but the grist mill was deep inland, situated, as it had to be, on a fast-flowing stream. There was a lot of grain because of the hard work completed by him and his sons, and there was a vast quantity of straw, and it wasn't long before the old man began to long for a real barn in which to store it all, a barn made of hewn beams and sawed lumber. Had he been able to afford the lumber, this would have involved another series of difficult journeys to a saw mill, also located inland on another fast-flowing stream.

His neighbour was the son of an original Upper Canadian settler; the family had been in the vicinity for two generations. Their crops were healthier, their house was bigger, and they had what my uncle called a "real beaut" of a barn built on a foundation made up of a quantity of fieldstones that had been removed from the acreage over the past thirty years. Great-great used to look across the two fields that separated them, at the neighbour's barn, and wonder if he would live long enough to have one of his own, concluding, sadly, that this wasn't likely going to be the case. On certain days, when he was able to take a small vacation from the endless work that filled his waking hours, he would walk across the two fields to talk to his neighbour about the building of barns and the acquiring of sawn lumber, and during one of those visits the neighbour announced that he was selling out and opening a harness shop in the village that was beginning to grow, albeit in a ragged fashion, two miles to the north.

Great-great bought the barn, my uncle told us, by trading the two fine workhorses he had raised from colts, angering his sons because they knew they would now have to manage with only the two elder parents of these young beasts. And there was another problem: my ancestor had not bought the land the building stood on, intending, as he announced, to move the barn to a foundation he would build with the fieldstones so prevalent on his own property.

More laborious effort ensued. A sledgelike vehicle, something called a stone boat, was used, I think. And when the foundation was ready, the wooden structure of the barn had to be moved across the fields on log rollers by the animals with the aid of something called a capstan. A kind of architectural drunkenness took place as the structure swayed precariously in the dips and hollows of the meadow or stood, obstinately refusing to be moved, when it rolled into a rut. Things could have been worse: the project had been undertaken in late August so the ground was as dry as it was ever going to be, and eventually the barn reached its destination. Then, of course, winches had to be devised and used to lift the structure onto its new foundation, and mortar had to be mixed and applied to cement it into place, all this going on while the women of the house hauled tables and chairs and buckets of food outside to feed the men once the job was completed. My uncle was a little vague on the details of the winching, but he gave a precise picture of the menu of the feast: roast turkeys and chickens and ducks, turnips and potatoes and cabbages, twenty-four loaves of fresh-baked bread, thirty apple pies, and thirty jugs of cider – one for each man – made from the farm's first apples. Much chanting of Protestant prayers, and much singing of Protestant hymns, and general good fellowship occurred at this banquet. The barn, firmly situated and looming over the celebrants, looked as if it had always been there, "as if it had grown there," my uncle was fond of saying.

The next day, Old Great-great and his sons filled the barn with grain and straw and led the two aged horses into the stalls. "When your barn is well filled, all safe and secure / Be thankful to God and remember the poor," my uncle always recited at this point with a knowing irony in his voice. The men hung harnesses on wall hooks and carved their initials on the rafters. The younger sons leapt from various heights into the straw of the hay mow, and cats from the house were coaxed into taking up residence in the barn to discourage mice. The few iron implements they owned, a couple of spades and a plough, which until that moment had been rusting either out of doors or in the damp of the log barn, were brought into shelter. In spite of extreme Protestantism, a barn dance was planned by the older sons and sanctioned by their father, who was anxious for these sons to court and marry and, most important, to mate in order to produce more young males.

Now weather enters the story, as it always seems to do whenever a story involves the great-greats. There followed two days of excruciating heat and "crippling" humidity and a lot of talk about how fortunate it was that this heat and humidity had not been part of the barn's relocation. And on the evening of the fourth day, just before sundown, a magenta cloud – unlike anything anyone had ever seen – crawled over the eastern horizon, trailing a powerful windstorm in its wake. Old Great-great enjoyed only a few moments of gratitude for the barn's shelter before the building exploded and then vanished as if it had never been there. No one in the vicinity knew much about tornados, but almost everyone had heard rumours concerning the wrath of God. They went through the list of sins in their minds and eventually concluded that it was the sin of covetousness that had brought this wrath down upon the family. To the end of his days, however, the old man himself believed that it was the sanctioning of the barn dance that had brought about the building's destruction, and, consequently, none of the subsequent Butlers were permitted to attend even the most innocent of dances. Not until my mother and uncle's generation was the ban lifted. Old Great-great never again allowed the word *dance* to be spoken in his presence. And, just to be safe, he never again coveted anything, as far as anyone could tell.

One of the horses in the barn had been killed outright. The other, however, was found the next morning calmly grazing in a neighbour's pasture, five fields away, with no gates open between him and the place where he was last known to be. And the only fragment of the barn that remained in Old Great-great's custody was the one board that had crashed through his kitchen window and that had his own initials freshly carved into its surface. The board was kept in the family attic; Great-great's descendants must have been superstitious about discarding it. My uncle hauled it down from there one evening after telling the story, hauled it down and nailed it up above the fireplace. He did this in spite of my aunt's protestations – even she did not have the power to stop him once an idea of this nature had firmly lodged itself in his mind. He wanted, I now think, to change the status of the old board to that of a holy relic. But you could feel the will draining out of him as he searched for nails and for the struts in the wall in which to pound them. In the end the whole act became faintly ridiculous, embarrassing those of us who had been ordered to stay in place until the ceremony was over. It took too long and was too fraught with ordinary difficulty to qualify as a mythic gesture. The ancestral initials were all but invisible to the naked eye, and my aunt's disapproval was palpable in the air. When he had finished, my uncle looked at his audience as if he were going to say something we would all be required to remember. Then he turned back to the fireplace and removed the flakes of plaster his hammering had scattered all over the mantel, pushing them, quite carefully, with one hand into the cup of the other. "I've made a mess," he said, maybe to himself, maybe to my aunt. Then he closed his fist around the fragments and left the room.

"He wanted to be called an orchardist," my mother once said. "As the years passed, your uncle was never entirely comfortable with the term 'farmer', at least in relation to himself."

The view from her windows at the Golden Field, as I've said, was one of strip malls and row housing, neither fields nor orchards in sight in either direction. On this winter day, however, it was difficult to determine the shape of the landscape at all because the wind had come up and the atmosphere was thick with blowing snow.

"Sadie, you see, was always trying to get him to understand that what he was doing had more to do with science than with ordinary labour."

Yes, I thought, he had consistently described his activities in a botanical, chemical, or sometimes even an aesthetic manner: soil chemistry, blossom-to-fruit ratio, the transfer of cells after grafting, the sinuous line of branch growth after pruning. It was up to my aunt to take care of the practical, and the financial details, tasks she undertook with enthusiasm and ultimate success. She was herself ambitious: also not fond of the word *farmer* and all that it implied. But neither of them was able to come up with a substitute for the word *farm* and used it, unconsciously, all the time, unless one or the other was fed up with something or engaged in an argument, at which point the farm became "this place" or sometimes "this godforsaken place". Years later Mandy would hear this phrase in a country thousands of miles away. What kind of inner echo would that have caused in her, on that hot, dusty military base? Would she connect her parents, this farm, to the man who spoke the words?

The farm, of course, ground to a halt and faster than you might think as soon as my uncle was gone. The decade immediately following his disappearance was perhaps the oddest of the past twenty years, though none of those years seemed to have any kind of structure regardless of the way life insisted that regular maintenance take place, that new clothes and cosmetics and toothbrushes be purchased, and that various repairs be made to windows, faucets, roofs, cars. As I've said, sections of the waterfront property were sold off as estate lots. Large, ungainly houses were built by people neither my aunt nor my mother – nor I for that matter – ever came to know. I can see none of these houses from my windows as the farmhouse is situated midpoint on the shoreline of a small bay and the homes in question are located on the other side of what we, as children, called the Old Wharf. Sometimes this pleases me, as I like the isolation of the spot, that sense – entirely an illusion now – that I am alone on the shores of the great lake. At other moments, though, when I feel myself being absorbed into the past, I wish I had the ability to become part of a neighbourhood, as my mother hoped I would; had the knowledge of how one leans over a back fence to discuss the goings-on in a village or township, or even to participate with some interest and enthusiasm in the art of gossip.

Sometimes I feel the past will eat me alive, will devour me in the same way that the now abundantly overgrown cedar bush is devouring the pioneer rail fences on which, as children, we used to stand in order to watch the Mexicans work. I fear I will become one of those women you sometimes see buying groceries in town, unkempt, vaguely mad, barely present, and talking quietly to herself as she pushes the cart in a bewildered fashion toward the vegetable section, a woman not unlike the woman my aunt was in her last years.

"I wonder why he insisted on the term 'orchardist'," my mother continued, still thinking about my uncle. "He wasn't really a snob, you understand. Everyone he knew was a farmer. Everyone had a farm of some kind or another." She glanced at the clock on the wall. It was nearing lunchtime. "Either that or they did something on the lake. The trout was wonderful, you know, when we could still eat it. And then there was the shipping."

If you look at our small bay, you will see that its eastern arm is made up of boulders and mature willow trees. One of the old great-greats had a sizeable wharf built there so that he might ship his own apples across the lake to the markets in Cleveland, or Akron. But I doubt that any of my unseen neighbours, looking at it from the opposite side, think of it as anything other than a natural phenomenon, like the western arm, a series of limestone slabs pushing out into the lake, which we called Little Point.

When we were children, Teo and I constructed our paper boats on Little Point and set them afloat in the shallow water. I can recall the feel of the cool water on my ankles and the smooth stone beneath my feet, Teo's laughter, him teaching me the words *barco* – boat – and *naufragio*.

"Do you remember Teo and me playing with boats at Little Point?" I asked my mother now. "He used the word *naufragio* whenever one of our paper boats capsized."

She was still looking at the clock on the wall. She said nothing.

Strangely, that was the word my uncle had used. *Naufragio*, he had whispered, his voice broken. And though it had been several years since Teo and I had stood at Little Point folding my other uncle's auction posters into ephemeral watercraft, and though I had heard no one, neither my uncle nor Teo, utter the word since, I knew it was, at that moment, the only thing that anyone could or should say. The word *naufragio* uttered inside a temporary room, a half-finished bottle of wine resting on the kitchen table.

Since I have begun to read some of Mandy's poetry books, I have come across a translation of the Chilean poet Neruda's poem "La Canción Desesperada". In it the noun *naufragio* is used in such an angry, sorrowful way it becomes almost a verb. The poem itself is so full of blazing lighthouses and wharfs, islands and shorelines, departures and abandonment, it defines both our family and the geography of that night for me so precisely, that it tore into me and remained inside me, fully memorized almost the first time that I read it in English. I know, also, the dark inevitability of that truthful line: "*Todo en ti fue naufragio*." In the book on Mandy's shelf it is translated as "In you everything sank." But I prefer my own translation: "In you everything shipwrecked."

Our uncle told us stories of shipwrecks and other nautical miracles and disasters; tales of drowned sailors, men turning into seals, and mermaids emerging from the sea. He told these stories over and over on this farm until we half believed that all of these tragedies and transformations had taken place at the end of the lawn in the great lake water that shone there. The landscape of childhood is so limited and, in our case, was so beautiful we could think of no better combination of water and land where these tales should unfold. He told us stories of howling gales during which the courageous Butler keepers would successfully light the thousands of candles in the huge glass jewel-like lamp on the top of their towers. He told us about treasures coming in with the tide after such gales: diamonds and doubloons, leg irons minus the legs, a complete guillotine, intact, ballgowns without the dancers, canisters filled with tea, the leaves still dry, a cat and her kittens (alive!), and barrels of rum, whiskey, sherry, absinthe, port, Madeira, red, white, and rosé wine. After these sessions we would scramble down to the beach, returning later with pails of lake-worn glass, so colourful, but, like his stories, in the end so useless. Yet we instinctively knew, I suspect, that they were all that remained, years later, after an event where everything shatters: harmless, softened shards of cargo smashed and then smoothed by storms, they were forgotten evidence of a spectacular series of wrecks.

But there was one seminal Butler story, which was dark and

seldom told and all the more fascinating to us. My uncle was adamant in his refusal to tell the tale on demand, yet could not be dissuaded from insisting that we all listen when he felt the moment was right for the telling, that moment almost always occurring at a Butler funeral after which he had consumed a fair quantity of alcohol. The older Butler relatives, you see, were scattered like wildflowers all over the fields on both sides of the lake, living out their declining years in frame houses that, like the elders themselves, were in various states of dignified decay. After their funerals, all of the Butlers would gather either at this farm or at its double across the water, depending on the citizenship of the deceased. I don't remember hearing the tale on the American farm, however, so it must have occurred to my uncle only in the wake of Canadian Butler deaths.

It was the kind of story that moved steadily toward its conclusion, then paused and circled back to begin again in the manner of certain gloomy sonatas. And it was a story that, because of its references to steep rocks and ancient history and magnificent weather and strange architecture, we were unable to place in our own calm landscape. It seemed therefore quite reasonable to us that the setting for the narrative should be Ireland, the country the Butlers had abandoned. Also, it involved the death of children. Not one of us believed that a young life could be violently severed in a place as safe and settled as ours. Though our graveyards were filled with nineteenth-century girls and boys, we in the twentieth were, or at least we thought we were, exempt from catastrophic surprises. The Butlers we were familiar with aged quietly along with their houses, then died sedately and politely just before harvest.

"Do you remember the story of the Irish children at the lighthouse?"

My mother eagerly answered this question. "Oh yes," she said. "Indeed I do. It was Stanley's favourite, I think, though he would only tell it when he was good and ready to."

The first in the litany of lighthouses, or at least the first according to my not always accurate uncle, was situated on one of the two Skellig Islands that rise like temples from the sea off the most western tip of the south of Ireland. Everything about this lighthouse was improbable and exaggerated: its elevated position, the constant rain, the near impossibility of its construction, or of even landing boats filled with building materials on the island, the tortuous climb up the cliffs carrying cut stone, wrought iron, and glass. And then there was the monstrous wind that would pluck workers, as if they were insects, from the rising tower and throw them either onto the rocks below or into the sea from which their bodies were never recovered.

But there had been a precedent for this astounding feat of engineering. During the sixth century, on the highest peak of the landward side of the island, a small group of self-punishing monks had set up a colony. Surely, my uncle had said, the first generation of these holy men would have been entirely worn out and used up in the task of carving the steps for the three separate staircases, one of six hundred steps, out of the steep rockface that led to their monastic enclosure: a gathering of a half-dozen corbelled, beehive-shaped huts, a small medieval priory, an oratory, two wells, and some stone basins dug out of the same rockface to collect rainwater. There was also, of course, a graveyard, consisting of a half-dozen rough stone crosses.

My uncle took great pleasure at the thought of his forebear, Tim Butler, the one he named the dog after, making tea from the water he collected from the monks' stone basins. No mention at all was made, however, of his wife, who was undoubtedly washing clothes, bathing babies, cooking or cleaning with the water he called "the heavenly gift". To this day, when I think of the man the people of Kerry called Butler the Keeper, I imagine a family subsisting on tea while unimaginable winds roared around them. The supply boat from Port Magee would rarely, if ever, be able to land, and the ghosts of the first generation of monks would undoubtedly be blowing around the tower, sackcloths flapping and bones rattling in the gale.

Every second year, a mainland keeper would offer to take up the post so that Keeper Butler and his family could get back to Butler's Court for Christmas, and each time the second year came around, the weather would cancel that possibility with winds of increasing velocity. And Keeper Butler would have wanted to get back, I would think, hoping to stake out at least a bit of symbolic territory in that quite possibly fictional place because, as my uncle said, only one son could inherit the land and Keeper Butler was not that son. He was the bifurcating one.

Even as a child I remember thinking that I had been genetically affected by the serial division among my ancestors. The entirety of my early life was bisected by seasons. In the autumn, winter, and spring, my mother and I lived in the city, in the modest, square brick house that my father had bought and thankfully paid for before he died. But my true sense of home and belonging was activated only in summer when my mother and I settled into this farmhouse. I wonder now whether Butler the Light (a name given to Keeper Butler by the fishermen of Kerry) would have been visited by this same sense of belonging had he been able to "get off the rock" and return, even briefly, to the green fields of Butler's Court? Or was he fully owned by the sea and the wind and perhaps also by the phantom monks?

What eventually liberated him from this ownership, if indeed it existed, was a string of escalating tragedies of such dimension that no man or woman could possibly retain a sense of duty, never mind a fondness for the environment that was responsible for causing them.

First, the light that Keeper Butler had so faithfully kept burning was smashed by a two-hundred-foot rogue wave just at the moment when he had finished climbing the tower's hundred steps to inspect it. A hailstorm of glass shards descended on him and entered his flesh wherever it could, as well as his hair, his tongue and gums, and one bright eye from which he was never able to see again. Fortunately, the layers of wool and oilcloth that were required for warmth, or even for survival, on the island prevented the penetration of vital organs, and he was able to stumble back down the stairs and into the arms of his terrified wife, who spent the next two days plucking splinters from his head and mouth and hands.

A new light was duly and without doubt riskily delivered

and installed, and Butler the Eye, as the mainlanders now called him, returned to his duties. By now he had two sons, children so frequently storm-stayed inside the keeper's cottage that they would cry to be outdoors the minute the wind abated even marginally or when a stray shaft of sunlight broke through the clouds. Six and eight years old, they played most often in the one small startlingly green meadow called Christ's Saddle, which the monks a thousand years before had probably made by hand with layers and layers of seaweed in order to support a cow, a donkey, and a goat, and which, surrounded by sloping rock, provided as much outdoor shelter as could be hoped for on the island. How did they play? What kind of island games were invented by them? These were the kinds of questions my uncle would ask us when we were bored or whining for some new toy or for the television. "C'mon," he would say, "those kids out on the Skelligs had absolutely no toys, and weather was their only television." The weather indeed! What kind of unusual games did absorb them, I wonder, before they heard the extreme howl of the fatal wind that tossed them both out of that man-made meadow and into the waves below? "Like coins into a fountain," my uncle said, relishing the metaphor.

But they were not tossed so far that their bodies were unrecoverable, and poor Butler the Eye found his sons bumping up against the shore the following day as he made a frantic tour of the island. First one – the eight-year-old, my uncle said, making the story more precise than it needed to be – and then the other. Only a hundred yards apart, they seemed unharmed, their bodies free of mutilation, their eyes staring.

Both children were buried in the monks' graveyard, the ground of which had not been opened for centuries, and after the burial Keeper Butler wrote a letter to the Commissioners of Irish Lights, requesting a transfer to the mainland. This transfer was accomplished and Butler the Eye lived long enough to father two more sons, who, like their father, became lighthouse-keepers: one on the tamer and much larger Kerry Island of Valentia, the other on the relatively serene east coast of Ireland. The son of the Valentia resident would, in turn, become the American keeper who eventually migrated far enough north to staff the lighthouse at what is now called Sanctuary Point.

But for me, the story, thrilling as it was, really began with the burial of those island boys in the monks' graveyard. As a child I developed the theory, though this was never suggested by my uncle, that those children would have become ghosts almost immediately in such surroundings and that they would have been instructed in the rights and obligations of the spirit world by their neighbours, the shades of the monks. I imagined, or tried to imagine, what shape their conversations might take and whether as ghosts the whole company might be affected by the wind. Sometimes I still dream of flapping sackcloth and shards of glass.

Once, during that last summer, I told Teo the story of Keeper Butler. He listened intently, then said that, although he couldn't remember hearing it, he somehow already knew the story of the two drowned boys and the community of monks who had settled there so long ago. At the time I wondered if there might have been a Mexican lighthouse with a similar story attached to it. But now I realize that my uncle's stories took paths we never knew about and were repeated in rooms we would never see, heard like a dream whispered uncertainly on the edge of sleep, used, perhaps, to buy time or affection. Is there anyone alive who remembers these tales? I now wonder. Shane and Don and I have never spoken of them. Is this recounting to be their eventual destination? Perhaps you will tell them to someone, sometime, and they, in turn, will tell someone else.

———

My uncle, I have now come to understand, rehearsed his own final desertion almost every year. At the end of summer, when the final bushels of harvested apples had been shipped and the last of the Mexicans had been bussed to the cargo terminal at the airport, my uncle would simply disappear – sometimes for two or three days, sometimes for a week – with no one telling us where he had gone or why – if they knew themselves. My aunt would call my mother, and we would return to the farm for a subdued weekend, the mothers talking quietly just out of earshot and completely silent when we, the children, were in their midst. Anxious telephone calls would be made. Sometimes my aunt, always so intractable, would alarm us with utterly uncharacteristic weeping, more, it seemed, in anger than in sorrow.

It was always a disturbing and transitional time. The birds from the sanctuary were beginning to migrate; chevron after chevron appeared over the lake, heading south. The only crop that remained to be harvested was the faintly ridiculous yet fascinating pumpkin. I had already begun my life of school and after-school lessons. Teo was gone. His mother and the other Mexicans were gone. And then my uncle was gone as well, though, until that last time, he would always make a dramatic reappearance, after which my mother and I returned once again to the city.

Once, when we had all become teenagers (I was about fourteen at the time), my uncle stunned us by driving the Volvo at full speed into the quiet warmth and slanting light of the autumn afternoon. He motored straight into the white wooden garage and out the other side. The tasteful board-and-batten construction, with its period windows and flower boxes full of chrysanthemums, snapped apart, became airborne, some of it landing on the veranda roof, the rest of it scattering all over the yard. And then there was the lacerated car steaming near the lake, and my uncle sitting calmly in the driver's seat. To our amazement, delight, and relief, he kicked open the metal door, struggled to his feet, and walked out onto the beach. There he sat quite carefully down on the rocks, removed his jacket, folded it into a pillow, and, placing it behind his head, lay down and went to sleep. To my mind, this was a brilliant re-entry, and my impulse was to run to his side to both minister to him and to congratulate him.

But my aunt swept by me and got to him first, so I knew better than to make an approach. I stood watching as she pulled him up to a seated position by his hair, using words I wouldn't have thought an adult had any knowledge of, and then shook him by the shoulders – all this going on while his head jerked back and forth on his neck. He was completely unresponsive; everything about him was so absent from the physicality of the argument it was as if he were a bundle of loose cloth, a puppet rather than a human being. After only a few seconds, she abruptly stopped, let go of him, stood, and walked back toward the house, where my mother waited on the other side of the screen door. My uncle fell back on the beach stones like a dropped rag, and for a moment or two, until he moved one leg, I was worried that he might actually be dead. A few hours later, once it was dark, my mother went out to him. I could hear the sound of their voices through the open window of the room I shared with Mandy but not what they said. Soon we would go back to the city. But for now my mother was once again coaxing my uncle down from his ladder of anxiety and despair.

"Poor Stanley," she said that winter day, looking out the window as if she might catch a glimpse of him wandering aimlessly near the convenience store. "I'm sure he never meant –" The lunch bell rang then, interrupting her sentence. I walked with her as far as the dining room and continued down the hall and out the door.

During the course of that period I've already told you about, when my mother and my aunt occasionally lived alone together in this farmhouse, they were not, I now realize, nearly as old as I thought they were. I was an undergraduate, then graduate student, and eventually a lecturer at the university in the city during this time, so almost everyone in my daily life – professors notwithstanding – was young and walking steadily toward some eventual future or other. My mother was only just emerging from her fifties, and my aunt, her second cousin, as you remember, was in her early sixties, but it was simply impossible to envisage any kind of changed future for them. Day after day, they occupied this house like two elderly ladies from a previous era: thin, prim, sedately dressed in tweeds and sensible shoes, using the good family china and silverware at each meal, preoccupied by the cleaning and polishing of objects from the past, the same objects, as you can see, that surround me now.

They had few callers. The people in the town didn't quite know what to make of them, and Aunt Sadie's boys, professionals by now, had drifted to the coasts of this country and rarely visited. Instead of visitors, the women we called "the mothers" had their little tours of duty. My own mother worked two days a week in a charity shop, and, until it became impossible for her to do so, my aunt sometimes drove elderly people to medical appointments. But they made no real connections this way. My other uncle and aunt would ask them for Sunday dinner now and then, until that uncle stepped down for the last time from his auctioneer's box, sold his collection of tin toys and cigar-store Indians for a good price, and moved with his wife to Florida.

Mandy, who was enrolled at the Royal Military College and was later posted to Petawawa, was not so far away, and very occasionally would stop by for the afternoon – though she never stayed the night. She once told me she hated going home. I didn't ask why because we both knew the answer to that question, and it wasn't something we could easily speak of the way that, a few years later, we could talk about the man she had met and the anguish he was causing her. So, in the early years, I was put in the position of making the obligatory visits, arriving three or four weekends a year – sometimes with a boyfriend in tow – and dutifully appearing, alone, at holiday time. During these occasions we would sit right here at this beautiful old dining-room table and talk about nothing at all except my work as an entomologist, which my mother could never completely understand but was nevertheless curious about. My uncle's name came up very rarely, and when it did, my aunt, who by then had completely lost her intractability, would begin a sentence and then trail off as if there were nothing at all she could state with any certainty. "Stanley always said that there were more insects near the . . . oh I don't know," or "When Stanley and

I were first married, we would sometimes, well, not often, no, not even sometimes . . . there was one time, perhaps." Then she would look through the window and out over the lake or rise and start to clear dishes from the table. Sometimes my uncle figured as the subject of a question that was never completed, never mind answered. "I wonder why Stanley built those fences so far from . . . ?" I refused to utter his name during those years because I was still convinced that I hated him. My mother, on the other hand, kept a framed picture of him as a very young man on her bedside table, along with a photo of my father, a fact I noted but never commented on.

All the other images had been put away, including the framed aerial shots of the farm in its heyday when the Mexicans still came each summer. I was not unhappy with this: memory was not my friend, even though I was so young. I now believe that memory is rarely a friend to anyone. Always attended by transience and loss, often by anguish, the very notion that the elderly spend their days wrapped in the comfort of pleasant mental journeys into the past is simply absurd, in spite of what my mother wants to pretend when I visit her. Perhaps, after all, it was better to be my aunt, who was officially divorced from memory before her death, than it is to be my mother staring out the window at a parking lot, trying to puzzle out the riddle of all that was lost.

And yet, while my mother and my aunt still lived here, and in spite of my reticence, there was something mildly consoling to me about returning to an intimately known place situated on a lake so large that the shore of the lake itself, and therefore the place where you stood, was visible on a map of the world in a way a city street could never be. Comforting as well were the rituals my mother and my aunt still participated in, attending to all the Butler graves in anticipation of Decoration Day at the town cemetery, for instance, both of them being blood Butlers by birth, and myself as well, I suppose.

That graveyard! There they all were, the antecedents who were heroes of my uncle's legends, the old farmers, and the old lighthouse-keepers, all the great-greats and the ones who were once or twice removed and therefore vaguer to me, though, remembering the stories, no less interesting. The ones who went to the Klondike, the ones who went to the wars. The ones who died in childbirth, though they were surprisingly few, leading my mother to announce that the women in this family were strong and healthy, a statement that would seem ironic when it was recalled a couple of years later at my aunt's funeral. The ones who died in farming accidents, and logging accidents, or as the result of an incident with a horse. The small curved stones of the many Butler children who died in the early years following the migration from the south after the American War of Independence. Flowers were planted and placed at all these graves. My uncle wasn't there, of course, so we brought with us no flowers for him. And once, only once, during that period did my mother bring this sad fact to our attention, though without using his name. "He can't be buried anywhere else," she said. "Everyone was always brought home."

"You mean you think he is still alive?" He had been dead to me for years. Completely gone.

"Yes, of course. He would be brought here, if he were dead."

"And how exactly would that happen? No one knows where he is. And," I added, "no one wants to know."

I could see that my mother was close to tears, but nothing in me was willing to relent. "He is my brother," she said. "I want to know."

My mother was silent then.

"Do you have any idea what bringing him back would do? What are you *thinking*?"

"He is my blood and . . ." She stopped speaking, sensing the approach of my aunt.

I walked angrily away from them both. As far as I was concerned at the time, my uncle had lost his citizenship in the ancestral geography. He had given up the luxury of being able to claim an easily identifiable place for himself on a map of the world, and I wanted even the memory of him erased. Dead or alive, there would never be any flowers for him, not if I could help it. Nor any legends either. I wanted nothing to do with the kind of custody the past enforces on those who continue to remember. And yet, here I am, all these years later, talking to you, detailing history, solidifying legends. Day after day, I allow myself to be taken into custody, my life an anachronism lived in the vicinity of that chair, this table, the polished walnut of Old Great-great's important-looking desk.

My mother sometimes talks about this dining table where we are sitting; its superiority to the functional tables at which she is forced to eat at the Golden Field. "It was brought by water from Ohio," she tells me, "to the wharf, along with all the other furniture. Interestingly, the good dishes in the house had to be ordered twice because a November storm sank the ship carrying the original set."

I remember the china shards that we as children so often found along the shore. Their numbers have diminished in recent years. I think of all the tableware and glassware that, during the previous century, must have sunk down to the bottom of the lake only to be broken apart by seasonal storms, then tumbled, softened by the company of stones.

Sometimes around four o'clock on a late-fall afternoon, the grey, leafless trees beyond the window become black silhouettes against the backdrop of lake and sky, and there is a bruise, purple and strange, on the horizon, a lake-effect snowstorm, I expect, though the day will only now and then show evidence of the famous and deadly squalls of November. Each time I look out this window, the season surprises me. I have overwintered for two years at this place, which as a child I believed was where only summer lived, and still I cannot fully accept the slow, darkening onset of winter.

I recently read a diary I kept when I was nine years old during one of my city winters: a litany of piano lessons and ballet recitals, sessions of skating in city parks with children whose faces I have completely forgotten, and tests administered by teachers whose names I barely recognized now. How could so much of my life have meant so little to me? The only vivid memories cling to the summer territory of this farm and the past that built it.

I have one very clear memory concerning a school lesson, but even that connects with my summer life. We were studying the Aztecs and then the Spanish invasions in social studies, reading from an illustrated book entitled *The Explorers*. The heroic explorers, looking like circus performers in their brightly coloured tights, striped bloomers, and silver armour, often met a sad end at the hands of "the natives", who were, it seemed, consistently ungrateful for the word of God and the European flags the explorers had taken great trouble to bring to their shores. There were maps in the book, and among them was a map of Mexico, twisting like a funnel cloud at the end of British North America. I knew that this country was where Teo lived when it wasn't summer, but I never once associated him with the ungrateful natives.

———

We were in and out of the house and in and out of the lake all day long in the summer, always running, often together and joined by a gaggle of my cousins' friends, the screen door banging behind us and driving the mothers mad. Fly swatters were handed out to us before dinner each evening – a red one for me, blue for Mandy, dirty white for Don, and yellow for Shane – because, as the adults reasoned, we were the ones who let the flies in and should therefore assume the responsibility of getting rid of them. All these sounds I recall from the end of the day: the bang of a door, the slap of a fly swatter, the churning noise of the great lake negotiating with the shore, the footsteps of the Mexican workers on the gravel path leading to the bunkhouses, adult voices, the clink of ice filling a tumbler.

One summer afternoon, Mandy and I – about ten and twelve at the time – burst noisily into the silent house, looking for our swimsuits. This was during a time when the mothers were visiting Aunt Sadie's family on what I, having been there once or twice myself, thought of as our twin farm in the state of Ohio, and we and Mandy's brothers were left, therefore, in the somewhat abstract care of my uncle. We hardly noticed him as we hurried through the living room, he was sitting so quietly at the varnished walnut desk that had belonged to his father, and his father's father before that. But as we were running past him on the return trip, he intercepted us, holding up an old brown school scribbler in his hand.

"Stop right there," he shouted, though we were only a few feet away. "Stop!" he commanded. "Look!" he said, holding the notebook aloft. "Listen!" We knew we could not object, though the day was hot and we had found and put on our suits and longed to be in the lake. This may not have been the first time I'd seen him like this, but I do not remember previous episodes, only the conviction, strongly felt, that I did not wish to provoke him by stating our case.

"Mandy," he said, "you like poetry." He waved the book back and forth in a faintly menacing way, as if he were going to toss it over his left shoulder. "This is your goddamned great-grandfather's poetry I have here," he said, a belligerent tone in his voice, "and I'm going to read you his goddamned poems."

I doubted the existence of such poems but was instinctively fearful of this side of my uncle. I wanted out but dared not move. Mandy stood beside me, tense with apprehension and interruption, as if quivering on the edge of flight, a towel hanging from her arm.

He pushed his chair back and began to read aloud in a slow,

deliberate voice. "'Milkers and milking,'" he began after a meaningful pause.

> Milkers should be kind
> Neat and clean, milk rapidly
> Systematically, regularly

He looked at us to make certain we were paying attention. Then he continued.

> The udder is filled with veins
> Arteries, fat and flesh
> The periods for feeding cows
> May be divided in two
> Winter. Summer.

He looked at us again, distrustfully, over the top of his reading glasses. I could feel myself wanting to giggle at the word *udder* and sensed Mandy would share the impulse. I determined not to make eye contact with her and looked instead at my uncle, resentment rising in me for reasons I barely understood. And yet, and yet, cutting right through the resentment and the fear of his bewildering anger toward us was a slender, taut thread of love that was tied to him and whatever his anger was trying to express. There were tears in his eyes. I hoped, and I knew that Mandy hoped, he would put down the book and come back to us, but, even though we were just children, we were aware this wouldn't happen. Not yet.

He began again, in a subdued fashion, and less declaratively, as if he had forgotten his audience, though we knew better. "'Dairy stables should be light-filled, well ventilated, have tight floors, comfortable stalls, and should be handy to work in. There should be two rows of cows facing each other for company.'" He looked toward the ceiling. "Christ!" he said. "For company!" He looked down again at the book. "'The stable should be wide, with a place overhead for hay and straw, meal bins within reach, a silo and a root cellar nearby. The tether, if needed, should be as comfortable as possible, and mangers should be cleaned out daily.'" He was reflected in the glass of the nearby door that led to the porch as well as in the mirror on the opposite wall, as if there were three uncles in the room. Why do I remember this, these ghost images of him?

"Christ!" he said again. "Who uses the word 'manger' now?"

"Baby Jesus," Mandy offered.

He ignored her. "Or the word 'tether'," he continued. "Who talks of stables?" He brought his fist down on the desk, causing both Mandy and me to jump nervously. "One cow!" he shouted. "One cow could produce three hundred pounds of butter!" His voice softened. "'Guernsey, Jersey,'" he recited solemnly, then, "How many pounds, Amanda?"

"Three hundred," she said uncertainly. Her answer was barely audible.

My uncle pushed his chair back, his hands on the armrests as if he were going to spring into action. "Speak up!" he commanded. "Enunciate!"

"Three hundred." Mandy could not control the quaver in her voice.

"All right," he sighed as he sank back into the chair. Turning from us, he began to fumble in the pigeonholes of that old dark desk. We could see the flask, but he was having trouble finding it, and we wouldn't have considered giving him directions of any nature. "Ah well," he said, his hand finally coming to rest on the beaten silver container that also likely belonged to his grandfather or his great-grandfather. "And what do we keep in that godforsaken wood lot out back?" He gestured vaguely to the north with the hand that held the flask.

"Holsteins," said Mandy. "Three of them."

"Who milks them? Who writes poetry about them?"

Mandy and I were silent. I suspected there was no right answer to this question.

"Who the *hell* milks them?"

"Nobody," whispered Mandy.

"Exactly." He waved us away. "Write your own poetry then, swim in your own lake!"

The argument in him had mercifully collapsed, and we knew we could get out of the house if we did so quietly. We did not look at each other as we moved toward the door in which he was reflected, as if both of us were ashamed of something we had done or were about to do. "Swim in your own lake!" we heard him call from the house as we silently crossed the grass toward the beach, towels hanging limply in our hands.

By dinnertime he was jovial, playful, inclusive, cooking wieners and beans over a fire on the beach, insistent afterward on somersaults and cartwheels in the yard, games of tag, badminton, baseball in the twilight with Teo ferreted out of the bunkhouse to participate, and Teo's mother encouraged to observe the goings-on. A few other Mexicans, whose names we never troubled to learn, would stand on the fringes at times like this, their bodies as muscular and sturdy as alert engines, primed for labour and waiting to be put into gear.

Teo's mother, Dolores, was taller than most of the men she worked with but only slightly, and like them she was made of smooth firm flesh; no part of her body moved independently when she walked, as I had noticed my own mother's did. And when she stepped up behind her son and draped her arms over his shoulders and across his chest, those arms looked to me like polished wood or some other solid matter, completely unlike the soft freckled flesh on the arms of my mother and my aunt. I believed then that everything about her was other, though she spoke our language well and operated as a kind of messenger between the bunkhouses and the farmhouse, the fields and the gardens. Teo, at least, had the fact of being a child in common with my cousins and me and therefore inhabited a space I could partially understand. But she, his mother, walked alone. I don't recall her ever laughing, for instance, though now and then, looking at her son, a slow smile transformed her face, and that, combined with the angle at which she held her head at such times, made her almost beautiful. Once, standing in the kitchen preparing a picnic of peanut butter and jam sandwiches to take to our fort, I asked Mandy where Teo's father was. "He doesn't have a father," she told me while pouring water into a plastic pitcher containing the pink powder that would magically transform into raspberry Kool-Aid. She glanced at me to gauge my reaction, her expression, for a fleeting moment, not unlike her mother's. "Just like you," she added. Though I was somewhat stung by what she said, we were soon too busy in our playhouse to think about parents at all.

But those twilight games! My uncle was an enthusiastic participant, a joyous collaborator. Somewhere in this house I have the photos: all of the cousins and sometimes the boys from the neighbouring farms, my Uncle Stan, Teo, and occasionally my other uncle frozen in gestures of anticipation or avoidance, bracing for a blow, it would seem, or an attack, or stretching and opening up to receive an airborne object into their arms. Everyone's concentration in these pictures is so fierce, it is impossible to believe that whatever was coming toward us was not life-changing, profound, or at the very least much more meaningful than a simple ball thrown in play. The yard was as huge and significant as a battlefield – it would never look that large again – the lake surprisingly less important than the earth until, near dark, we crashed into the water for the evening swim, which was followed by flannelette on cool skin and a sleep so deep we would be unaware of the presence or the absence of adults in the many rooms of this house.

A week ago last Sunday I passed by the walnut desk where my uncle had intercepted Mandy and me all those years ago. It was a clear day. The low winter sun plunged through the windows facing the lake and crossed each object in the room at such an oblique angle details normally invisible insisted on being noticed; dust, for example, and the places here and there where my sleeve had, unknown to me, brushed dust aside. And there, on the wooden surface of that desk, pressed into the soft wood, were hundreds of incised words, the residue of sentences written on what must have been thin, single sheets of paper. I found the magnifying glass my aunt had sometimes used for identifying the manufacturer's marks on a certain piece of pressed glass, and later used for reading fine print, and began a tour of the wide polished board that was the flat top of the desk, hoping to find ancient family history until I realized that only a ballpoint pen would require the kind of pressure that would leave such a mark. The sentences overlapped and latticed one another in ways that made the words impossible to decipher, except for two fragments, written in my uncle's awkward backhand script. "What I mean to say . . ." one truncated sentence began, and then another, the phrase "farther than everything", followed by a jumble of superimposed loops and swirls in an unfamiliar hand, and then his hand again, and one word: "winter". How like him, I thought, unfairly, I suppose, how like my summer uncle to leave behind only a partial record of a cold season. He was *farther than everything*. He was completely beyond my understanding.

By the time of my tenth or eleventh summer, Teo and I had developed an unspoken, intermittent alliance and sometimes broke away from the others in order to be on our own. I see now, that even in the midst of a gang of children, there was an undefined yet quietly understood apartness about us. We were the same age, which united us in a way. But there was more to it than that. Arriving each summer as we did from somewhere else, and then departing again at the end of the season, we were migratory in nature, the differences in our migrations being those of direction and distance and the fact that while I was away from "home", I was still in what could be called my natural habitat. Teo, on the other hand, had landed in unfamiliar territory, a temporary and artificial location, one where, in the not too distant future, he would be required to join the adults working in the fields and orchards, rather than continue to play with me. And yet, in spite of his obvious dislocation, to my mind he was so firmly planted on that summer farm, I simply couldn't imagine him in any other place. He never joined us in the car when my mother took us into town for ice cream or pop, or when Aunt Sadie went to my other uncle's auctions. It was only my uncle who would invite him to come along on expeditions, and those were infrequent because Uncle Stanley was fully occupied by this place in summer and hardly ever went shopping in any season.

Because Teo's English was not yet fluent (and because it had never been suggested that it would be a good thing if I learned Spanish), most of our games involved elaborate gesture, and I came to love both the silences and the signals he and I sent each other. I was an only child and, when in the city, a bit of a loner as well. I could play quietly for hours and with great concentration, and there were times when I would be, at least mentally, quite absent from my surroundings. And although I also loved the sense of belonging that blossomed in the company of my cousins, bouts of mute, episodic imaginings were something I could ease into without appearing to entirely break away from the world. Sometimes when Teo and I played together, he was almost like an imaginary friend.

Now and then there would be a silent agreement between us to withdraw well back of the orchards (where, toward the end of summer, his mother could be seen working with the other Mexicans) to the forested acreage my grandfather and great-grandfather would have called the wood lot. Those former patriarchs had both timbered and maintained the trees on that property but, by the time Teo and I were exploring it, my uncle had pretty much let it go back to bush. Had it not been for those three Holsteins it might have been impossible to enter without hacking out some sort of trail. But, as it had been opened up by grazing cattle, Teo and I were able to look for things there, a jack-in-the-pulpit, mushrooms, tree fungi, puffballs. Earlier in the summer we searched the remaining abandoned meadows for the monarchs' cocoons, which hung from the milkweed plants in those ignored acreages.

On occasion we played on the edges of the stream, which we called our river and which meandered through the wood lot toward the lake. One whole summer, I remember, we occupied ourselves by making islands – miniature feats of engineering that required us to cart boulders and branches into the water, then to cement them together with quantities of dripping mud dug out of the creek bed. We worked silently, side by side, on these projects, then toward the end of the afternoon sat on the mossy bank admiring our creations. To stop the paper boats we had made from escaping too quickly, dams were built in roughly the same manner, as wharfs were at various points upstream. The water always reclaimed the results of our efforts but sometimes not until a day or two had passed. Then, undiscouraged, we would either reconstruct the frail, ruined remains or begin something new.

The whole process became an unstoppable fascination for us. The materials were always close at hand, as were the curious small brown trout, nosing around the obstacles we placed in their path in an unconcerned fashion, as if appreciative of the reorganization of their waterway. Paper boats were folded and launched from one of the miniature islands. There was something strangely compelling about all this attention to arteries of water that lived in such close proximity to a lake so huge in proportion. We both knew the streams we played in were fatally drawn to the lake and would shortly be engulfed by it. Making the dams and islands that prevented or at least slowed down this process, both for the water and our boats, I sometimes felt like a benign giant engaged in a doomed rescue mission.

None of the other children was as interested in the wood lot as Teo and I were, and because we were among the youngest of the group, they were likely just as happy not to have us around all the time. And, besides, the boys had not yet become comfortable with Teo's presence among us – a presence my uncle insisted upon and put emphatically in place. I remember him saying angrily to Don and Shane that Teo was a kid, just like the rest of us. When the language issue was brought up, my uncle yelled at the boys, "Who cares about Spanish or English. Just start running! That's what kids do, for God's sake, they run! They don't sit around having intellectual discussions."

Unknown to my uncle, there had been one particularly cruel incident during the first summer that Teo and I had begun to explore the wood lot. A complicated game of hide-and-seek had been developing all day among the boys: my cousins and a couple of their friends. It had already lasted for hours and seemed to be driven by that very compulsion to run that my uncle had referred to. There was no need for explanation. The assumption that this childhood activity based on hunting, camouflage, and stealth would be instinctively and universally known proved to be true, at least in Teo's case, and he joined joyfully in the searches.

Mandy and I were on the porch, washing our dolls' clothes in an old galvanized tub loaned to us by my aunt in advance of her painting it white and filling it with geraniums. We had also strung a

clothesline from a porch pillar to a nearby tree and several miniature dresses flapped like pennants in the breeze coming in from
the lake. Mandy was fully absorbed by suds and cotton, but I was
distracted by the boys who had come from neighbouring farms to
join my cousins. Not having brothers of my own, it was always in
me during those summers to wonder what those boys were thinking, how they arranged their days among themselves, what led to
their ability to cooperate, to be of one mind, moving in a group
from one part of the yard to another like a small army, with Teo
hovering nearby, just out of range. That particular morning I saw
Teo's face become alert with pleasure when it was explained to
him, through single words and various hand signals, that it was
his turn to hide. He must have liked the notion that he would be
looked for, that he would have a turn at being the centre of things.
Hiding would make him dynamic and essential.

I watched him slip between two cedars and disappear into the
woods we knew so well while Don and Shane and the other boys
faced one another and counted to one hundred, then two hundred,
then three, chanting the numbers aloud, "two hundred and *one*,
two hundred and *two* . . ." Finally they broke ranks, turned away,
and walked quite casually around to the other side of the house
where I couldn't see them. Soon, however, I heard the crack of a
ball hitting a bat, then shouting and laughter.

The anxiety I began to experience mounted in intensity each
time I heard the smack of the wood connecting with the skin of
the ball. There was no yellow cotton doll's dress, edged in blue
piping and floating in warm suds, that could remove me from the

suspicion moving like a finger up my spine. Maybe they were just giving him a better chance, I thought, more time to find the perfect hiding place, an opportunity to win the game. But then once again the brutal sound of an oaken bat smacking leather, and laughter and even clapping reached me. Why were they not looking for him? "Aren't they going to *look* for him?" I asked Mandy. "Shouldn't they look for him *now*?"

"Who?" she said, her hands twisting damp cloth, and then remembering, "Oh . . . I don't know. It doesn't matter." The boys she lived with every day apparently didn't interest her. Neither did their friends. "Stupid boys," she said absently.

He'll come back, I thought. He'll come back and try to reach home base before being tagged. But a boy I didn't know, one slightly older than the rest, was sitting at the foot of the designated tree reading a comic book. He was there, I realized, for the purpose of preventing that small victory from ever taking place.

An hour or so after lunch I finally went out alone to look for him. The boys and Mandy were swimming and the neighbouring boys had ridden their bicycles home to various chores. Shane shouted my name from the lake and my mother turned in her deck chair to look at me, confusion on her face. "Raspberries," I called to her as I walked away, forgetting that I had no pail. If she noticed this, she made no indication of it and waved me away with her hand.

The forest floor was punctuated with small boulders, likely left there when the larger, older great lake had pulled inward to become the stable basin on the edges of which our family lived and farmed and played. I knew the wood lot so well by then the bark of several trees was as familiar to me as houses on a residential street. I followed the paths the Holsteins had made from one part of the forest to another, calling Teo's name. I looked under juniper and sumac bushes. There was no answer, no sound at all except that of the wind in the tops of the few remaining big hardwood trees and the soft noise of branches brushing my sleeves. Occasionally, these branches were connected to the wild raspberry bushes I was supposed to be looking for and I would have to disentangle my clothing from their barbs. This impeded my progress and made me anxious. It occurred to me that I might die if I didn't find Teo, if he were lost. Not that he would die from being lost, but that I would die from losing him, and even then, at ten or eleven years of age, I recall thinking how strange, inappropriate, and desperate that feeling was. Then, instinctively, I knew he was nearby.

He was hidden in a spot I had passed three times without noticing, leaning against the trunk of a Jack pine whose lower branches almost touched the ground and provided concealment. His arms were folded one atop the other and were placed on his knees, which he had drawn up toward his chest. His dark head was resting on his arms and, at first, I thought he was asleep. But he wasn't asleep, and when I crawled under the branches to reach him he lifted his head and looked at me with such innocence and such sorrow. Never again would I see such a pure expression of either of these states. His small brown hands were clenched, and a line of dried tears on each cheek made it clear that he had been crying. Even his boots, side by side on the ochre-coloured pine needles, looked sorrow-laden to me.

"It doesn't matter," I said, quoting Mandy. Drops of sunlight fell like rain through the trees and onto his shoulders. The breeze shook the branches over his head.

"*Abandonado*," he said.

I knew the word *abandoned*. My mother had used it quite recently in relation to three kittens we had found in a ditch when we were walking down the Sanctuary Line looking for wildflowers. Until this moment I had thought those kittens were the unhappiest things I could imagine. And I knew the word *humane* because that was the name of the society to which we had taken the kittens. There was nothing humane on that particular day about my boy cousins and their friends.

"I think they forgot," I said, wishing it were true, knowing it wasn't.

He wouldn't look at me. His humiliation was palpable. "*Me aparté*," he said.

"No," I said. And when he didn't reply, "Okay then, me too. *Me aparté* too."

Why is it that everything freezes right there and I can't remember how we got out of the wood lot and back into our lives? I would have been called in to supper on the sun porch of the house, and Teo would have veered off in the direction of the bunkhouses; it had to have been so, but I remember nothing of our return. When I think of that day, there exists in my mind the insane belief that if I walked out the door right now and over to the wood lot, and if I searched hard enough and long enough in those woods, if I followed the paths made by the Holsteins, I would find those two children crouching under that Jack pine, and that when I found them I would be able to make everything turn out differently. Mandy would still be splashing in the lake with her brothers, her blonde hair a nimbus around her head. Teo and I would be building dams in our river, and he would be free from the notion that no one wanted him. My uncle would have been planning the harvest of peaches, or walking through the grassy orchard examining the growth of McIntosh apples. But it is almost impossible to get into those woods now. The Holsteins have been gone for years, and scrub brush has obscured the paths. Are the creeks still being pulled toward the lake? Do the small brown trout still twitch in the watery shadows? And the children, if they are still there, are they able to go home?

As I've told you, my uncle loved to talk about the bifurcating lighthouse-keepers of our family, those who kept the "lights" of Ireland, as well as the later nineteenth-century American Butler keepers, as he called them, in spite of the fact that the most significant member of their ranks had ultimately migrated to Canada and settled not at all far from the farm on which the tales were told. "Born American," he would say, if anyone dared to correct this detail, "came here only in defeat." My mother, having sat beside her brother while the previous generation's adults told these stories during the course of her own childhood, still maintains the belief that American lighthouses were bigger and better than their Canadian counterparts, whiter, brighter, their lamps travelling further into a storm, more successful, and the keepers, except for one notable exception, more dependable. The Irish-American Butler farmers had similar gifts, apparently. They were taller, stronger, had better horses, more sons, endured fewer crop failures, built more attractive houses, and stuck to their guns, literally and figuratively. They had a prosperous and rewarding nineteenth century, their lives unfolding near calmer waters or on richer soil, already well established while their brothers, the Upper Canadian Butlers, chopped wood and dug wells and threw up hastily built dwellings. "Except for our beautiful stone house," she would add, "built by my great-great-grandfather, who, though foolish in his allegiances," meaning his loyalty to the Crown, "at least had some sense when it came to housing his family."

There is hardly anything left of the nineteenth century now on the north side of the lake. The remaining barns in our township have been reduced to skeletons; you can see their graceful beams and rafters, the gaping spaces that would have been their wide entrance doors, and sometimes a last load of hay in a sagging mow, placed there years ago by a farmer who either lost heart or died or both. Occasionally an oxen yoke can be seen fastened between two upright boards, or a harness hanging from a nail on what would have been a stall. These old essentials, of no use now except as objects of curiosity, seem almost to have become part of the decaying structure simply because they have not been moved or touched for so long. Most of the old frame houses have been replaced by newer models, or torn down and not replaced at all, their foundations ploughed under the huge fields of factory farms. Other, smaller fields go back to bush if they are of no use to the agro-industry, or if they have not caught the eye of a developer. And in the villages, shops and stores, still vital in my own childhood, have either become boutiques or pizza outlets or have no life at all, their windows boarded, the signs above their doors fading.

What remains is a network of roads brought into being two hundred years ago by the land baron Colonel Talbot and a surveyor called Mahon Burwell, whom Talbot hired to complete the task. Burwell tramped through the bush with his crew and his instruments and provided the territory then known as the Essex-Kent District with three distinct roads and hundreds of more or less well-ordered plots for settlers, who, in return for the deed to their land, were required to build the concession roads that fronted their farms. The concessions, which run in an east–west direction, are – like the frontage of the plots they define – 1.25 miles apart, moving inland from the north shore of Lake Erie, or the front as it was then called (as if it were an unsettled weather pattern, which, indeed, it sometimes is). Moving at right angles to the concessions are the lines, named for the places to which they lead or after the early settlers who farmed the original acreages and who fill the graveyards scattered here and there at intersections. The road running two fields back of this farm is called Concession One, but the one heading toward the lake is called Butler's Line or Butler's Sideroad, depending on who you are talking to. It wasn't until 1930, when the birdlife on the Point, five miles to the east, was deemed worthy of preservation that the name of the old Point Road was changed to Sanctuary Line.

My great-great-uncle Gerald Butler, having left the southern States in what my uncle called "a paroxysm of shame", would have ridden down old Point Road to reach his new post, and there were some interesting tales associated with his tenure there. But it was the story of why he chose to leave America that my uncle told, more than once, probably because, as he once stated, the Butlers were in love with both irony and tragedy.

The two remaining sons of Butler the Eye, discouraged, apparently, by the poverty and misery of the sparsely populated post-famine world of County Kerry, had set out from Tralee to seek their fortunes in the New World. The crossing had been difficult enough that by the time they landed in New York, they had survived homesickness, near starvation, ship cholera, and a series of such wicked storms on the open sea, their fear of weather, originally engendered by the knowledge of the fate of their siblings, was increased a hundredfold. One of the brothers, my great-great-grandfather, would eventually depart for Upper Canada, where he had heard there was good land to be had on the shores of Lake Erie. Another, a great-great-uncle who, like my cousin, was called Shane, had stayed on similar and as it turned out better land on the south shore of the same lake, where he settled and established the American Butler line. The third, Gerald, had decided to pursue his father's calling. Knowing the south of the continent was warm, he believed it must also be calm, and so, in spite of his reluctance to face the fury of the elements, he accepted a post as assistant keeper of the light at Mosquito Inlet in Florida. He was not to be principal keeper (that position was held by a fellow Irishman with an increasing wealth of children) but a keeper nonetheless who would, on occasion, be fully responsible for maintaining the light while the principal keeper took time off to deal with the demands of family life.

Gerald was a reader, and, had been encouraged in this activity by the Church of Ireland pastor on Valentia Island, a literary man who wrote poetry and had a sizeable library, which he was happy to share with any young person interested in books. The bloodlust and romance of Walter Scott's novels particularly appealed to Gerald – he was very fond of *The Heart of Midlothian* – as did the eccentricities of the characters invented by Charles Dickens. For a while in his teens he was drawn to Trollope, especially to those novels set in Ireland. But by the time he sailed, he was deeply affected by the tales of James Fenimore Cooper's Leatherstocking series and by the – mostly imagined – Aboriginal and colonial world this series revealed to him, page by page.

"Reading was the perfect pastime for a lighthouse-keeper," my uncle always told us. A book could be easily held in one hand – a lantern was likely in the other – and the stories it contained would cut the boredom of the long hours at the post. When Gerald finally settled in at Mosquito Inlet Lighthouse, therefore, he was pleased by his discovery that the tower he would spend so much time climbing and descending had been designed by one Frances Hopkinson Smith, an artist, engineer, and author of such titles as *Old Lines in New Black and White*, *Well-Worn Roads*, and *A White Umbrella in Mexico*. As I've already said, Gerald had acquainted himself with American literature and, while on board that grim ship on which he travelled to the New World, he had been engrossed in the stories of Washington Irving, coming to love Rip Van Winkle for his solitariness and his aversion to wives, qualities that Gerald himself shared.

Women utterly terrified him, my uncle said, unless they were characters in books. Over the years he had been briefly in love with Scott's Flora McIvor, Green Mantle, Rachel Geddes, and Rose

Flammock, and also with Estella from *Great Expectations*, Nancy from *Oliver Twist*, and for a moment or two after his mother's death with Peggotty from *David Copperfield*.

So, after he settled himself into the routine at Mosquito Inlet, he began to read American literature in earnest, subscribing to *Scribner's Magazine* once he had heard of it and ordering as many books as his salary would allow.

Reading the magazine he became familiar with the works of Lee Bacon, Charles G.D. Roberts, W.H. Henderson, who wrote about the sea, and the small poem "Parting" by Emily Dickinson, with whom he fell briefly in love. He came to adore the magazine and was distracted from it only by his reading and rereading of Melville's *Moby-Dick*. Tales concerning the sea were a kind of home to Gerald, spending, as he had, countless hours looking over its surface toward the horizon and countless other hours, before he came to Florida, huddled against the chill of its squalls in a corner near a turf-burning stove.

In 1897, after Gerald had been in Florida for about a year, Principal Keeper O'Brien decided to take a ten-day leave at Christmas in order to visit some relatives in Georgia, and my great-great-uncle was left in full charge of the light and all the other duties associated with it. Having been a principal keeper on Valentia in Ireland, Gerald Butler knew these duties well. In addition to ensuring the light was lit, he would be required to be on constant lookout, to make use of Morse code communications if there was anything to report, to make weather observations and report the same in a log, to start the fog alarm on misty nights, and finally, if necessary, to call upon rescue services and, upon occasion, provide sanctuary.

He was fully engrossed in *Moby-Dick* at the time, had entered its territory in every way that it is possible to enter the territory of a book. "Amanda! What are the four ways that a person can enter a book?" my uncle would often ask at this juncture. "Emotionally, aesthetically, intellectually, and philosophically," she would dutifully recite. "Gerald," my uncle would continue, "had come to that stage of rereading where it becomes possible to identify certain feelings simply by seeing the shape a remembered paragraph made on a page." And, yet, apparently, he was still able to be surprised, even shocked, by something Ahab said, or even by a fractional gesture made by a minor character. He had become very interested in pastimes of whalers and had even begun a few scrimshaw projects of his own. He thought deeply about "The Whiteness of the Whale" and "The Spirit-Spout" chapters. He had come, therefore, to a stage where the fictional sea seemed more thrilling and interesting than the actual sea that he should have been examining but often wasn't. He reasoned, I suppose, that these January days and nights in Florida were so utterly calm, a cursory glance now and then away from the page toward the horizon would be all that was needed. The waves were breaking half a mile or so from shore as they almost always did, and it seemed to him the winds were gentle and constant, certainly in comparison with any wind that had visited Ireland, and indeed much lighter than those that pounded the *Pequod* on various pages.

He was delighted by his literary discoveries, which were

becoming those of one well read, although in a somewhat haphazard fashion. He noted, for example, that the first paragraph of "The Counterpane" chapter brought to mind two of Robert Louis Stevenson's poems for children, "The Land of Counterpane" and "Bed in Summer", and he wondered if Stevenson had read *Moby-Dick* and whether that reading might have affected his subject matter. He thought that the community on board the *Pequod* was not unlike that of the soldiers whom he had encountered in Stephen Crane's *The Red Badge of Courage*, which he had devoured on arrival in America because he wanted to know more about that country's civil war, but also because the book had compelled him to devour it. Sometimes, in spite of the fact that he was alone, he experienced the camaraderie of the crew as if it were going about its business in the room where he read, and he felt the sway of the ship beneath his chair. When he had spoken to no one for over a week, he began to believe that he knew more about life aboard a whaling vessel than he did about life inside a cylindrical tower.

Eventually, Principal Keeper O'Brien returned, his loud and noisy family along with him. Gerald Butler enjoyed the children and was not entirely indifferent to Mrs. O'Brien's meals. Moby-Dick, though not entirely absent from his thoughts, became more ephemeral and ghostly. The children's squabbles and their competitive games, the chaotic dinners and boisterous mornings, had brought him back to dry land.

But, of course, he continued to read. Six months later, when he opened the June issue of *Scribner's*, he was struck by the opening sentence of a story by Stephen Crane. "None of them knew the color of the sky," it read. Why not? Gerald wondered, glancing at a cloud passing the window. He turned back to the page. There followed a description of waves, of emerald green and amber water, of a faraway shoreline, and of a small open lifeboat on the sea. And then a bit of dialogue that included a reference to Mosquito Inlet Light. His own Mosquito Inlet, his own light. Gerald looked out over the sea for a moment, allowing this reference to register in his mind and savouring the experience of finding a place with which he was intimate immortalized in print, then he plunged back into the story with even greater enthusiasm.

Gulls arrived and withdrew. The men in the boat detested them. The sea tossed the small vessel, slapped its side, spilled over its gunwales. Seaweed slid by. Sharks loitered in the vicinity.

"See it?" said the captain. Gerald stopped reading and looked out at the ocean. See what? he wondered, knowing the answer. He turned the page and one of the other men in the boat saw what the captain was referring to. The lighthouse was "precisely like the point of a pin". The boat, on the other hand, was practically submerged. "A great spread of water, like white flames, swarmed into her."

Gerald's heart was banging in his chest. The lighthouse "had now almost assumed color," he read, and then the lines he had been dreading stood out in terrible black on the white of the page. "'The keeper ought to be able to make us out now, if he's looking through a glass,' said the captain. 'He'll notify the life-saving people.'" Gerald tore through the magazine to the contributors' notes at the back. "Mr. Stephen Crane wrote the story on page 48, having survived 36 hours in a dinghy after the sinking of the ship *Commodore* off the coast of Florida on January 3rd of this year." On his watch, Gerald realized with horror, on his watch.

He dived back into the story. "'No,' replied the cook. 'Funny they don't see us!'" Tears sprang into my great-great-uncle's eyes. Moby Dick swam into and out of view. He dared not read further, but a sense of inevitability and the beauty of the prose held him. "Slowly and beautifully the land loomed out of the sea," he read. "The wind came again. It had veered from the northeast to the southeast. Finally, a new sound struck the ears of the men in the boat. It was the low thunder of the surf on the shore." Gerald had heard that sound, had listened to it night after night for months. "'We'll never be able to make the lighthouse now,' said the captain. 'Swing her head a little more north, Billie,' said he."

Stephen Crane was alive, thought Gerald with great relief. The prose – even the contributors' notes – could not have been written had he not been alive. The story had a positive ending, not one that included him, of course, but happy in spite of everything.

He read further in a marginally better state of mind, sickening only when he came to the penultimate sentence. "The welcome of the land to the men from the sea was warm and generous, but a still and dripping shape was carried slowly up the beach, and the land's welcome for it could only be the different and sinister hospitality of the grave." He wondered, briefly, what duties the dead oiler had performed on the ship, then he put his head in hands and wept. He loathed *Moby-Dick*. What did it matter if Queequeg's tattooed arm resembled a quilted counterpane? Who cared about

"That ghastly whiteness . . . which imparts such abhorrent mild-ness"? He had failed to carry out his own duties. He had failed to provide either rescue or sanctuary.

All night long he paid attention to the light. And when it did not need attention, he looked out at those parts of the ocean that the light revealed and into the utter blackness beyond its beams, and listened to the sound of the waves and the wind until he was almost mad. North, north, north, the surf seemed to be saying. "'We'll never be able to make the lighthouse now,' said the captain. 'Swing her head a little more north, Billie,' said he." Whether he was polishing the bull's-eye lenses of the celebrated Fresnel Light or whether he was staring out into beams and blackness, he contin-ued to repeat these sentences until he came to believe that the gentle command contained in the statement was intended not only for the cook at the oars but also, and more particularly, for himself. "'. . . a little more north,' said the captain." By dawn, Gerald was holding a telescope, scrutinizing the surface of the ocean for the appearance of a small, endangered boat, praying that an opportu-nity for redemption would present itself. But he had already decided what he would do. He would go north and join his brother on the far side of Lake Erie: he would look for work there. A lake cannot kill men the way an ocean can, he mistakenly concluded. He decided to leave that very morning.

And that, according to my uncle, was how my great-great-uncle, sometimes known as the ex-reader, came to man the light on the furthest point of what is now the sanctuary. "He had failed to provide sanctuary," my uncle concluded, "and so there could be no real sanctuary for him. Once it became clear to him that more shipwrecks took place within view of his lighthouse than anywhere else in the great lake system, he would not believe that it was the dangerousness of that part of the lake rather than his own negligence that caused the tragedies to occur. In the midst of a particularly stormy November, when the owners of shipping companies were once again attempting to move one last load of goods with fatal results, he walked down the curved stairs, filled with grief and guilt. Then he locked the tower door behind him and stepped into the waves.

"Like the oiler in 'The Open Boat', he was found 'in the shallows, face downward'. And, like the oiler, 'his forehead touched sand that was periodically, between each wave, clear of the sea.'

"Those are two important words," said my uncle, who would himself eventually reveal his own "abhorrent mildness" with an inability to take action at a moment when everything was at stake. "Rescue, sanctuary," said he.

My uncle was always breaking things, casually or deliberately, by accident or sometimes, I think, with unconscious intent. There were the rocks on the beach, smashed open with a hammer when he was looking for fossils. There was that garage I told you about. A tyre on my summer bicycle exploded once, when he filled it with too much air. When he tried to replace a windowpane, the result was often shattered glass. And then there was the day he broke the house.

A long, V-shaped crack had appeared between the chimney and the outer west wall where the chimney stood, and my uncle had taken it into his head that it was the fault not of the leaning chimney but of the house itself. The building had settled somehow, he explained to us, in a way that was causing it to separate from the chimney, which he swore was plumb, straight as an arrow. "This old house," he said to us, "needs to be straightened, and I think I know just how to accomplish that." More than once that summer he could be heard mumbling to himself about the house and its state of repair, almost as if he had taken what the Irish call a scunner to the building, or as if the very structure of the place had betrayed him in some indefinable way. "Post and beam," he said to my mother once in exasperation while she laughed at him and shook her head. "It's nothing but a great big slowly rotting box!"

The mothers were gone for the day, a shopping expedition, I expect, or perhaps a round of visits to the elder relatives in the remote dusty villages of the back townships. Mandy and I were in the last stages of our childhoods by then. She had moved beyond *The Children's Treasury of Poetry* and into the likes of Edna St. Vincent Millay and Carl Sandburg – the fog comes on little cat feet, and all that – and I had already begun to pay attention to bugs. I had filled several jam jars (with holes punched into their tin lids) with desperate, small crawling things that lined the glass, searched for escape, and ignored altogether the leaves I had dropped into their transparent prisons for sustenance.

It must have been a Saturday: I remember the workers were absent from both field and orchard. The boys, Teo among them, were called away from their games to help, as was Teo's mother, who was foreman and lived alone in an old trailer near the bunkhouse. Her son was now, apparently, old enough to sleep with the other male workers in what my aunt preferred to call "the dormitories" but that the rest of us still referred to as the bunkhouses.

My uncle brought a heavy length of rope, thick as his arm, into our afternoon. Then, with our assistance – we were placed at regular intervals and at each corner – he surrounded the house with this rope and dragged what remained of the coil out to the lane where the tractor waited. Once the vehicle was started up and began to move, I remember my hands burning while the hempen cord was yanked, unexpectedly, out of my grasp, and then the smell of diesel fuel, a soft groan, and a slight shift. My uncle inserted three or four wooden shims and slapped two inches of the cement he had mixed earlier into the space that had appeared between the floor beams and the foundation on the east side of the house, while we all stood nervously by. All except for Teo, who was handed a trowel and encouraged to apply the wet, grey paste in the spots my uncle said he had missed. I remember thinking my uncle wanted to miss spots, wanted Teo to work alongside him. "You're the filler-inner," he said to the boy.

Fooling around with something as large and permanent as a house was as amazing to my cousins and me as Peter Pan's flying ship or the wind-tossed farm in *The Wizard of Oz*, or as amazing as the painstaking relocation and then the explosive disappearance of Old Great-great's barn. We knew that only our uncle could have arranged this alteration of the ordinary, the stationary, this miraculous though hardly seismic displacement. He walked with us back to the west side of the house and posed for Mandy's new camera in front of the chimney, which now hugged the outer wall in the way the great-greats had intended. Then he invited us inside for what he called refreshments.

The kitchen was serene and unchanged. Looking through the door that led into the parlour, however, we saw that my aunt's treasured pine floors had snapped like kindling during the course of events. Once this piece of information had registered among us, Teo and his mother hastily withdrew to the bunkhouse. I and my cousins also left the house, all joy wrung out of us as we sat in a line on the picnic table, facing the lane, waiting for our mothers' return with a combination of anxiety and fear. My uncle did not join us. He just stood in the broken parlour, self-removal and distance all around him, a drink in his hand.

He did not come back outside. He did not ask us to help him return the rope to the shed. He did not drive the tractor back to the barn. He just left those physical manifestations of his wrong-headed conceptions visible and in place, as if he were trying to say, "Look at what I tried to do. Look at my failure."

Yes, I think now that he must have been in some way courting the anger my aunt, an hour later, would so vehemently express. Something in him wanted his wife to see exactly what he had done.

I recall how quickly Teo and his mother vanished from the scene once they knew there would be trouble, interesting, perhaps, to realize how attuned they were to the notion that trouble was always there, waiting like an offstage understudy for an opportunity to perform.

Maybe all the workers carried this kind of prescience with them. But if this was so, we would never know. I'm ashamed to confess that my cousins and I paid little attention to the Mexicans, with the exception of Teo, of course, who had been thrust into our midst by my uncle. Always in the orchards and the fields, clothed in various shades of cotton like a multicoloured crop, their movements were as dependable and overlooked as the dance of vegetation under the touch of an indifferent wind. What had they been thinking? What secret pleasures or sorrows did they keep close to their hearts as they bent down to the ground or reached up to the branch, over and over, filling the waiting baskets? They did this all through the long summer days, while we ran, or swam, or read, or hung our doll clothes up to dry.

The majority of the workers, as I've said, were men, but there were a few women as well, mothers mostly, whose children, unlike Dolores's Teo, had stayed in Mexico with a grandmother or an aunt. My own aunt had insisted that if there were to be women, they would have to be mothers, assuming, I suppose, that their status as such would make them less interesting to the men. (I heard her tell my mother once that in the early days of seasonal workers, there had been some goings-on that she didn't approve of.) What variety of maternal worries those women might have had to stifle while they laboured in a foreign country for less than that country's minimum wage was not considered. Neither was the possibility they might resent Dolores because she was able, as a result of her elevated status of foreman, to have the company of her child. But, as my aunt said, all the workers respected Dolores. "She's worth ten of them." I remember her saying that when my mother had questioned the appointment of a female supervisor. "And the men respect her as much, maybe even more, than the women do."

We would see the Mexicans on weekends in town. On Saturdays they posted letters and bought some personal items in the stores, and on Sundays they attended an early Mass, performed in the basement of the Legion Hall, in Latin, the closest language to their own, by the local priest, in advance of what my mother called the real service at the town's Catholic Church. Always moving in groups, through the park or on the streets, in the proximity of the faux-classical architecture of colonial Ontario, they seemed much more foreign than they did on the farm. We children stared in a way we never did when they were in the fields or orchards. We noted the patience with which these two dozen strangers waited their turn at the pharmacy counter on a Saturday morning or stood in line outside the glass box of a phone booth, after their own special Mass. We did not think about the possibility that the special Mass meant they were not made to feel welcome to join the local congregation. We also did not think about their yearning to hear a faraway voice in that phone booth, their need, perhaps, to whisper endearments to a lover or seek assurances concerning the well-being of a child.

And then there was Teo. In the absence of their own offspring, he became every Mexican's child, and it was obvious that he was universally adored, even the most closed faces coming to life as he walked by a field or down a line of trees. He was a small light to these people, brightening the middle of a day worn thin and meaningless by drudgery. It was his quiet courtesy, his grace, I suspect, and this indefinable light that caused my aunt to relent when my uncle wanted him to play with us.

I was not immune to his grace either. And even though I couldn't define the experience, I had been touched by his luminosity. And yet, never once during that last summer did I ask him to tell me the name of the town he came from, never once, in spite of the way I was drawn to him, did I ever ask his last name. Even if it were possible for me to look for him now, I would have no idea where to begin the search. No, I never requested the simplest details of his life because, as far as I was concerned at the time, it was as if Teo was born anew each summer, like the blossoms, like the fruit, and, yes, you're right, like the butterflies.

———

There were a few evenings during that last summer when I would be alone for part of the night in the room I shared with Mandy. She had friends in the town two miles up Sanctuary Line and would sometimes slide into the Volvo with her brothers for a night out. I went with them once, to a dance at the Sanctuary Pavilion, but was so self-conscious in the face of teenagers who had known each other since grade school that I never wanted to go again. Out of place and out of context, I conjectured that I slipped from my cousins' minds the minute they walked onto the dance floor, or perhaps even before that, if they had spotted someone they were interested in lounging against the wall on the opposite side of the room. This was perfectly natural, if it was in fact true, and I knew even at the time that there was no unkindness in it. I stayed in the shadows and waited to be taken home, a mask of indifference on my face. I remember the double-screened doors of that now disappeared pavilion, and the silhouette of the one pine tree that could be seen through them, the moon on the water beyond that. And

I remember the beads of moisture on the pop can I held in my hand because these were the kinds of things I concentrated on while my cousins draped themselves over a boyfriend or girlfriend and appeared to stagger under the weight of physical contact.

I remember one particular night in the dark at eleven o'clock when I was alone in the bedroom, sitting up in bed, my arms around my knees, Mandy's books and her Mötley Crüe posters that had been on the walls since she was twelve all around me. The window beside me was open, and I could see the lit bunkhouses in the distance. It was early in the summer; we hadn't been at the farm for more than a week, but the workers had been installed in their long, low quarters and Dolores in her trailer since mid-April, when the hard labour of tending the orchards and preparing the fields had begun. Warm yellow lights lit some of the windows and made a series of rectangles on the ground beside the planks of the outside wall of the bunkhouses. I knew which window was Teo's because when he was late for work in the cherry orchards, he would remove the screen and climb out over the sill rather than walk down the length of the bunkhouse to the door. There was something about the awkwardness of the exit that made me smile because unlike almost every other movement he made, there was no grace in it. Late in the day I would on occasion glimpse him working in the trees, his T-shirt wrapped around his head as a sweat band, his skin gleaming. He stretched and twisted on the ladder in order to reach the fruit, then after a while unclasped a full twelve-quart basket from the harness that he wore and carried the cherries down to the ground where an empty basket waited. He was more like a performer than a labourer. The strength and fluidity of his efforts were a wonder, and sometimes I just stood and watched him, if I was certain he did not know I was doing this.

We were less comfortable with each other than we had been during the previous summers and I still believe, even now, that neither of us knew why this was so. Gone were the long days of unstructured time we had enjoyed when we were young children, the sessions of play. We were less comfortable but in an inexplicable way more drawn to each other. Teo spoke English fairly well by then, and so instead of inventing games, we talked in a shy, hesitating way – about driving the car, which I was beginning to do, or about what the city that I lived in was like. So far, he had told me nothing of his own place or his own schooling; the distant other world where he spent the autumn and winter was so unreal to me my imagination failed in the face of it and, as I said, sadly I never questioned him. Once, hitching a ride with me partway into town, a letter in his hand, he mentioned his grandmother and grandfather. He was sending them money, he said, because they needed it. One of them was sick, I don't remember which. I didn't ask him about this either, though I recall being surprised in some way, not by the need but by the existence of further family connections. Until then, in my mind, his was a family of only two: himself and his mother.

This night, it was Dolores I saw when I looked through the window. She walked out of the dark and passed through the rectangles of light, moving along the wall until she reached Teo's window, which she gently slapped once or twice with her hand. He raised the sash and they spoke for several moments. Then, just as I began to hear faint music coming from somewhere in the dark, Teo vanished and reappeared a few seconds later at his mother's side. They stood entirely still, facing each other, framed by light. The tension in their bodies made me think that perhaps they were going to start to argue, that she was going to chastise Teo for something he had done, or that he was refusing to do something she wanted him to do. Then, abruptly, they began to dance in a way I had never seen anyone dance before. Dolores circled her son, her arms moving toward and around his upper torso and head, as if she were about to tie him up. She never once touched him, but it was as if she was drawing almost visible lines of energy from him as he stood motionless and appeared to control the choreography of the dance.

No teenager I knew would have wanted to dance with a parent, particularly in such an odd location. Maybe at the daughter-and-father night at my private school, or at a wedding, but not alone and never by choice. And as far as I knew, mothers and sons didn't dance together anywhere, not even at a boys' private school. I thought briefly about that, and then about the embarrassment I had experienced in the face of my own school's daughter-and-father night because I was without a father. Not that I missed him – as I've said, I barely remembered him being in my life – but because, even though my uncle had come to the school that night, taking my father's place, I felt that the rumour of my semi-orphaned status had been telegraphed through the crowd.

Once Teo began to actively enter the dance, I realized that there was a repetitive pattern to what he and his mother were doing, that they knew the steps of the movements well, and I thought that they might be practising, keeping the skill honed. Once Teo began to move, his mother took two formal steps away from him, standing to one side with her head high and her face averted. Then, when he came to a sudden halt, she took over once again as if they were passing authority back and forth between them without ever relinquishing connection or control. Then, abruptly, she entered a furious solo that went on and on, as if it had no end. It was during this phase that I began to hear another noise unattached to the music, a high-pitched yelping, almost like a coyote baying at the moon or a dog announcing the arrival of a stranger. Though Dolores appeared to be ignoring the sound, I could tell by Teo's posture that it had interrupted his concentration. I think Teo and I likely discovered the source of these cries at the same moment because, as soon as I had discerned that it was my uncle's silhouette framed by the lake about five hundred feet away, I looked back to the scene. Teo was gone, but his mother was still dancing. My uncle made one or two more of those weird caterwauls, then put his hands in his pockets and walked back toward the house, in a casual sort of way, as if nothing out of the ordinary had happened. And maybe it hadn't.

But now I think that perhaps those slightly mocking sounds had dismissed Teo from the dance, that they had replaced him somehow, and that my watching uncle had moved into his territory, becoming a shadow partner. And was I not a partner as well: silent, unacknowledged, watching behind the glass?

Heading north from here, away from the Point that gives it its name, Sanctuary Line crosses the Middle Road, an old Indian trail appropriated long ago by the surveyor Mahon Burwell. Ten miles further on, it passes over the highway that connects the towns and cities of this province. I took this highway a few months ago to visit our sister sanctuary at Presqu'ile Point on Lake Ontario for the beginning of the late-spring butterfly migration and was very aware that after passing through Toronto I was once again on the Highway of Heroes. How disorienting it was to be travelling along that stretch of road, yet heading in the opposite direction. So disorienting, in fact, I almost believed that if I could only drive far enough I would be able to undo Mandy's death and rediscover her, alive and well, at the air base, grinning on the tarmac.

As I drove, I remembered the first overpass we saw the day that Mandy's body was driven to Toronto; how all the local volunteer firefighters and the few sad old veterans who had fought in previous wars, along with dozens of civilians, had gathered to pay tribute. There were duplicates of this makeshift honour guard on all the overpasses we slipped beneath in the long black cars, but the first one was somehow the most consoling. Some of the people held flags, and because it was a breezy day, the colourful banners of cloth fluttered in an almost celebratory way against a clear blue sky. The veterans, their medals gleaming in the sun, the firefighters, and now and then a couple of police officers saluted. From below, in the back of the plush cars that drove us away from the air base, we noticed this gesture because the police and the firefighters stood on top of their vehicles, backlit by the afternoon light. In spite of the distance that grief had put between me and the world, I remember viewing all this with an odd sense of relief, as if in the back of my mind I had feared that this one time the spontaneous gatherings we had been told about and had seen on the national news might not take place, that Mandy's death would not be acknowledged.

These assemblies, as you know, are in no way official. They simply came into being once it was discovered that each fallen soldier would be driven along that stretch of the highway after the repatriation ceremony at the Trenton air base. I remember Mandy telling me she found the government decision to put up official signage renaming the highway to be faintly ridiculous, that, to her mind, there were roads in Afghanistan to which the word *hero* could be more aptly applied. And she wondered about the peace-keepers, why there had been no fanfare when they were brought home in coffins, as they often were. Because of her reaction, I decided at the time that I would never stand on an overpass that overlooked someone else's misery. I could simply not allow myself to believe that it might be my own misery that would someday be briefly acknowledged from a small cement bridge.

Once during that week I spent at the Presqu'ile Sanctuary I found myself driving to an overpass on that highway. Another soldier had been killed, and, of course, there would be more to come. I realized as I waited that I had now become one of those who stand and wait for a glimpse of tragedy. And when the dark line of cars passed beneath, like the other civilians, I wept, though whether I was weeping for Mandy, or myself, or for the unknown young person in the long black car I can't really say.

———

A few weeks ago, after struggling for an hour or so with the poetry of Wallace Stevens, I came across a book I hadn't seen for years, not since the people I still refer to as "the adults" – my uncle, my mother, my aunt – were in full residence here and in full control. Decorated in the Victorian manner with a gold-embossed title and twisting flowers on its bright green cover, it is a collection of poems written in the last half of the nineteenth century by the town's Baptist minister, Reverend Thomas Sanderson, and quite probably published at his own expense. As children we loved this book. We could find poems in it about places that we felt were ours simply because we recognized them: the little park in the town with its cannons from the War of 1812, the then brand-new Baptist Church, which is now an antiques store, the town itself, and the nearby lake. We recognized occasions as well: Dominion Day, Victoria Day, or the Queen's Birthday, as the reverend called it, being a contemporary of the queen in question. But most thrillingly, there was a poem about visits the reverend made to our very own shore-line on summer afternoons more than a century before. "We dwell in the fullness of summer," the poem, which was entitled, simply, "Butler Farm", began. Often his verses opened in this fashion; he was not a gifted poet. "The point and the bluff and the island," it continued, "make aspects more pleasing each day / The lighthouse, the schooners, the freighters / we see in this beautiful bay." Nothing affirmed our place on the planet more than that one unexceptional poem.

But when the adults read the collected poems of Reverend Sanderson, they did so with a considerable amount of merriment. On occasions when my other uncle and aunt were visiting, and drink had been taken, my uncle would often threaten to recite "Dominion Day 1878," "Dominion Day 1879," and "Dominion Day 1880" in sequence unless the gathering agreed to become more lively by, say, arguing about politics. "'Our vast Dominion,'" he would begin threateningly while all around him recoiled in mock horror.

To us, the children, however, he sometimes read the "Nellie" sequence. Nellie was the reverend's five-year-old child who had died of one contagion or another and who, according to the reverend, slept "beside Lake Erie's shores". The Baptist churchyard had been thoroughly searched and not one adult had been able to discover Nellie's grave, so the family came to assume that there must be another secret graveyard somewhere, one that was much closer to the lake. On days when we children were too much under-foot, we would be told to go outside and look for little Nellie's grave. Until I was an adolescent, the humour implied in this was lost on me, though the boys, eager to please, would laugh dutifully before setting forth along the shore and through the fields, looking for toppled gravestones in the long grass or in nearby wood lots. All the boys, that is, except for Teo. Teo did not laugh; he simply looked confused. He and I lagged behind on these excursions, pausing often to look for puffballs or butterfly chrysalides. I was uncertain about searching for anything, afraid that, because she had no known address, we might actually discover little Nellie's tiny bones.

Looking back, I wonder what my uncle's preoccupation with graveyards and dead children was all about. Everything and everyone he spoke of had vanished, in the way that all children eventually vanish into the past or vanish because they have been snatched by death in the midst of their childhood. He has his own dead child now. Do his cells, assuming they are still quick, recognize the horror of that fact? Dear beautiful Mandy. Like Nellie, you "sleep beneath your native earth, and in the land that gave you birth." But, unlike Nellie, your death occurred in unfamiliar terrain. You felt entitled neither to the love you were giving nor the ground on which you were walking. Away from your much-changed home, disoriented in the midst of a tour of duty, blindsided over and over again by physical love: each facet of your life was an improvised explosive device leading to a final, catastrophic detonation.

I noticed a few monarchs on that spring day while I waited for the first, and perhaps the only, time for a military funeral cortege to appear beneath me. The butterflies were feeding on the milkweed growing on the grassy slope that bends toward the highway. This was unusual. It was the middle of May. They should have been heading toward the lake by then, preparing to mate, lay their eggs, and die.

It is odd, now that I think of it, that the name of a destination is sometimes used to define a thoroughfare regardless of the direction in which you choose to move along it. Sanctuary Line, for example, bears its title whether you are driving toward Sanctuary Point or leaving it behind and travelling toward the town, the highway, the rest of the world, as if you are pulling one known place with you further and further into unfamiliarity.

The summer I was sixteen and practising for my driver's test, I drove that road so often there wasn't a bump or a pothole I was not intimately familiar with. The car, my mother's Buick, was painted a soft yellow and had bucket seats and air conditioning that flowed from two vents into the interior. I, however, preferred the windows to be rolled down so that I could hear the crunch of gravel beneath the tyres and feel the way the incoming air moved the hair at the back of my head. I also liked the way the sound of that wind changed, became surflike, as the car passed by the honeysuckle and sumac bushes that appeared in generous clusters here and there along the route.

If you turn left at the first intersection and drive in a northerly direction away from Sanctuary Line, you pass through two minor intersections before eventually arriving at the old Talbot Road, or the King's Highway Number Two as it was then called. If you drive in a westerly direction, the line itself bends to the north, eventually travelling over the freeway I just spoke about and into the back townships. I was not permitted to drive north. My mother had a healthy respect for those two intersections as well as for the law: I did not yet have a driver's licence and shouldn't, therefore, have been driving at all. If I chose, however, I could drive south, and then southeast to the spot where the line turns to enter the sandy lanes and marshes and beaches of the sanctuary. This part of the road still feels like home to me because, all through my childhood, I had explored these areas on foot and by bicycle. I knew it so well, I could have written an essay about the various gradations of gravel, how there were two firm tracks created by the passage of cars, and how the fine dust at the edges softened the wildflowers and weeds that grew there. I could also have described the irregular rectangles of the fence wire and the rough cedar posts this wire was attached to. Various animals in the fields were familiar to me as well – those patient herds that turned to regard us when we were children, walking or cycling by, our peanut butter sandwiches in the carrier baskets between the handlebars of bikes that ultimately were left to rust behind the wood lot, and may still be rusting there for all I know.

One Sunday in mid-August of the summer I was learning to drive, I found Teo standing on the side of the road about a half a mile from the farm. He watched the car approach and then lifted his hand, palm outwards, the gesture more like a blessing than a request. I came to a halt, and without speaking he opened the door and climbed inside, changing the atmosphere of the interior completely with his entry. There was nothing I could think of to say. He would have known I wasn't permitted to travel far, that the drive would not take either of us anywhere in particular. I turned on the radio to fill the silence. Songs about hunger and pain and lost love played as I drove, looking straight ahead, aware all the while that this boy was staring at my profile. Despite the rolled-down windows, the temperature inside the car became uncomfortably warm. Shafts of afternoon sun moved from his side to my side as I slowly took the curves of the road, until, on one of these curves, Teo's brown hand covered my white hand on the wheel. When I pulled away, he said he would like to learn to drive, and that he would be careful.

Even now, I find it difficult to understand why I was so shaken, so disturbed by that one brief touch. Was it the trance engendered by the increasing heat in the car? Was it the songs on the radio? As if I had known I would always do this, I relinquished my place at the wheel and all of the power that attended that place. I stopped and we opened the doors, stepped out of the car, and crossed each other's paths behind the vehicle without making eye contact in the exchange.

He was a natural, though an exaggeratedly cautious driver – I wondered if it was his first experience behind the wheel, but I didn't ask. There was something about his complete focus on the road, his utter absorption coupled with his nervousness, that made him seem older and more impenetrable to me, almost ancient. I looked at his hands, strong and thick. In the intense light I saw that dust from the fields had covered his smooth neck and beautiful forearms like down. His perfect skin caused me discomfort, almost fear, though I wouldn't have been able to say where this discomfort and fear came from or what it meant. I hoped that we wouldn't pass anyone I knew.

After about five minutes he very carefully manoeuvred the car over to the side of the road, a soft grey cloud rising behind us. "We will change back now," he said, though he did not take his hands off the wheel and neither of us moved. He was looking straight ahead, as if he had seen something in the distance that pained him. "I am sick with love for you," he said.

"No," I said, and the word sounded loud in my ears. "No, you're not."

"Full of love illness."

"No," I repeated.

He did not look at me. He left the keys in the ignition, opened the door of the car, closed it quietly behind him, and walked away.

Back at the house I crashed into the bedroom where Mandy was reading and angrily shook open and then kicked closed drawers as I looked for a swimsuit. I could feel Mandy's eyes on me and her unasked questions in the air, but I ignored her as I yanked on the suit when I found it and walked quickly out of the house toward the cold shock of the lake. I swam with strength, moving away from the shore, for ten minutes or more before I began to tread water. Looking back at my uncle's farm I could see the neat rows of fruit trees, the fields behind them, and, in the distance, the flat, dusty townships where some of the elder relatives lived. I was far enough away that the blue roofs of the house, the barn, the bunkhouses, and the other outbuildings were miniaturized and contained, as if the whole farm were a picture on a wall. The four trucks lined up neatly beside the storage barn looked like toys, the lawn furniture as if it were intended for a dollhouse.

The words that Teo had so awkwardly spoken had separated me from the collective embrace of that well-ordered demesne: from my cousins and aunts and uncles, from the bins of apples and the multiple trees on which they grew, from the rituals of bedtime, and the calm that always visited me when I woke beside that familiar window on summer mornings. Even the slight elevation of land that my uncle had told us was once the shore of some ancient and unknowable great lake, a forebear of the lake I was moving in now, was withdrawing into an irretrievable prehistory. It all seemed sad and distant and locked forever in a past I would now only remember and could never again experience. I told myself I had no idea what Teo had meant, and yet everything about me was responding in an unfamiliar and alarming way. I knew I was changed, but I could not, would not, name the cause of the alteration.

How much of first love – perhaps any love – is developed in isolation and absence. You could completely remove one of the players from the table and nothing much would shift, imagination being what it is. And how strange that early love becomes, once it enters the house the imagination has made for it. It turns and turns in the mind; the young person it attaches itself to becomes lost, unreachable. Had it been simpler for me, less sudden, with the daily-ness of ordinary events to ground it, I might have been able to remain present in my own life. But, as it was, everything around me was going to be remote, I could feel it, for the remaining weeks of that summer. I both resented this and was astonished and awakened by it. Eleven words and one touch and I was taken hostage. My self, as I had believed that I had known her, was never going to be available to me again.

And yet, when I myself re-entered the bedroom, there was Mandy, as curious and engaged as ever, and as watchful and knowing. I had been in the lake too long, had swum too far, my dark hair was darker now, pasted to my skull and clinging to my neck. And Mandy, bathed in the yellow tranquility of her room and in the late-afternoon sun, was golden in a way I would never be, her mother's perfect features just slightly rearranged on her face so that her expression was generous and inclusive. She invited everyone she cared about in. She kept nothing out.

"What's with you?" she said, examining me closely.

Whatever this new distance was, even Mandy, someone I had talked with in this room about everything, sometimes almost until dawn, was not going to be able to break into it. *Me aparté*, I thought, remembering the child that Teo used to be. "So what are you reading?" I asked, glancing at the book that lay open on her long, tanned legs.

"Next year's English . . . a book for that. *Lord Jim*. A boy book, I think. But I like it."

There would come a day when I would lose Mandy to her own darker seclusion; to ambition and to love; to what I would come to see as her own love and someone else's ambition, though she herself would never present it to me in that way. But for now she sat on the bed in her cutoff shorts, her legs crossed, a quizzical look on her face, and a book about the poison of ambition and invasion and colonization resting on her lap.

Mandy, articulate and poised in every other facet of her life, was brought to silence and uncertainty in the presence of the man who meant so much to her. "Silenced" was the way she described it to me, the listener, the one with whom she was never silent. "Silenced," she added, "because there is one place I will never be able to go with him, something elemental and essential about him that I will never have any real access to."

I often wondered if everything she said to me might not better have been said to him, that she could have given him at least a chance to know the one part of her *he* had no access to: the anguish, the grief. Impossible, she said, when I mentioned this once. His life was cluttered and complicated. He was already concerned about the military's rules about intimate relationships. Added to this were war strategies, the movement of troops, staking out the enemy, statements to the press. All of his mental and much of his physical energy went into this. What was left over he hoarded for his extended family, who, though most often far away, brought their own troubles and triumphs to his table.

He had once told her that she was his oasis, an apt metaphor for a desert warrior, this man whom I came to think of as Mister Military. But what can an oasis do but remain silently in place, reflecting the sky until, now and then, it is required to act as a mirror for the one who comes to drink there, sating his thirst and blocking out the light? I was convinced she was blinded and darkened by him, then left alone, disoriented in the stark desert daylight with everything around her in sharp focus. A knife glinting in the sun, a rifle in her hands. And the responsibility for her own platoon of cocksure and frightened young men was in her hands as well. How did she deal with all that in the midst of her absorption? It seemed to me from what she said that he tossed her aside like a rag, but in serial fashion, over and over again. Yet when he returned to her, and from what I understood she was never sure he *would* return, he would be fully present, as if he had never discarded her at all. She knew he was able to carry this engagement with him wherever he went: into friendship and into the theatre of war. There was a tense alertness about him, she said, which was as necessary for staying alive in the life he'd chosen as it was necessary for advancing forward. She wanted to develop her own skills of vigilance, but the fact of him broke apart her concentration. She was always attached to him in her mind; rerunning endearments, lovemaking, quarrels, entrances, exits, while the whole world exploded around her practically unnoticed. It was not the best recipe for survival.

"At least tell me his name," I'd say to her in exasperation during phone calls in the middle of the day or the night, or here at the house in the room we had shared since childhood.

She told me she couldn't do that. When I asked her why, she said she had promised that she wouldn't. I concluded he was married but couldn't bring myself to ask her.

What she did tell me was that they were rarely together unless they were together in a darkened space. The intimacy was so intense it could only unfold within the parameters of a rented and utterly neutral room. Dozens of these meetings took place across the Middle East, inside the walls of American hotel chains, which resembled to a fault the rooms of the same American hotel chains they had visited when she was still at the Canadian Forces Base in Petawawa, where they'd first met. Nothing ever changed, she said, presenting this, to my astonishment, as a positive thing. There could be an ancient city under aerial bombardment or a snow-filled meadow in serene Ontario outside the window, but it was still the same room, the same relationship. It neither advanced nor retreated, so any time they met could have been the previous time or the next time. Except, I suspected, when she demanded more from him, and then it would have become a bad time. He would have closed completely, I imagined. This man who minutes before had been holding her and touching her with great tenderness would no doubt gather up his things and leave the room as if there was nothing at all between them. She told me that with the exception of one significant time, he made certain that their leaves did not overlap so there would be no question as to whether he and Mandy might have two days or even a meal together. He didn't believe in love tokens. You're not a child, he told her. You're an adult and an officer, insinuating that she had chosen this as much as he had, which was of course true and therefore would be more humiliating than an unfair accusation. But Mandy admired his candour. I want him to be brutally honest with me, she said. Sounds like he's just being brutal, I replied.

He made it clear that she could talk about this with no one, not knowing how much she talked about it with me. Perhaps he wasn't even aware that I existed. This was a secret, apparently, that made all military and state secrets pale in comparison, a piece of information so volatile, according to him, that it defied classification. None of Mandy's fellow officers and no one in the lower ranks knew anything about it, though I suspected, in spite of the rules, a not insignificant percentage of them were likely involved in affairs of their own. But not with a senior officer, she said when I pointed this out.

I told her I didn't care who he was or how far he was up the food chain, he was using her.

For the past year, since Mandy's death, whenever I see a military spokesman on the television – they are always men – I've wondered if it was him. I've scrutinized the features of man after man on the screen, uniform after uniform, searching for the kind of coldness of purpose that would override any kind of personal relationship: a single-mindedness that would rule out warmth, connection.

"So, he's married," I finally said. "Mister superior officer is married."

"If only it were that uncomplicated," she told me, ignoring my obvious disdain for rank. "If he were married, or if I knew for certain he was using me, I could live with it, or maybe without it. As it is . . ." She didn't continue the sentence. She would never define what it was.

And yet, in spite of all this, in spite of the uncertainty, Mandy clearly believed he was a saint. Both men and women were mesmerized by him, she told me, and obeyed his orders without question or complaint. And they talked about him, she told me. They talked about him all the time while she stood in their midst. I pictured her, clothed in regulation camouflage khaki, appearing to be as prurient and detached as anyone else. So she would hear the gossip about what he might or might not be doing with other women, about who among the young officers had become his latest discoveries, who was the best new strategist, engineer, or warrior. He knew who would go far because he was part of the decision-making process that determined who would go far, and she came to feel she would never be among the chosen. But standing in close proximity to the chosen, eating and drinking with them in the Officers Mess, she watched them grow and blossom under the warmth of his attention. And his affection, she added, defending him.

When someone, anyone, died, his empathy and stalwart grief unified the whole corps, and when he spoke about the particular death it would be as if no one had ever died before. His reaction was utterly personal and heartfelt, a crack in his voice, the large heart of him remarkably visible. It was impossible, Mandy said, not to be moved by his words, his demeanour, the sudden humility in him. It was impossible not to want to throw oneself back into the fray. And, I suspected, impossible not to want to die so that he would talk about you with his voice broken and his heart exposed.

She told me that they did take one unofficial journey together. He wanted to visit the Canadian battle sites in Italy where their company, the Seaforth Highlanders, had served in the Second World War. Their leaves had somehow overlapped, and she had flown to Rome and taken a train from there to some village or another, far enough from Canadian war graveyards that there was scant likelihood that anyone from home would be there, though, as she told me he had said, there was always a chance. It wasn't perfect, she confessed. It had rained the whole time, and the place itself, bombed in the Second World War, though interesting in spots, was so filled with cement apartment houses, she said it had the feel of an ancient town being eaten alive by the present. That was the poet in Mandy speaking, and I wondered whether she had conveyed this observation to him.

He had become increasingly tense as the two days passed, although, as always, she said, smiling, there had been some moments of authentic connection. Mandy described the church filled with reliquaries they found, some on intricately worked silver pedestals, and some even fashioned in the form of ships, hanging from the ceiling. The finger bones and shards of skulls contained in these works of art intrigued him, and some of the fading, damaged wall frescoes as well, which, according to Mandy, showed vestiges of the Last Judgment. He became absorbed by the wall paintings apparently and told her he would return alone some day to study them more closely when he could.

Was it simply carelessness that made him tell Mandy he would go back without her to what she was trying to think of as "their" village – a place far from the celebrated monuments and therefore singular in its own, prosaic way? Or was he as intentionally cruel as I was beginning to believe? Alone, she'd wept on the trains and planes that returned her to Kandahar, carrying with her not the intimate moments of the trip but that one small remark across thousands of miles back to the theatre of war.

An official military letter addressed to my aunt arrived in the mail the week after Mandy was killed. I feared that because he was a "superior officer", the man I was increasingly thinking of as Mister Military might have been required to write it, and I despised him more for the idea that he would agree to do so. I hated even more that the military hadn't taken the trouble to know that her mother was dead, had died, in fact, during Mandy's tour of duty. I threw the letter into the fire unopened, but when I cleared the ashes from the grate the following morning I saw the bottom quarter of the page was unburned. Only the words "my deepest sympathy" and a signature remained. I remembered then that all through our talks, not only had Mandy refused to reveal the name of her lover, she had never once even described his face.

But the name was unimportant, really, as was the face, the rank. He would always be Mister Military to me. As far as I was concerned, he was the whole operation, the whole war, the camaraderie and the fear, the abject gratitude for the good days in the face of the arbitrariness of the bad, the seductiveness of all that. The way she had wanted to please him, to demonstrate her courage, self-control, and discretion, broke my heart. She was so accomplished, such a good soldier. In spite of what she believed, she could have achieved all that and more even, had he never existed. Instead, she was forced to endure an emotional life where he appeared and disappeared, reappeared and disappeared again, while the improvised explosive device with her name on it was waiting in the shadows to become the eventual resolution. How did he react to the news of her death? Would he have run from that as well? At the time, I couldn't help but think so because, whenever I pictured him, this man whom I had never met and whose name I firmly believed I would never know, he looked exactly like my uncle.

There had been only one tale of love among my uncle's stories. It involved one of the great-greats: a great-great-uncle to us, a son to others, a brother to some, but a husband and father to no one. He had fallen in love with his schoolteacher, a woman my uncle described as tall and thin with a high-necked collar and a head full of ideas surmounting that collar. It was the ideas that he fell in love with, though her long neck and willowy body, admittedly, may have played some role in the attraction he felt. Still, there were other long necks and willowy bodies in the neighbourhood, my uncle said, but none with access to the ancient history, classical mythology, and poetry that the schoolteacher brought into this farm boy's life for the very brief season when he had the time to go to school.

She was older than he was, of course, but not by as much as you might think because in the rural schools in those days, the teacher herself was often just seventeen or eighteen, having only to graduate from high school to be eligible for the job. Our young ancestor's farm work was so all-consuming and his school attendance so sporadic that he was sixteen years old when the new teacher arrived. He was determined to finish grade school in spite of his age and the fact that his height made him feel uncomfortable and exaggeratedly out of place. He became even more determined once he had seen the new teacher and heard her recite "La Belle Dame Sans Merci" by John Keats, an affirmation, my uncle told us, of everything that Young Great-great instantly felt about the woman who was standing at the front of the room.

That focus: a beautifully formed female monument placed against the dark, horizontal emptiness of the blackboard, the grace of her arm, making sentences like white fences on a landscape of slate, or holding a book out in front of her as she read. "Oh what can ail thee, knight at arms / Alone and palely loitering?" A potent mixture. Young Great-great never would have heard anything like the story that poem tells. Yet something in that narrative would be weirdly familiar to him once he saw the teacher. Like his lighthouse-keeping, bifurcating relatives, an interest in literature would take root in him, an interest that would forever be connected to the teacher, and he would begin to borrow books, first from the two small shelves at the back of the schoolroom and later, when he had finished grade school, from the lady herself. He read all of Keats this way, and a not insignificant amount of Shelley and Byron. And he thought about that poetry and that young woman all the time he was hauling stumps through rough pasture to make a fence or when he was felling timber. He would be all wrapped up in thought on the one hand, and concealment on the other, for she was engaged and about to be married to someone else. And even if she not been, this love he had would have been, according to my uncle, a private possession – something that set him apart from his brothers – and he never would have dared, or perhaps never even have wanted, to confess it.

This privacy, however, did not prevent him from brooding at great length when she married and also did not prevent him from continuing to borrow books from her once she was someone else's wife. But it did prevent him from moving forward when she became a childless widow – the perfect moment, my uncle said, for the young man to have approached her as, by then, he had his own farm, and one that was doing fairly well.

Men, our uncle told us, are not good at expressing their feelings. And the stronger the feelings, he assured us, the worse they are at expressing them. Hardly an original observation but interesting in that my uncle expressed it. Instead, as the years went by, when certain strong thoughts about the woman haunted Young Great-great, he would ask to borrow a particular book from her, one that he hoped might echo those thoughts. Maybe this was a peculiar language between them, though more than likely the lady, now in her thirties, would have assumed that he wanted only the books. The important thing, however, was that he wanted the books given to him by her, even though by now there was a perfectly good library in the town where they lived. He could have just as easily pulled Coleridge or Robert Browning from the library's shelves, but it seemed that unless the teacher had herself turned the pages of a volume, he did not feel compelled to read it.

After her husband died, the woman – her name was Alice Simmonds – had not gone back to teaching in the little schoolhouse. Instead she developed a curious talent, that of writing poetry for greeting cards. This was ironic in and of itself, my uncle said, because often she was required to write verses about relationships she (beyond her short marriage) had no real connection to. Her speciality was the sort of cards exchanged by courting couples. *To My Sweetheart on Her Birthday*, or *A Valentine's Greeting to the One I Love*, and a number of poems meant to be from a secret admirer.

> To him your hand is like a dove
> Your face is like a star
> He will not tell you of his love
> But worships from afar.

And things of that nature.

Young Great-great did not know about the greeting cards for several years until one day, purchasing a card for his mother at Christmas, he was startled by the storekeeper musing aloud as to whether the verses contained therein had been written by Alice. Alice Simmonds? he asked. Yes, the storekeeper said, and let on that this was how she made a living now, writing up these cards for a company in Toronto.

Always, after that, our ancestor spent a good deal of time browsing in the small greeting-card section of the store, paying close attention to any new secret-admirer cards that appeared on the shelves. The sentiments expressed in those cards, though admittedly not as complicated or fraught as those brought to light by Byron or Shelley, were very familiar to Young Great-great, and though he couldn't be sure which ones had been written by Alice, he began to believe that, all-along, she had been able to read his thoughts and that this, in fact, was her way of communicating with him. He bought one or two of the more discreet versions. He dared not mail a card to Alice, however, for fear that the verses had not been written by her and that she might take offence at receiving a card with a poem composed by someone else, even though he had absolutely no intention of identifying himself.

Now, while he was behind the two workhorses ploughing a field, or feeding his animals, or pruning the orchard, he tried to puzzle out a method of discovering just which cards had been written by Alice. He thought of writing the Toronto card company, but likely there was more than one, and anyway he believed that taking such drastic action would be too intrusive. And then an opportunity presented itself.

In the post office one day when he was collecting several packets of seed he had ordered from a catalogue, the postmistress handed him a parcel addressed to Alice. Oh, she had said, realizing her mistake, that one's meant for Alice, some of her cards. She pointed across the street in the direction of Alice's house and said, She works on them in the morning. I can see her there at her table near the window, working away.

Young Great-great knew what he had to do. He was to begin harrowing the north field that week, a job that began at dawn and ended at dusk, but he would put it off for a day or two. Instead he would go in the mornings to borrow a book. He would go every day until he could catch a glimpse of a poem she was writing at that table.

He brought home an edition of Shakespeare's sonnets that way and a collection of Wordsworth's verse, but it wasn't until the third morning visit that he managed to get close enough to the table to be able to gather two lines:

> My love's a secret no one knows
> Except my lonely heart

And those two lines shook him to such an extent he forgot what it was he had come to borrow, so he stood in her kitchen, hat in hand, with nothing at all to ask for. Alice pulled a collection by Robert Burns from the shelf, though he had already borrowed the book several times in the past. He was able then to put his hat on and say goodbye, which he did, my uncle said, with the knowledge that he had missed a significant moment, one when he might have spoken to her. "'Wee cowering, timorous beastie,'" he muttered to himself angrily all the way back to the farm.

Still he had those lines she'd written, and they seemed like a gift to him. He haunted the stationery section of the general store so often after that, reading every card, including those wishing a Happy Christmas, that the storekeeper finally asked if there was a particular kind of card that he wanted to order. Finally, in spring, he found what he was after: one with a cream-coloured background, and violets making a border around *To My Secret Love*. And inside, at last, the words he was seeking. Purchasing it, however, was a different matter. It's meant as a joke, he eventually said, for my sister. We've had a quarrel.

He mailed the card, unsigned, the following day.

Perhaps, my uncle said, the sending of the card was all that Young Great-great wanted at the time, or perhaps he had hoped Alice would guess that it was he who had sent it and would send some kind of signal of her own, and when she didn't, he felt foolish and humiliated. Either way, he stopped borrowing books after that and applied himself fully to the timbering he had begun in his woods, making a good deal of money in the process, and nothing further happened until one year later when he heard that Alice was gravely ill. It was then, and only then, that he resolved to marry her.

He appeared at her door on an autumn evening, dressed in his only suit, with a bouquet of the last roses of the season in his hand and a diamond ring he had purchased in Toronto in his jacket pocket. A woman opened the door, looked at him questioningly, then introduced herself as Alice's sister-in-law. She led him through the kitchen where all that poetry had been written and into the parlour where Alice sat with a rug over her lap and a shawl around her shoulders.

Neither spoke until she roused herself enough to ask if he had come to borrow a book. He handed her the roses then and looked at her drawn face, where traces of her beauty and of her intelligence remained visible in her expression. By the time he gathered the courage to produce the ring he saw that she had fallen asleep. So he left the small box on her lap and crept from the house. When he returned the following day, the sister-in-law told him that Alice was too weak to leave her bed but had left an envelope for him, an envelope that contained a card. Alone in his own kitchen, he opened the envelope and looked at this card, on the front of which, embossed in gold, were the heart-stopping words *To My Fiancé*. He could hardly bear to read the verse inside – *Our courting days are over now / We've found our joy at last* – or bring himself to look at her name written in a faltering script at the bottom of the page. But on his next visit he brought the card with him, showed it to the sister-in-law, and was permitted to enter Alice's bedchamber.

It was instantly clear to him that she was dying, my uncle told us, and that if he were going to marry her, he would have to work fast. *A wedding gown*, were the only words that she was able to say to him. Perhaps it was the beginning of a verse she was making in her head, but Young Great-great knew that he would be expected to produce this article of clothing.

Her sister-in-law gathered together the ladies of the church, who spent the next day and night working on the gown and who also provided the veil, which, in his haste, he had forgotten all about. The ladies of the church also put the minister on high alert, and his mother withdrew her own gold band from her finger so that it could be used in the upcoming ceremony. Three days later, my uncle always said at this point in the story, a middle-aged great-great finally married the middle-aged love of his life, and she died, six hours later, of tuberculosis.

In the end she had been too weak to put on the gown; this was the part of the story that Mandy and I liked the best. She had been too weak so the veil was put on the pillow behind her head and the gorgeous satin gown was laid over the blanket that covered her body.

Drifting in and out of consciousness, she was just able to nod her consent when asked the pertinent questions by the minister. Young Great-great slipped the gold band on her finger and held her hand, the only time they had touched. It was said that her youthful beauty returned once she was dead and the women were able to fully dress her in the wedding gown she wore in her open coffin. He went on to build sawmills all over the county and became tremendously rich. He wore a black armband, however, for the rest of his life, and never again read poetry after he found one of her cards with what he considered to be the perfect verse for her tombstone.

> She lies beneath her native earth
> And in the land that gave her birth
> A multitude of flowers wave
> In sadness o'er her early grave.

The only time I remember Mandy speaking about her disappeared father was in reference to this story. She said she couldn't believe that he had put all the romantic nonsense into our heads when . . . But she didn't finish the sentence, adding instead, Well, it wasn't like that for him, was it? I think my mother may have ruled him after all, or tried to. And his job, as it turns out, was to find ways to escape her custody. It was almost a decade ago in early spring when she said this. She was making one of her rare visits from Petawawa, and I had come down from the city to see her. Outside the house, melted snow had created a water meadow in the orchard. Through the window I could see that the few remaining trees were reflecting exact doubles of themselves in sheets of silver liquid.

Nothing romantic about an escape from perceived imprisonment, Mandy said.

I agreed, trying to keep the bitter edge out of my voice, nothing romantic about any person trying to control another by any means. I was thinking about the command-and-control theory Mandy told me she studied during her officer training program.

For Mandy herself, of course, romance would have had nothing to do with command-and-control theory. Instead it would have been the mystifying poetry she sometimes read to me pushed up against discipline, uniforms, physical training, and military strategy while she was still at college and talking about the honour of serving her country. Her college days were followed by postings to less than glamorous Canadian locations, and then eventually a journey into the chaos of a desert war so debatable in its intentions that even Mandy, who, like her colleagues, was fully committed to duty, once said if you look at history, it could be said that one man's terrorist is often another man's freedom fighter.

And then those hotel rooms. How much poetry could she have possibly brought with her into such spaces? How much of this farm, the lake, her father's stories, and the terrible way her father tore himself out of all that? She was – I was certain of this – both imprisoned and displaced. Where was the fight for freedom in all that?

Just last month, when we decided it was time to choose what to

engrave on the stone we chose for Mandy, her brothers and I immediately thought of poor Alice, of Alice and of our own Young Great-
great, who, because of her, had come to love the sophisticated
poetry she loaned to him and the banal commercial poetry she
wrote. We wanted there to be two headstones with that unsophisti-
cated verse concerning emplacement incised on their surfaces in
the little country graveyard. But in the end we changed our minds
when we discovered the military had already prepared the standard
headstone for Mandy's grave. A maple leaf surrounded by a circle,
her name and birth and death dates.

My mother and I spent brief periods of time around Christmas and Thanksgiving at the farm as well, all through my childhood and adolescence. During the long days of summer when I awoke each morning to the sound of the Mexican workers making their way to the orchards and the unfurling of waves over the pebbles on the shore, it was possible to believe that the orchards and the lake were the beginning and the end of the world, my relatives and their workers its only inhabitants. Not so the autumn and winter holiday: then the visit was more like an interruption of city life with its regulated hours of school and after-school lessons. Still, it was at those laden tables decorated with gourds or mistletoe that my uncle shone in the presence of his wife, his sister, his brother, and his brother's wife. Lengthy, articulate speeches flowed out of him. The ghosts of the great-greats were evoked and toasted, and the old worn book that contained the collected works of the Reverend Patrick Sanderson was pulled from the shelf and read aloud for the amusement of all.

The reverend had not only written about civic holidays, summer afternoons, and his own dead child but had penned as well tributes to the curling, lawn bowling, and literary clubs of Kingsville. These latter poems were considered to be howlingly funny by the adults, but I couldn't see much difference between them and the Robert Louis Stevenson poems that had thrilled Mandy so much she had committed many of them to memory as a child.

> When I was young and by the sea
> A wooden spade they gave to me
> To dig the sandy shore.
>
> My holes were empty like a cup
> In every hole the sea came up
> 'Til it could come no more.

Mandy's interest in lines such as these bewildered me, though I am beginning to understand their wisdom now.

Consumption of large amounts of alcohol was fully sanctioned for the adults during the winter holidays, while the children were both overindulged and blissfully ignored. I remember my aunt's cashmere sweaters – she always expected my uncle to provide her with a new one at Christmas. I also remember her competence in the kitchen, and how tastefully she had decorated the house. She insisted on real holly bought from a florist, rather than what she called "dusty plastic", and boughs of fir cut from the wood lot, the tree with its red and silver bulbs and tiny white lights.

My mother always felt she had to find the perfect piece of pressed glass to present to her sister-in-law, and was visibly nervous when the time came for the opening of gifts because she was never entirely certain that what she had chosen was not a reproduction. Unlike my aunt, she often could not work out how to tell the difference, and there were plenty of dealers who were happy to prey on that weakness. Not long ago she told me that my aunt would show no signs of disappointment if the goblet or compote turned out to be a fake, but that once or twice during the subsequent summer she would notice that the Christmas present was not evident on the shelves where my aunt kept her collection. A sad, little attempt to please, followed by a small cruelty.

My uncle encouraged physical activity during the two or three days of festivity. One year he bullied all of us children away from the television – or in Mandy's case away from her book – and out into the fresh air, where he insisted that we build not just one snowman but a full army of snowmen in the yard. Those ancient terracotta Chinese warriors had just been unearthed, and he was intrigued and impressed by the discovery. Adults and children alike had more than once been forced to look at the *National Geographic*'s photos of the horsemen, row upon row of them. And then he had taken it into his mind that we could create something similar, though certainly not as permanent, just steps from the door.

Even my uncle had to admit that the horses would present a problem, that conventional snowmen would have to do. He would be satisfied, he told us, with just over a dozen. Only three, for each of you, he promised. I'll do three as well. There wasn't really enough snow for this project, but he was determined, and sent the boys off into the orchards with wheelbarrows and shovels once it became clear, by evidence of the emerging grass, that we had used up what was available in the yard. The boys went willingly enough for the first few loads, but there was never enough snow and they were sent back again and again, even after the light began to fail at about four in the afternoon. By that time we were all cold but still more or less game.

Then my uncle revealed what seemed to us, at first, to be a wonderful plan. Up in the attic were a number of clothes worn by the great-greats. Mandy and I knew all about these costumes, of course, having thoroughly explored their possibilities as soon as we were able to do so, and even the boys were familiar with some of the more masculine apparel, which they had worn at least once at Halloween. We all thought that maybe a cape or a top hat would be just the thing for our snowmen, who were now nearing completion. But my uncle's ideas, like his harvests, were nothing if not bountiful, and he made trip after trip to the attic, returning with his arms filled with dark cloth and his face as rapt as if he were the subject of a magnificent conversion. And then I knew that, under the spell of some ridiculous combination of humour and ancestor worship, he was going to try to resurrect the great-greats, right out there on the dismal December lawn. He draped the clothes over the picket fence that surrounded the yard, then took off his soggy gloves and pulled the old beaten flask out of his pocket, as we had seen him do several times before in the course of the afternoon.

The silver glinted in the light that was being thrown from the house. "What do you think?" he said.

"I'm cold," Mandy offered, a bit sullenly. "What I think is, I'm cold."

He ignored her. "What do you think, should we have some girl warriors as well as boy warriors?"

"No." Shane was stamping his feet on the ground, trying to keep warm. "There's no such thing."

"And anyway," Mandy said, "they wouldn't wear dresses, even if there were."

"Let me tell you . . ." My uncle was screwing the lid back on his flask, not looking at us. "Let me tell you, the women warriors in my life wear dresses."

He actually used four-inch spikes in order to get those garments to stay on the snowmen. By the time he had gone to fetch the mallet, we had been called into the house and he was angry. Angry with his wife, I imagine, for once again interrupting one of his projects, angry with us for succumbing to the pressure of women and abandoning him, and angry with himself for not having figured out in advance that a snowman could not be manipulated into either a velvet jacket or a silk dress. Inside, watching him through the window, I remembered the schoolteacher poet our ancestor had loved, how, like the snowmen, she could not fully wear the costume the moment demanded of her. My uncle, meanwhile, had marched out of the house and within minutes had our car, his car, and a truck all idling along the fence so that he could use the headlights to illuminate the task he was about to undertake.

My aunt pushed open the door. "Stanley, for God's sake, stop," she yelled. "Get in here. Don't be a fool."

An orchardist in winter can be a desperate animal, even if that orchardist has lofty, progressive notions and a cultured wife. In order to produce, the peach, apple, and cherry trees must enter a lengthy dormant period. For this to happen, they must be cold and quiet, so that the developmental process can move at the slowest possible pace. If the temperature is too high or too variable, leaf bulbs will not receive the signals they need to make them grow, and the tree may not produce at all during that particular year. It would be like expecting a caterpillar to become a butterfly without the encasement and calm of the cocoon. I've now come to think that, like the fruit trees he nurtured, it was essential for my uncle himself to enter a dormant stage so that he would be prepared for the chaotic work that would make up his spring and summer. The trouble was that he could never accept the notion that rest would enable him to cope with any kind of season ahead. His whole being was focused on engagement of some kind or another. It was simply impossible for his mind or his body to remain still. There was no middle ground with him. He believed that the opposite of vitality was death, and from a scientific point of view, of course, he was right. Vital statistics, vital signs. But his own vitality was extreme, exhausting. I never saw him sleeping, and still can't imagine him asleep.

He worked on those white ghosts in the yard for an hour, spiking aprons and frock coats into their flesh. Child's play, really, but the kind of child's play that even the children could no longer bear to participate in. We sensed something sombre and funereal about those clothes, and we withdrew from the process altogether, settling instead into the safety of board games and an easily understood set of instructions while my uncle laboured with snow and rags in the evening chill. The thing about my uncle was that he made all the rules, clarified them in our midst, then in that extreme way of his changed them or broke them. It is both heartbreaking and enraging to think of him out there in the dark and cold, stubborn and alone. It was as if he had been trying to make us witnesses to his awkwardness, his discomfort, the fact that there was never going to be any respite for him.

Sometime later that night, the temperature rose above freezing and it began to rain. It rained all the next day and the day after that. No one, including my uncle, mentioned the snowmen, who began first to sag, then to diminish by degrees. I tried unsuccessfully to forget about the disappearances that were occurring in the yard, and more than once I caught Mandy anxiously looking out one window and then another, as if she believed the snowmen could be resurrected simply by changing one's point of view. On the second night, the freezing rain set in, and my mother and I were forced to stay for an extra twenty-four hours. By the morning of our departure, the clothing lay in dark puddles all over the lawn, as if the great-greats themselves had lost substance in the last three days and their shadows had been fixed in place forever by a half-inch of ice.

The last summer my uncle operated the farm, he appeared to be filled to capacity with energy and physical warmth, and because he was always up before dawn, his laughter would awaken Mandy and me each morning from the depths of adolescent sleep. He was bursting with jokes, often at someone, anyone else's expense. His delivery was so slapstick and essentially so affectionate, his arm flung around his victim, a bantering tone in his voice, one couldn't help but be warmed by the attention. We grinned and blushed when he teased us about imaginary boyfriends, or when he tried to sing the songs of our favourite rock groups. Even Sadie could be caught secretly smiling, her back turned in feigned disapproval when he reminded her, in our presence, of their courting days, of a certain night in a tent by the Ohio River, or that time in the canoe. We teenagers loved this. "What tent?" we would cry. "What canoe?" But our questions were never answered. His attention span was so short that summer, he would be wrapped up in something or someone else before we could press him any further and, of course, we knew better than to ask our aunt for the details of those occasions.

But right in the midst of this good humour, once we had entered the last two weeks of summer, the twilight games we always played began to change, becoming, for want of a better word, more vigorous. My uncle had discovered the English game of rugby and would gather as many of us as he could out in the yard to divide us into teams. No more touch football: these innings involved full physical contact, sometimes edging toward violence. Teo and I arranged to be on opposite sides, or perhaps it just happened that way and this is something I have since invented. But it was often Teo who tackled me when I had the ball, and I remember his arms around my hips or the hardness of his thighs against my own, and then a delirious tumble in the grass. This was to be the only time in my life when I would fight competitively for a ball. Although I never could have admitted this, it was really Teo I was fighting for, his proximity, his arms.

My uncle could sometimes be quite brutal with his boys during the game, enthusiastically crashing into them, dragging them across the grass, and once or twice I thought I saw real anger in his expression. Don's wrist was sprained in one of these skirmishes, and then there was the trip to the hospital: all three parents were involved; my mother, no doubt, trying to both comfort Don and placate Aunt Sadie, who would have been furious at her husband. The neighbouring kids who had joined in the game trailed home, and the rest of us were left alone in the fading light. Mandy and Shane went indoors to watch television, and Teo and I walked out to the beach, where we sat throwing stones into the water and very occasionally and surreptitiously allowing our hands to touch.

I have no memory of what we talked about, perhaps we merely discussed the stones and the water, but I do remember how the shyness slowly evaporated between us. Our speech became less halting and awkward as the days passed, and the sense of dislocation I'd been feeling began to be gradually replaced by a new emotional landscape. Without making any formal promises, we met at that spot, in full view of the house, the next evening and the evening after that. We were easing ourselves into this intimate companionship – neither of us spoke about the afternoon in the car – as if we were learning a vocation, the skills of which we had not yet fully acquired: a glance, the touch of a hand, the sound of a voice. But each of us knew, I think, that those skills would become comfortable and familiar to us as the days went by, and that eventually we would own them as if they had always been ours.

Her husband gone, her sister-in-law still in the city, her grown children moving deeper and deeper into the preoccupations of their own separate lives, my aunt lived alone in this house for a number of winters. I can imagine her standing at various windows watching the leaves fall from the old maples or the build-up of ice along the shoreline while her elegant face began, almost imperceptibly, to lose its particular definition, softening with age. During this period she seems to have become engaged in an odd and disturbing activity, one I would know nothing about until I moved here a few years later.

When I arrived at the Sanctuary Research Station, it was the time of the late-summer migration, so my work with the butterflies kept me there for most of the daylight hours. Eventually, however, the monarchs departed and I was left with some empty mornings in this room, with its shelves still filled with my aunt's collection of antique pressed glass goblets, tumblers, spooners, compotes. The late-September sun, I remember, plunged through the windows, having lowered since full summer, and made the dust on all forty of these highly collectible vessels visible, even to me. Recalling the meticulous care that was lavished on each glass item by my aunt, I decided to wash them. As soon as I placed a dozen or so goblets in hot, soapy water, piece after piece, pattern after pattern – Bull's Eye, Grapevine, Daisy, and Button – fell apart in my hands. I was mystified by this and believed that perhaps the temperature of the water was responsible for the breakage. I removed the shards, filled the sink with cooler water, then added several more pieces. I was astonished that again the glass separated into fragments. I pulled a compote from the shelf and held it up to the light. I noticed a couple of seams and the odd tiny bulb of dried china glue emerging from them. I examined the rest of the collection, and then I knew. She had broken all of it and then glued it, object by object, back together again. I had to assume my fastidious aunt had for some reason destroyed one piece at a time because the jigsaw puzzle created by a sudden, full demolition of the inventory would have been impossible to solve, and clearly she had made the effort to repair the damage. For a while anyway, she had been able to keep up appearances.

It wasn't the destruction that confused me but rather the painstaking reassemblage. Thinking of this aging woman, alone in her house at night with a broken treasured item and a tube of china glue, caused me to feel an uneasy compassion for my aunt. This was particularly true as, aware of the irony, I watched the interlocking circles of her favourite pattern, Key and Wedding Ring, fall to pieces again now in this oddly gentle manner.

She didn't replace the rose bushes, however, the ones that had been torn up and thrown into the lake. And as for me, I never was much of a gardener. I planted nothing at all during my first month in the house. Instead, I spent my time wandering from room to room arguing with ghosts. In the end, I filled two clear plastic recycling bags with that antique glass. Then I dragged those clinking bags out to the road, where they awaited the arrival of the garbage truck. If Mandy or the boys noticed the collection was gone, they never spoke about it.

———

Mandy used to talk about the bond that developed over there among the soldiers. I knew that in the vicinity of Canadian Forces Base in Kandahar there were literally dozens of men, boys really – young, bright soldiers, some of them just as dead as she is now – who would have been more than content to spend one hour speaking quietly with her across a table, consoled by the vitality of her conversation or simply by watching the changing expressions on her lovely, intelligent face. She knew this too, and responded to the attention in the same way that she blossomed in the midst of her schoolmates all those summers ago at the pavilion. In the beginning, many of these young soldiers became her friends. She could talk to them, and they to her. She told me that just being there made it seem as if everyone, men and women, had known each other since childhood. Brothers and sisters, she said. And then she added the word *cousins*, acknowledging me.

Tall and strong, her wealth of blonde hair pulled back from her face, she looked good in anything. But her undeniable attractiveness was so natural, so unstudied, it would facilitate rather than interfere with any kind of interchange, and I am certain she could talk to a homesick boy from Hamilton, or a lovesick boy from Nanaimo, or a young married man from Quebec, frantic with worry about a sick child, with full empathy. And, I imagine, all of the soldiers would respect her military judgment as well, her perceptiveness, the way she could cut through the complicated intricacies of military language right to the core of a particular manoeuvre, the choreography of any planned diplomacy or violence, if it came to that. They would talk to her about the chaotic events of the day before and ask her to tell them her thoughts about what she felt might unfold next. She would be a comfort to these men, many of whom were frightened or angry about things they barely understood. She brought a focused energy with her into any room and a sense that each man's troubles were as important to her as they were to them. It was a gift she had, this power of shared talk. At least in the early days.

But I came to know that she could not talk this way to the man she loved, and what she saw as her own failure in this caused her to withdraw even from those men and women of whom she was so fond. Oh she still went through the motions, but, as she said, eventually all her relationships became pure performance, and she hated herself for this. I could barely hear their voices, I remember her saying, but by then I was skilled at hiding absolutely everything, including the fact that I was hiding. One half of me never left the room where I had last been with him, while the other half of me was dressed in the costume of the day, saying my lines, playing the role of the sympathetic, understanding officer. Even when there was danger or horror, she told me, her reactions were studied, not real. It was as if she couldn't feel anything except the feelings she had for him.

I told her this was crazy, that she certainly felt something for me, for her mother, her brothers. And who was this man anyway? What did he give her? How could she be willing to accept his reticence, his ambivalence? He could make it clear that he is committed to you, I said. He could at least do that. He must love you. He's been with you for years.

No, I don't think he does love me, she said. He has never once told me so.

Mandy, back home on leave, was wearing the same pyjamas she had worn almost two decades ago, at the time her father disappeared. I wondered if she was aware of that.

She turned away from the fire, which she had been studying while we talked, and gazed directly at me. There was such a helpless look of exhaustion and sorrow on her face. But, she said, aren't people like him, the smart, powerful ones, the ones everyone is drawn to, aren't they always almost monsters? They are an exaggeration, and everything around them becomes an exaggeration. As a commander, he is composed, stern, and then for one moment . . . one moment only . . . he will give evidence of feeling, and that moment moves like a tidal wave through the company. I've seen people weep because he closed his eyes once, in pain.

I ignored this for the time being. Mandy, I said, it's time to stop. You can *not* keep doing this, allowing it to bulldoze your life. I tried to remember how many years it had been. Five? Six?

What life? Her voice was shaking. It makes no sense really, but the only time I feel authentic in my life is when I am with him. This, coming from a woman who had held dying children in her arms, had lost friends and colleagues in battle, a woman who knew every kind of authorized and unauthorized weapon, and walked on the edge of death every day of her working life. This statement came from that woman. But it also came from the girl I had known, the one who was so gracious and so sociable. Every one of us had basked in her light: her brothers, her cousins, all her schoolmates. And now these soldiers, who not only adored her but needed her. Surely there would be something in that, some antidote. She quoted a poem by Emily Dickinson then, something about the soul choosing its own "society" and ending with a line that struck even me as powerful. "I've known her from an ample nation. Choose one; then close the valves of her attention. Like stone." Mandy and her poetry, I thought. What the hell is she doing fighting any kind of war?

She turned back toward the fire. In the face of this, of him, she told me, I am utterly powerless. She was twisting her long blonde hair around and around her wrist. They had wanted her to cut it off when she was in active service, but she had been able to wear it in a knot at the back of her head, covered by a net. And I know he's leaving me, she added, or preparing to leave me, slowly, by degrees.

Why, *why* have you chosen this? I said to her. I know now my tone was that of a person full of exasperation. I was almost angry with her. I should never have been angry with her.

I didn't choose it, she said. It chose me. Her cellphone rang then and she answered it, walking into the adjoining room, looking at the pine floor and engaging in some kind of brief, intense talk. A call from Kandahar, I suspected. Apparently, the arrangements for their meetings were as anxious and secretive and deadly as any kind of undercover military operation in which she had been involved. Right on cue, I thought. But then I realized she would have been thinking about him all the time, wherever she was: any conversation with him would have been right on cue. In her life there would have been various grounds: the pine floors of home, the tarmac of the air base, the linoleum floor of the troop planes, the tiles of Shannon airport where the aircraft refuelled, the hot dust of Afghanistan. Had her cellphone rung in such places?

I asked what they had talked about. Nothing, she told me. Mostly we exchange pleasantries. You know, she said, the usual. Are you well? Is everything okay for next Thursday?

That or nothing at all, she told me. Sometimes the phone would not ring, and the emails she sent would remain unanswered. She would settle for the pleasantries.

Clearly, she would have given up anything for him, or so I thought: her career, what remained of her family, her life. I asked her again and again, What about *you*, what about your *life*? She would look at me with blank defiance. I think, she once offered, that he is what makes me want to solve whatever problem presents itself on the ground over there. I know this sounds like a cliché, but it is as if he has some kind of appointment with destiny . . . you can't imagine what this mission means for him . . . and when we are at our closest I can feel some of that in myself. I've seen Afghans build an entire life around the disintegrating fragments of the kind of social order we take for granted. And once I'd seen that, I knew that I could build an emotional world around the smallest splinter of him, the idea of him, perhaps even the memory of him. I perform well because of him. Her voice lowered, and she admitted, with what seemed to be a hint of embarrassment, that she felt affirmed when he noticed she had been insightful or courageous in some way or another. I perform on a mission as if . . . as if he were watching me and this, well, this gets me through.

Approval, I thought, the one thing she was never going to fully receive from him. It would make her take more and more risks. Her focus had narrowed so completely, she was like a slender artery clogged by romance and by war. Seizure was inevitable. I'm so thirsty all the time in this godforsaken place, he had told her once. Yes, he was referring to Kandahar. You can't imagine the heat, she had told me. Ninety degrees is a chilly day.

But, she said, now he wasn't just referring to heat and thirst. He was also talking about her. In his mind, she believed, she had become that godforsaken place.

An older man, she had told me, by five years. Not that much older. But old enough that he should have taken some responsibility.

She disagreed. And anyway, she said, he does take responsibility. He keeps it private and safe. And, she said, he's so tender when he's able to be with me.

It was late at night and the wind had dropped; every detail of the view outside the windows had disappeared into darkness and nothing at all seemed to be moving. Still, I could hear the faint sound of the lake nudging the beach stones, making a fractional readjustment.

What was wrong with this man? Protecting himself, I decided. And throwing her to the wolves. Emotionally, even physically to a certain extent; perhaps more than I knew. She was not safe and she did not survive. And, privately, I blamed him, I blamed him.

I once believed that nobody but me would ever understand her pain, how she couldn't break the threads that braided them together, ones that I imagined as heavy links of iron but that she must have – at times – envisaged as golden. And even now I can understand it only in the way that I understand butterflies; I know what they do, but I am at a loss to explain why they do it. Perhaps we are drawn to the beauty of difficulty, the limited access to a sacred space, the arbitrariness of one species surviving while another vanishes overnight, a magnificently complicated relationship.

Mandy once said that if she let the difficulty go, her belief in poetry would disappear, along with her belief that her presence – and the presence of the others – in that faraway country might finally cause something good to happen. She said that the belief was a kind of poetry in itself. How could I argue with that? I have never been moved to participate in impossible situations. I have never fully understood poetry. I have never been a soldier. I have never been a butterfly. I have never loved in the difficult way Mandy loved.

I remember that on that final strange night lights from all the downstairs rooms of the house were spilling out onto the grass. There were outside lights as well and a moon bright enough that my cousins and I – and Teo – were playing Monopoly on the picnic table near the beach. I remember the *plonk, plonk* of the wooden pieces being moved from property to property. I also remember Teo and I looking at each other across this board game that I had had to explain to him because the monopolizing of urban property as a game was something he couldn't quite comprehend. Why would someone want to own a street? We sought each other's gaze with frank affection and seriousness during this interchange of information and with something else that I did not yet understand and would never name. I recall his brown eyes and thick lashes, the generous sweep of his eyebrows, the way he was able to concentrate both on me and on the game. It is somewhat startling to find how well I remember his face after all this time. And I remember that Monopoly board as well, how it remained in place for weeks after, curled by moisture, baked by sun, until all the properties and their streets – Boardwalk, Pennsylvania Avenue,

Park Place – faded and their names became lost, unreadable.

The previous day, after my uncle and the boys had moved what furniture they could into the living room, Mandy and I had spent a couple of hours washing the kitchen walls in preparation for the painters who would be arriving later in the week. While my aunt and my mother carefully lifted the glass collection from its shelves, my aunt said she had doubts that things would go as planned with her not there to oversee things. There was some family problem concerning the farm across the lake, and she was leaving that afternoon to spend a couple of days there. Was it something to do with estate matters? I can't recall now, or perhaps I never knew. She said that my uncle was given to interfering with her decorating plans and could quite possibly come up with ideas contrary to what she wanted. He'll be busy outside, my mother said, adding that she would keep an eye on him, though I could tell that my aunt didn't believe for a second that my mother would stand up to him if he took a notion to get involved. I was looking out the window at my mother's car while all this was going on. I wanted to be inside it.

I had spent many more hours of that summer practising how to drive. Teo would join me now whenever he could, though he never again asked for the keys. But mostly I was alone at the wheel and in the landscape through which I drove. The lake glinted on the left- or the right-hand side, depending on which direction I was going, and then there were the apple trees. Because it was late in the season they were filled with the Mexican pickers, Teo among them, their cotton shirts splashes of colour through the branches. Sometimes I could spot him on a ladder or in a field, other times he was hidden.

Recently I have become aware of how far this house really is from Sanctuary Line – the public road – of how long the lane is. I drive it each day and watch the old sugar maples cruise by the car windows. I drive it at night and see the two paths of the narrow track picked up by the headlights of the car and wonder if on that particular night the headlights were illuminated or if the driver navigated by the light of the moon.

Without making a statement of withdrawal, Teo and I abandoned the game. Neither of us had properties worth defending anyway, so we sold out to Mandy, her brothers, and a couple of their friends. Mandy, I think, had all the railroads. Shane had Boardwalk and Park Place. Neither of us could win, and we knew it, but that wasn't what made me want to walk away. I had lost interest in everything but Teo's face across the table, the intensity of his regard. The days were growing shorter and we hadn't much time.

Walking up the beach, he told me about his grandfather.

"An old man," he said, "very old. And always poor. We are, all of us, very poor." He spoke the word *poor* in two syllables. "But a great man," he added, "a fighter for the revolution."

He said the word *revolution* with such vehemence, it made the term electric and meaningful to me. But this was something so far from my own small realm of experience there was nothing I could say about it.

"Neither one of us has a father," I said. "I don't really remember mine."

"No." Teo stopped walking for a moment. "I can't remember either. But my mother said he was a good man."

I was pleased that Teo couldn't recall his father. It made what was developing between us feel even more important, less accidental. The fact that we were semi-orphaned was a link between us, one that could never be broken. "And your school?" I asked.

"There I am good." He smiled. "I will go to agricultural college. This" – he moved one arm back toward the fields and orchards – "this is how I will make money for that."

"Will you come here then, to go to college?" I had been gradually gaining a bit of knowledge of his life in a country that, until only two weeks ago, was connected to sombrero hats and what I had learned about certain vanished tribes when I studied the explorers in grade school.

"No, no, I will not come here. Here I can only be a worker." We had taken off our shoes and were walking on the edge of the sand where the cool water touched our feet. I remembered our little paper boats but did not bring that memory to his attention.

"You dance with your mother," I said.

"Yes," he said, "we dance. She has taught me, and sometimes we dance for tourists, for money."

"With your mother?"

"No, she has only taught me. At home I dance with other young people she has also taught. We have special clothing. And shoes."

I imagined there might be girls involved in this dancing, and this troubled me a bit, so I didn't ask. He would be graceful: the dancing would be electric, like the revolution, but I didn't want to discover any more about it. By now we had come to the rocky part of the shore. I stumbled, and he held out his hand and clasped my bare upper arm to steady me. The first moon of the autumn was rising, large and orange in the sky. A silence fell between us, and when he dropped his hand I moved in front of him and continued to walk along the shore. We rounded the point where the platforms of ancient limestone moved out into the lake, and eventually we came to a large smooth area where the sand was more plentiful than it was near the house. There was a log here where one could sit, and the cold remnants of a half-burnt campfire made by Shane or Don sometime earlier in the summer.

Teo wandered through the moonlight collecting kindling, and when he had found a fistful of twigs he dropped them on the partly charred wood and produced a packet of matches. I knew that he sometimes smoked in the bunkhouse with the men, and I remember the glow of the lit match in the shelter of his palm, how adult and masculine the image seemed. Once the fire was blazing, he sat beside me on the log, his arms on his knees and his hands clasped in front of him. The moon had diminished in brightness because of the fire, and now everything outside of the circle of warmth had become darker. Teo began to hum softly, and then he sang:

> *"La Chamuscada" le dicen 'onde quera,*
> *porque sus manos la pólvora quemó*
> *entre las balas pasó le pelotera,*
> *la "revolufia" sus huellas le dejó.*

I asked him to tell me what the words were saying.

"'La Chamuscada.' The Burnt One. A song from the revolution about a woman. A *soldadera*. A woman fighter. The burnt one, they call her everywhere," he translated, "because gunpowder burnt her hands. The revolution left its mark upon her."

His grandmother fought, he told me. It was how she met his grandfather. "He was only my age, she a few years older. Now she is dead." He hummed the tune for a moment. "My grandfather was only fifteen when he went to fight. The rest of his life, the rest of their lives were not so important because they remembered always this fighting. My great-grandfather too. He went with Pancho Villa in the mountains when the Americans were looking for him, for Pancho Villa. And my great-grandfather, he took his son with him." Teo turned to look at me. "My grandfather was younger than you and me are, and he was in the mountains fighting to keep some small bit of land for a farm." He stopped talking and threw a stone he had found in the sand into the path the moon was making on the lake. I wanted to ask who this Pancho Villa was, imagining him, because of his name, as a Mexican covered by a blanket and wearing a sombrero.

I wanted to ask, but I didn't, out of embarrassment, I think. The history I knew was so narrow it concerned only the British Isles, their kings and queens, their wars; that and the folk history of my own family. Instead, I told him that my uncle, too, had gone to be a soldier when he was very young, that he had had to run away to do this. "He didn't go with his father," I added. "And there wasn't any war then."

"You see, we are not so young." Teo seemed almost defensive. "We are not too young to have love."

"No," I said, though whether in refusal or agreement I wasn't sure.

He kissed me twice after that; once when I said the word *no* and again a few moments later. It is foolish and sentimental to suggest that something like that can alter one's outlook completely, but it seems to me that that is what happened. There was a whole life in those kisses, I think now, or at the very least a full young adulthood. There were the letters we would never get to write to each other. There was next summer and the one after that. In my weakest moments, barely awake at dawn, I think there may have even been the possibility of us operating this farm together in those kisses, tending the orchards and planting the fields, and perhaps some children waiting to be born. I realize that this is all an indulgence. How would we have managed it, after all? The immigration papers, the long road of schooling and changing ahead of both of us before immigration could even have been thought of. There would have been his family, and mine, both objecting vigorously, the complete incompatibility of our winter childhoods. His Catholic religion. My utter lack of any religion at all. Any one of those things could have left us staring at each other in the cold light of day; the combination of these factors, any rational person must admit, would have made anything I imagined impossible.

And yet we keep these things, don't we, these unresolved

touches in the dark? I bring the girl I was that night back to life as I tell you this, her astonishment in the face of shared love. She walks right up to my elbow, completely empty of the hard knowledge she would gain only hours later, and for a moment or two I am able to see everything through her eyes, the way the beach looked, and the smooth surface of Teo's palm when he held my hand as we walked back to the house, my sudden awareness that the keys to the car were still in the pocket of the shorts I was wearing and had been wearing when I drove up and down Sanctuary Line that afternoon. I bring that girl back and with her comes Mandy, innocent of love or war, asleep in her yellow bedroom in the house, her dreams a concoction of summer dances, disturbing poetry, and new fall fashions.

The car was parked at some distance from the house, which was a good thing because, careful as we were about closing the doors after we slid into the front seat, and in spite of the fact that I didn't turn on the lights until we reached the end of the long drive, I feared the noise of the engine starting up might have alerted someone, though I knew the one most sensitive to noise, my aunt, was safely across the lake. As it was, we drove undetected down Sanctuary Line until we came to a public boat launch where we could park. Teo put his arm around me and I placed my head on his shoulder, aware that if he had been a boy from the pavilion and not from Mexico it would have been him, not me, behind the wheel. We caressed each other and talked, comfortable now with the affection that was growing between us. The radio softly played the songs that were popular at that time, and among those songs were lyrics describing the end of summer and the separation of lovers. We were quiet when songs like this played. Neither one of us spoke about our own impending separation, the miracle of the present, this intimacy taking precedence over anything that might happen next.

"He never went with Pancho Villa to the mountains, my great-grandfather," Teo told me. "I said that because of all those stories your uncle tells. I think you will love me if I have stories too." He put his hand on the back of my neck under my ponytail. "Maybe you cannot love me if I tell you only we are poor and my grandfather did nothing but work till he died of a cough, and my great-grandfathers had no barns that blew away or lighthouses, or even any land." There had never been any gunfights, he confessed sadly. He said their lives – the lives of everyone he knew – were unimportant replicas of other unimportant lives being lived all around them. The people simply worked and then they died. And, surprised to find myself feeling womanly and adult, I ran my fingers over his cheekbone. I didn't care about the gunfights or the mountains. When I had said the word *no* down at the beach, it must have been in response to a premonition of what would happen later that night because everything I felt sitting beside him in the car was simple and natural and affirmed. He opened my blouse and placed his face and then his mouth on my small breasts and, though I was startled by this, nothing in me wanted to stop him from doing it. He kissed my hands and placed them under his shirt on the silk of his own skin near his waist. Then he carefully closed my blouse, button by button, with his mouth on my mouth.

I was aching under the spell of this transformation, this evolution of feeling. For the first time I knew that there existed a state of being that was both unbearable and hungered for.

There have been a few men in the intervening decades, and I have known physical pleasure and satisfaction, but the ghost of Teo – a boy I was just beginning to know – has always stood between those men and me in any room we entered. Maybe I was hoping to resurrect his ghost in them, or maybe that's not it at all. But I have stayed with no one I have touched for longer than a few months because not one of them, in any real way, has truly touched me.

Later, when we returned to the farm, I slowly eased the car back into its spot near the end of the lane and we walked hand in hand across the lawn, skirting around the picnic table where the Monopoly board glowed in the moonlight. There on the grass, Teo tried to teach me to dance in the way that he and his mother danced, but I was awkward and stumbling and finally he threw his hands up in mock despair and laughed at me. Then we danced in the slow way that teenagers at the pavilion had been dancing all summer long, while Teo quietly sang once again the sad song about *la Chamuscada*. I asked him if the Burnt One had died, and he said no, she didn't die, at least not then. The house was dark and silent. Everyone is asleep, I thought, and Teo and I had no business being out here in the dark alone together long after he should have been in the bunkhouse and I should have been in the narrow bed across from Mandy's in her room. Tomorrow Teo would have to be back in the trees; the harvest was in full swing and each evening trucks filled with produce departed for the city. Tomorrow I would begin to pack up my summer clothes in preparation for my return to the red brick house and to school. Still we stood with our foreheads touching and our arms around each other swaying in the dark as if this were the most natural thing to do at one o'clock in the morning in the vicinity of orchards. From the window beside this table I can see exactly where we stood, though the fences have fallen into disrepair and the trees are mostly dead and choked by weeds. He kissed me once more, and this time his tongue began a slow exploration of the inside of my mouth. It was in the middle of this kiss that we became aware of lights in the drive and quickly drew apart, hurrying behind a cedar bush beside the house as my aunt's car came to a halt ten feet from where we were standing.

I will never know exactly why my aunt decided to make the return trip in the middle of the night, but at that moment I thought it was because she couldn't bring herself to believe my uncle would be able to properly oversee what was going to take place in the kitchen. She doesn't trust him, was the thought I recall passing through my mind. Teo was still holding my hand when we saw their bedroom window blaze with light, then close down to darkness again. My aunt reappeared in the moonlight and hurried across the yard, passing within three feet of us as she moved toward Teo's mother's trailer.

What happened next is almost too painful to describe. The trailer windows flooded with light, and then there was yelling and commotion, a terrible howl and Dolores's voice pleading for something – could it have been mercy? – in Spanish. Instinct should have kept us, the children, out of the fray, but instead it propelled us directly into it, where we saw everything. My uncle standing there naked, slowly turning to the wall. Teo's mother, also naked, with her hands clasped over her skull as if she were being brutally pushed toward execution. And my aunt, her mouth twisted into a hard silent line, unleashing all the fury she had bolted inside her, bringing her fists down over and over again on Dolores's brown flesh, her breasts, her thighs, while my uncle stood motionless, his back turned, doing nothing. Though it must have been only seconds, all of this seemed to go on for hours, and I remember thinking first that my uncle would stop it and then, when he remained silent and still, that it would never stop, that Teo and I would be standing forever inside a trailer while this collision of outright violence and brutal immobility unfolded before us.

It was when my aunt turned to lift a chair from the corner of the room that Teo intervened, ripping it from her hands, then pinning her by her shoulders against the wall. She struggled for a moment or two, then wrenched herself from his grasp and fled into the night. Silence entered the room. The only sounds I remember were Teo's sharp breath and the ironically peaceful lapping of the great lake. Then Dolores removed her hands from her head and looked toward my uncle, who was stepping into his trousers. "Stanley . . ." she began, "Stanley, *por favor* . . ." Her voice left her and she sank back onto the bed. He looked in her direction. "*Naufragio*," he murmured, shaking his head. His face was grey, his expression almost empty, and without looking back, he moved into the dark, following his wife.

He had done nothing. He had said nothing but that one word. He protected neither his lover nor himself. Instead he followed his wife back to the house to receive the full force of her rage, leaving the woman he had been making love to in the custody of her son. I was still reeling from the brutality that had exploded out of my aunt and that seemed to be reverberating in this small space. I was also processing the fact of adult nudity with what I believed then to be the ugliness of that mature flesh, and the ugliness of what I realized must have passed between my uncle and Dolores, and I knew that Teo would have been trying to deal with all of that as well. He was on the other side of the table now, closer to where his mother lay.

"¡Yo la mato!" he said, breathing hard. "¡Yo la mato!" The anger in his voice terrified me.

"No," his mother said. She had a pale blanket around her. I couldn't stop staring at the swelling around one of her eyes. Teo was speaking rapidly to his mother. After one statement or another, he would hurl himself at a wall, either with his fists or with his body. Dolores said nothing except the word no and then more urgently, in English, "No fight!" Even humiliated and wounded, she was proud, and there was something pitiless in the tone of her voice; she didn't seem to pity herself and, she did not appear to pity her young son, as if she felt that he had no right to the fury that was coursing through his blood. No right at all, even after he had seen his mother as no child should ever see his mother, beaten, dishevelled, and in the immediate aftermath of love.

"*Amor*," she was saying to him now, as if to answer the question he kept asking, a question I would have been unable to understand. "*¿Por qué?*" he had kept saying. "*¿Por qué?*"

Teo stopped at the sound of the word his mother had spoken and stood completely still. Then he looked, just for a moment, at me. I was standing on the left side of the door, having moved not one inch since we both plunged through the cedars my aunt had planted and into the insane adult world contained by the four walls of that old rusting trailer. "*Amor*," Teo repeated, with bitterness in his voice.

"The keys," he said, thrusting his open hand toward me. "Give them to me." And then more softly, "Please."

"I won't," I said, now starting to cry.

"Please!" he said again, begging. "I ask you to give them to me."

"No," Dolores said. Was she speaking to me or to her son? "No."

Perhaps he was going to drive into the town to find the local doctor. Maybe, just maybe, that is what he had in mind. Certainly, he could not have entered the house to use the phone. But, and this is what haunts me, what I can't forgive myself for: I could have done that. I could have shaken myself out of my own paralysis, walked right past whatever viciousness was unfolding in the kitchen, gone into the parlour where a phone sat on my uncle's desk, and made the call. I could have kept those keys firmly in my pocket.

It was Teo's helplessness, his desperation, and my own confusion that must have caused me to hand him the small sliver of power contained in the two flat fragments of metal I had in my possession. "I'm coming with you," I said, but even before I had finished the sentence he was out the door. I could hear the sound of tyres spinning on the white gravel drive and I knew he was gone.

The inside of that trailer has never left my mind, and it will never, I'm certain, leave my memory. It presents itself each time I insert keys into the ignition of any car I've driven. It surfaces when I am shopping for groceries or bending over a microscope in the lab, and it slams itself into my consciousness any time a man has tried to make love to me. Dolores appeared not to notice me. She lay down instead on her bed, under the picture of the Virgin that hung on her wall. She rolled onto her side, away from me, and pulled the sheet over her shoulders, but even through this sheet and the blanket that still covered her, I could see that she was shaking. The chair my aunt had lifted lay on its back like a dead animal. There were two glasses and a half-bottle of wine on the Arborite table, and one other chair, still upright. I remember wondering, pointlessly, whether my uncle had sat on the piece of furniture my aunt had later chosen as a weapon. Dolores's voice cut right into this thought. "Go," she said. "Just you go."

Halfway across the yard I found Mandy, still partly stunned by sleep, standing like a white pillar on the lawn. Unlike the others who had remained in the house, she had been blown right out of her room by the tornado of invective that had burst into the house, a storm that must have brought to her attention in fragmented detail the scene I had witnessed, and shards of her parents' relationship.

I had no idea where to place my own feelings, no idea who was guilty, whose heart had been more painfully broken, how this terror had been born or why it had chosen to visit us. The attacker and the attacked, the adulterers and the spouses all seemed like one grotesque, vindictive adult to me. But seeing my cousin in her pyjamas, so disoriented and forlorn, her face still smudged by sleep, her eyes filled with such terrible knowledge, what could I say then? What can I say now about that? Except that all this year I have wondered what Mandy's lover might have felt had he seen her right there, right then. What would he have said to that thin child who stood in the dark yard with her arms and legs shaking in reaction to the ugly words she had heard and the hostile faces she had seen. Would he have taken some pity on the human side of her and drawn her with real affection into the comfort of his arms? Would there have been something in him that could recognize her vulnerability, something that would cause him to want to console and protect her?

I took Mandy's hand that night and led her over to the picnic table where that useless Monopoly game still sat, its pieces in place on various squares of property as if we might simply resume the game. We sat together on the bench, facing the lake and waiting out the night, neither of us saying much. We were still there when the dawn began to appear over the water, still there when the police cruiser bringing news of Teo's death turned off Sanctuary Line and made its way down the drive.

Mandy and I sat in the back seat of my uncle's car late the next morning, waiting to be taken somewhere by some adult or another. Not my uncle, no, it wouldn't have been him. It was likely my mother, wanting to get us out of there, telling us to get into the car, then being detained by the emergency in the house, talking to her brother, her sister-in-law, trying to add calmness to what was by then an impossible situation. The boys were in their room. There was no way to know what they were doing, but hearing the sound of the little television set when we'd passed by their room suggested they were looking for ways not to have to think. Something in them would have been broken. My uncle was refusing to speak to any of us. When we had last seen him, he was in the living room, sitting at the kitchen table he had recently moved there, staring out the window at the lake and smoking one cigarette after another. My aunt, on the other hand, having dismissed the painters the minute they arrived, was standing by the counter in the empty kitchen, one hand on either side of the sink, her arms tensed as if she feared she might vomit or collapse. She was looking out the kitchen window toward the road at the end of the lane, waiting. Rain fell softly and covered the car's windshield with small bright bulbs of water, but I could still see my aunt at the window, her face blurred by moisture. For a moment only, I recalled being a child in the back seat of another car, one sold years before, how I had been placed in the back seat for safety, and how, when I wasn't looking out the window, I could watch the small crescent moons refracted from the face of my mother's wristwatch tremble on the fabric ceiling.

———

There is no misery like a young person's misery, no tears like a young person's tears, no thought that grief should be concealed: grief is the dictator of this small brutal state, and its edicts control everything. I don't believe I have wept in any significant kind of way since that late-summer morning, even for Mandy, my partner in early sorrow.

The police had arrived about six in the morning, had delivered their news, and had gone away again. The car, they said – the car with Teo in it – had crashed through the cement railing of the overpass that crossed the highway and had fallen, nose first, onto the pavement below. The two officers had taken Dolores with them when they left. Had taken her to see her only child one last time, at the hospital where the ambulance had delivered him. What my aunt was waiting for at the window was Dolores's return, though how she could have faced her under the circumstances was more than I could imagine. But face Dolores she would, with all the practical arrangements for her return to Mexico efficiently taken care of. The two plane tickets waiting at the airport: one for Dolores, one for her brother. The procedure for the transport of the body, the phone calls, the discussions with officials, had been interrupted by the heated and unanswered questions she flung in the direction of her silent husband.

The orchards were filled with empty ladders: the whole operation had ground to a halt. Not a single Mexican worker had left the bunkhouses that morning except for Dolores, of course, and her brother, who had walked with her to the squad car and had sat beside her in the back seat, his thick arm over her shoulder. I don't recall the police vehicle pulling away, but I do remember thinking for the first time that the man who was always referred to as Dolores's brother was also Teo's uncle. All those years he had had an uncle too. That one thought penetrating the wall of anguish inside me.

There are large patches of time from the days following the accident that are completely unavailable to me, but I do have a distinct visual memory of being in the car with Mandy. The older maples had begun to turn and their coloured leaves were slick with rain. Now and then a leaf would descend through the air and paste itself to the windshield of the car like some kind of bad-news propaganda that had drifted down from an enemy plane. The monarchs were nowhere to be seen, having begun their migration, I suppose, unnoticed in the midst of this human tragedy. Quite a number of them would never reach the south side of the lake, never mind their eventual destination. None of them, I have come to know now, would ever come back.

Strangely, I was thinking about "little Nellie's grave", how Teo could never understand the wit behind the adults banishing us from their day in such a fashion. *She is dead in a funny way?* Now I knew that no one was ever dead in a humorous way, particularly not a child. Poor old Reverend Thomas Sanderson must have written his bad poetry in a state of helpless grief. The fact that his child's carefully chosen resting place had gone missing in less than a century just added to the tragedy. I thought about the lost Nellie. I knew no one would write a poem for Teo.

Mandy was wiping her wet face on the sleeves of her shirt. "The Mexican whore," she said, echoing her mother's words.

"Don't," I said, the word torn from inside me.

"She deserves her son to be dead." Mandy's voice was flat, cold.

I stopped crying then and looked at my cousin for a long time. Everything was unfolding in slow motion and slowly, slowly I could feel the desire to strike her moving through my blood. Instead I put my hand on the steel handle, pulled it up, and kicked open the car door, slamming it behind me as I walked away.

On the beach I threw everything I could find into the lake: stones, driftwood, two lawnchairs, a magazine Mandy had been reading the day before that she had left out in the rain, a plastic bottle filled with suntan lotion. I wanted to throw the house and outbuildings into the lake as well, and one part of my brain was trying to figure out how to accomplish that while another part of me had spotted my aunt's roses, more accessible victims.

A considerable number of bushes were floating offshore by the time Mandy attacked me from behind, her arms around my chest in a weird embrace, pinning my arms to my side.

"I didn't know," she said over and over, her head beside mine, her voice coming directly into my ear. "I didn't know, okay? I didn't know!" Blood from my hands was all over my shorts, and when Mandy let me go and I tried to push the tears and rain off my face, there was blood all over it as well. Mandy grabbed a sodden towel from the line and tried to clean me up. "I'm an idiot," she kept saying, crying as she pulled the cloth across my eyes and mouth. "Nothing is ever going to be the same, nothing is ever, *ever* going to be the same." She opened my closed bloody fists, first one and then the other, to search for thorns. "Shit, Liz," she said, trying to remove a black barb, her hands shaking.

How frail each life is. We mow a meadow and kill a thousand butterflies. The racket of the mower, the sound of a fist hitting flesh, an American bomb striking a Middle Eastern city – perhaps in the way of these things the only difference among them is that of scale. We keep on walking toward clamour and then cannot accept what that clamour shows us. What did I do, after all, what did any of us do to interrupt the chain of events that led to catastrophe? In some way I have never really wished to acknowledge, my aunt, violent and disgusting though her actions were, was the most honest among us at the moment when everything she must have overlooked confronted her and outrage bubbled to the surface of her character. My uncle, standing naked with his face turned to the wall, betrayed everyone with his passivity. Full of fear and inert refusal, he may as well have been saying to his wife, mow the meadow, slam the flesh, take the responsibility. It is this lack of life's energy at one pivotal moment that can in the end provoke tragedy. He could not bring himself to say the word *stop*.

Mandy and I had still been in the yard when the police car drove back down the lane. As if they had never known us, Dolores and her brother, sheathed in sorrow, walked right past us on their way to the bunkhouse. We made no gesture to stall that short journey but followed the one police officer who had driven them back, walking behind him and into the house.

My mother, aunt, and uncle were all in the kitchen. Someone, maybe one of the boys, had brought a couple of chairs back into the room and there was a bottle open on the counter; the two women each held a glass in their hand. It was now my uncle who stood at the window, a shroud of cigarette smoke around him, facing neither his sister nor his wife. He did not turn around when we entered.

"Well?" my aunt said.

The police officer removed his hat. A cursory discussion concerning the kind of papers needed to take Teo home followed, the fact that the police had been able to contact authorities in Canada who, in turn, had spoken with their counterparts in Mexico.

My aunt said she had talked to the airlines, that tickets would be waiting at the airport. I realized that this would be the only time that Teo and his mother would be departing from the regular airport and not the cargo terminal.

"Good," the officer said.

My mother offered him coffee. She was on her feet, moving toward the stove. When he shook his head, she set the cup down on the counter. My aunt lifted her glass to her mouth. No one spoke. A momentous quiet filled the room, and I could feel the misery rising in me like dark water.

"At least there is something to be grateful for," the officer eventually said, putting his cap on his head and adjusting the angle of the visor.

"Really?" my uncle said, still not turning from the window. "And what's that?" These may very well have been the first words he had spoken all day.

"At least no one was killed." The officer had his hand in the lower pocket of his jacket. I could hear the jingling of his keys. "An hour later there would have been a number of cars on that highway. It could have been a disaster."

"But someone *was* killed," my mother said, distress on her face and in her tone.

"I mean, besides the car thief." The officer had the doorknob in his hand. "It could have been a disaster," he repeated.

He let the screen door close behind him and descended the three stairs of the kitchen stoop.

My uncle spoke one last time then, his voice broken. "I wanted to stop it," he said. "But what could I do?" He had turned and was looking at me as he said these words, but there was nothing I could say in response. He left the house a few minutes later. He didn't say where he was going, and no one leaned out the door to call to him, as we so often had in the past. We were no longer hoping to be taken along on an adventure. We no longer wanted to follow him. We no longer wanted to be in his company.

"Open the window, Amanda," my aunt said after he had gone, "and the one in the parlour as well. Let's get the smoke out of this place."

II

At the beginning of this summer, on a clear morning, the first Sunday of June and a full year to the day after Mandy's death, a car I didn't recognize turned off Sanctuary Line and inched its way tentatively up the drive. I was cleaning up after my breakfast and was doing the dishes from both that meal and the previous evening's dinner, staring out the same window my aunt, and then my uncle, stood at all those years ago. I was trying to think more about Robert Louis Stevenson than I did about Mandy, but I had recently read Mandy's fourth-year thesis on Stevenson's poetry, and even if I hadn't, the two subjects were now forever connected in my mind. The poignancy of a young officer-in-training at a military college – one who would later die in active service – doing her honours thesis, after all her reading of contemporary poetry, on *A Child's Garden of Verses* was almost too much for me to bear. She would have chosen this subject as a refuge, I expect, a revisitation of the time before everything changed and shattered. I remembered her saying that nothing would ever, *ever* be the same.

I was thinking about Emily Dickinson too – Mandy had written that Stevenson's sensibility, though more masculine and meant for children, was not unlike Dickinson's in its focus on smaller, more fractional images. She argued it was merely a question of a light or a dark palette, comparing lines such as "I dreaded that first robin so" with "A birdie with a yellow bill / Hopped upon the window sill" or "She died at play / Gambolled away / Her lease of spotted hours" with "When children are playing alone on the green / In comes the playmate that never was seen." But all those tombs and death beds, and all that hopeless love in Dickinson's poetry signalled from such distance, and death himself such a courteous and much anticipated caller, all this was making me edgy in spite of the walk I'd taken earlier in the morning. I had passed through the old neglected orchard where the twisted trees had once again erupted into the kind of blossoms that should make the heart glad but in my case did not. The blossoms, the tombs, Mandy, and Teo were all mixed up in the way I was looking out that window, watching the unknown car come slowly toward the house. By the time it came to a halt and an attractive, dark-haired man had emerged – he seemed to be all legs – I was on the path to meet him, arms folded across my chest, defensive, the words "Can I help you?" delivered, I admit, with a touch of sarcasm from my lips.

"You're Liz," he said quietly.

"Am I?"

He looked around the property, taking in the blossoms, the fieldstones of the house, the lake with the arm of the Point over it's shoulder. "It's beautiful," he said, glancing toward the beach. "There are fossils, of course. She said there were thousands of them. She called them stone snails." He was fumbling in one of his pockets. The sun was making him squint. Eventually I found myself looking at an ammonite curled in his open hand. I knew who had given it to him. I knew then. I knew who he was.

Mandy's distress, her suffering, standing there right in front of me: the utter embodiment of tall, dark, and handsome.

I held up my hand. "Don't say anything."

He touched my arm as I moved away from him, then immediately withdrew his hand. I was heading mindlessly in the direction of the beach. "Hold on," he said. "Please."

He was following me now. "Don't – say – anything – else," I warned. "I really think you should leave."

He did not say anything else, but he did not leave. He sat down on the pebbles by the shore and put his head in his hands and began to weep.

————

You should, at the very least, have arrived in full dress uniform, appeared on the lawn like the controlling authority I was certain you were. Or battle dress would have worked as well: jackboots, and weapons, and camouflage. "The brute, brute heart of a brute like you" was a line I had read somewhere in one of Mandy's poetry books. You should have had official papers in your hand, a search warrant, orders for my arrest, even your own commission would have been more appropriate than the one stone remnant of this place that Mandy had taken with her into battle. Instead you stood there in jeans and a T-shirt, your fist relaxed and opened, the fossilized memory of an extinct species resting in your palm, your expression pained, concerned.

And you looked far too young, in spite of the odd trace of grey in your dark hair, too young, almost boyish, your shoulders stiff and awkward, a peculiar shyness in the way you held your head when you glanced at me, then glanced away. Then you walked on to my beach, Mandy's beach, you sat down and wept, and I was a witness to your grief.

I said nothing. But you stayed.

"I went out to the graveyard earlier," you said, throwing one stone after another into the water, the way every male I have ever known has always done when confronted by that pebbled beach. You were too young, five years older than Mandy, middle-aged really, but nothing like what I had imagined. An amalgamation of hunger, curiosity, and sorrow was almost palpable in the air around you.

"You knew about me," I said.

"Yes, she talked about her cousin Liz." You glanced at me, and then away again in that shy manner. "She talked about you, your butterflies." You lifted your head and examined the air, but I'm sorry to say there was not one monarch in the vicinity at that moment.

"You knew that Mandy and I talked."

"She never told me you talked about me. But I knew."

I didn't respond to this, mistrustful, for a minute or two, of your motives. Had you come here to win me over?

"Second generation," you said, when you caught me looking at you. "So no accent."

I knew then that for years, whenever a look of suspicion crossed anyone's face, you would think it was your race they were questioning.

"What's your name?" I asked. "Major? Colonel . . . ?"

"Vahil," you said, ignoring my reference to rank. "My name is Vahil." When I was silent, you told me this was a Kurdish name.

———

We walked along the beach to the spot where Teo and I had sailed our paper boats and I pointed out the shelves of limestone and we talked about how the fossils came to be. You asked if you were keeping me from anything and I said you were not and took you inside and made some sandwiches for lunch. We sat on the veranda, ate, and looked at the lake. You smiled when I told you about Mandy and all the swimming, how she would stay in the water until her lips turned blue and her shoulders shook.

"She was like that on the ground, over there, as well," you said, "always staying in. Once she had taken something on, she would never give it up." You paused. "Even me," you said. "She wouldn't give up – even on me."

We both became very quiet then, you with your face averted.

"She was the one who was going to shine," I told you. "We all thought nothing was ever going to interfere with her steady intelligence, her full engagement." Nothing, I thought, but the love that blindsided her and left her breathless in the midst of combat duty. "Even the idea of battle itself intrigued her, the strategy, the team spirit. She talked to me about that."

You nodded. "But over there, there are no clearly defined battles. Nothing is the way you think it will be. There are no teams. Just people, and all of them being hurt in some way or another. Physically, emotionally . . ."

"Yes, she used to talk about that as well."

You pulled your wallet from your pocket then and showed me a picture of a kind-looking woman and two boys, their bright faces aware of the camera, anxious to please an invisible photographer. I didn't even ask you where that photograph was taken, where you lived, but I knew that you lived there, wherever it was. The woman was wearing a hijab and her arms, long like yours, encircled the two children.

"So you *are* married after all."

You laughed in surprise and told me that your father had taken the picture when you and your brother were children. As you returned the wallet to your pocket, you became serious again. "No, not married." You paused. "Muslim."

"Mandy never said anything about that."

"No," you said, "it was too complicated. Even *we* could barely talk about it. She tried, but there was this conflict in me, all the time, and my family . . . I asked her not to say anything. I wasn't the only Canadian Muslim there, of course. And not the only Muslim in Petawawa either. One of my cousins" – you looked at me and smiled – "and a couple of others, only acquaintances really, from the Ottawa mosque. But if they had known . . . it is a small community."

They wanted Canadian Muslims to join the armed forces, you explained, especially those who spoke Arabic, which you did, you do, a bit. You paused after telling me this, ran your hand over the surface of the old table that sat between the two chairs on the veranda, and picked up one white stone from the collection I had made there. "I joined as a peacekeeper. I was a high-school math teacher before." You smiled, and I thought, Here is Mister Military: a Muslim, a teacher. "And then, six months later," you said, "we entered the war." You told me that, in Kandahar, you had arranged informal prayers for the Muslims on the base. I was intrigued by this.

You were not yet an imam, you explained. "I never would have thought that it was in me," you said. "I wasn't even very religious before." You looked out over the lake. "But there was something about being over there." You ran your hand back and forth along the arm of the chair. "It wasn't long before I knew what I wanted, what I had to become."

"And Mandy knew too . . . that you were moving toward a decision."

"Yes."

"She went to military college because of the peacekeeping," I said. All that searching and rescuing, I thought.

"I know," you said. "I loved that about her. That, and the poetry."

———

239

I showed you the twisted trees in the orchard, pointed to the wood lot, explained how the land had been sold to developers of estate housing. You asked about the monarchs, and I told you about them as well. You said you already knew about the butterfly tree, and for the first time I thought about Mandy lying in your arms, painting a picture of this farm, the summers of our childhood, and wondered how she would have painted it. Would the palette have been bright or dark, or that combination of shadow and light she wrote about. Chiaroscuro.

———

Back inside the kitchen as I made tea, you mentioned the prayers again. "Over there," you began, "we . . . the North American Muslims on the base . . . needed something, some connection to our own world." The desire to tighten that connection kept coming to you, you said, over and over when you were leading those prayers, or in the midst of manoeuvres, or, sometimes, even when you were with Mandy. It grew larger as you walked up and down the Middle Eastern streets through the unimaginable heat, acknowledging the quiet devotion of people caught in the teeth of chaos.

Yes, I said, knowing that Mandy could only have stood outside that world, that desire.

And you said, as if sensing my thoughts, "Our worlds could only have intersected there, you know, Mandy's and mine, on some base or another. It didn't really matter where that base might be . . .

Petawawa, Kandahar. But, oddly, it was Kandahar that cracked me open spiritually."

I wondered why you said *oddly* and asked.

"Because I am a Muslim and there I was in a Muslim country. It wasn't until I was in the Middle East that I discovered that, no matter where I went, I would always be a displaced Muslim." And yet you told me, in the midst of that displacement, there was this music of communion. The call to prayer.

"And Mandy wasn't like you."

"How could she be?" You looked around the room, then outside the window. "This is what made her."

"So you couldn't love her." Mandy was vivid in my mind. *He has never once told me he loves me.*

You were silent, but your distress was visible on your face. "Of course I loved her," you said, "but we were never going to be able to enter each other's lives once our tours of duty were over." There were no tears, which that made what you were saying even more desperate. "How could I talk to her about that love and at the same time know that I would never bring her fully into my life? This stone house, these meadows, orchards full of flowering trees created her. That, and growing up without ever once having to ask yourself where you belonged." Your elbows were resting on the kitchen table and your hands were raised. You held them, palm inwards, about ten inches apart, as if you were indicating the measurement of something.

"I wish – and you don't know how much I wish – you had told Mandy that."

"Liz," you said, looking away from me, your voice soft, "I didn't have to tell Mandy that. She already knew."

I stood up and crossed to your side of the table. I took your hand, and you rose to your feet. "Look out the window, Vahil," I said. "The cultivated landscape of this farm has decayed so completely now it is difficult to believe that the fields and orchards ever existed outside of my own memories, my own imagination."

You turned and walked with me toward the kitchen window. You stood in front of the glass with me slightly behind you. You looked out, glanced back in my direction, and looked out again. "Yes," you said. "Mandy told me that after her father had left . . ."

And then I told you everything else, long into the night.

It is almost three weeks since you were here and I have been busy measuring wings, an activity that might seem to be exotic but that is in fact rather tedious. I'm ashamed to say that one monarch can seem much like another once a hundred or so have passed through my hands. Still, I know that the tags we use, which only very infrequently furnish the information we want, could prevent the butterfly from reaching its destination if that butterfly is too small or too frail to carry one, so these measurements are important. Chance, after all, is more powerful than destiny, or so it seems, and we scientists want to do everything we can to thwart risk.

A pileated woodpecker has taken up residence in the woods behind the research station, and during the day he spends his time not far from the window of my lab, doggedly and noisily demolishing the logs along the shore, searching for ants. Whenever a jet airliner flies far overhead, or if a small plane buzzes by, the bird stops working, looks up, and follows its path across the sky, as if he believes that he and the aircraft are part of the same species. With the exception of the ants in the logs, nothing moving at ground level catches his attention, only these noisy airborne machines.

The first phase of a monarch's mating behaviour is entirely airborne and makes up that lilting dance we have all seen in early summer, the two specimens circling each other, their wings astir, their movements so cadenced it is possible to believe that what we are watching is music made visible. They are caught in the enchantment of courtship and the spell is as beautiful and as transient as youth. The next stage occurs when the male brings the female down to the ground level, where the pair remain locked together for up to an hour. After that, the female causes the astonishing metamorphoses to begin. She lays her eggs on a milkweed leaf and a caterpillar is born, an uncomfortable organism that will struggle out of its own skin several times before beginning to spin the cloth in which it will enclose itself, entering the smooth, green, and gradually hardening season of the pupa. Each of these small, firm caskets is so seeded with genetic memory, the emerging monarch will, even as its wings are stiffening in the sun, know the tree where it must congregate with its fellows and the route of the migration it must make.

The butterfly tree on the edge of Sanctuary Line was empty of wings when I woke up this morning. In spite of my profession, the enormous number of monarchs had taken me by surprise a few days previously. As if some ancient god had passed by in the night, lighting ten thousand small orange tapers before disappearing once again into antiquity, all of earth's vitality was confined to that one tree. Everything else was filled with the kind of stillness that follows an early-September sunrise, the great lake reflecting the sky, the birds strangely silent.

I returned to the house to find the camera, but what you will see in the photograph I am sending may look to you only like the turning of the leaves, the arrival of autumn. There seems to be no way to capture and hold on to that evidence of the perfect communion among these creatures of like mind and similar purpose. Perhaps all this is not unlike the Hajj you told me about, the tree a mosque, and that one particular mountain in Mexico a kind of Mecca. The monarchs who have just left my shore will take their journey only once, but all through their development, perhaps from the moment of conception, their cells have known that they must make the effort required to reach that holy ground. The Mexicans who watch their arrival, I've been told, believe that they are witnessing the annual return of the souls of their beloved dead.

It is another clear morning. I have just returned from the wood lot, which is almost impenetrable because no animals, wild or otherwise, are able to graze there anymore. Nevertheless, it is somewhat accessible at the northeast corner where the stream enters it. So I took off my shoes and socks and walked in the water between the bank of what Teo and I called our river, just as we used to do so many years ago. There aren't as many small brown trout now, but I did spot one or two, darting away from my ankles, and once I swore I saw one of Teo's temporary islands, but it turned out to be merely a spot where a fallen branch had caused the stream to silt up to such an extent that the soil was visible above the water-line. I had no paper with me, could make no boats, but of course I remembered the boats.

I have found that it is almost impossible to read *A Child's Garden of Verses* more than once without unconsciously memorizing a poem or two. This is also true of me and Emily Dickinson. As I walked in that water, then, approaching the bright openness of the lake that glittered in the sun beyond the trees, these two nineteenth-century voices were, side by side, debating in my mind, neither wanting to win their argument. Stevenson said:

> Dark brown is the river.
> Golden is the sand.
> It flows along for ever,
> With trees on either hand.

And Dickinson replied:

> Adrift! A little boat adrift!
> And night is coming down!
> Will no one guide a little boat
> Unto the nearest town?

Neruda was in my head then. His shipwrecked love.

———

When I visited the Golden Field yesterday, I took along one of the photos of the tree at the end of the lane. My mother held it in her hand for a long time before rising to search for her glasses so that she could examine it more closely. Once she had settled back into her chair and had given the picture another long look, she gazed at me with an expression of sadness. "Once, when I walked down to the end of the lane to see the butterflies, I recall the Mexican boy, Teo, standing beside that tree. He was alone and so was I. 'From my country' – I think that's what he said – 'from my country.' It's astonishing how well I remember that. At first I wasn't sure what he was talking about. He was quite small then, hardly knew any English. I suddenly realized he was talking about the butterflies." She paused. "He was Stanley's child, you know. I suppose Stanley must have had real feelings for her . . ." She was silent again, for a few moments, seeming to search for Dolores's name. "And the boy," she added. "I am sure that he loved Teo."

Slowly I sat down on the one antique sofa my mother had taken with her when she left the house. I noticed that the curved piece of wood on the arm of the sofa was beginning to separate from the upholstery. That will have to be fixed, I thought. Some day, that will have to be fixed.

I hadn't known. Mandy's voice was a phantom in my ear. *I didn't know, okay? I didn't know!* Her own lack of knowledge at the time was about the beginnings of a hidden teenage love, and yet something as simple as the way I slammed a car door could bring all that hiding and all that love to her attention, even in the midst of her own distress. How could some part of me not have known about this: the shared cells, the genetic inheritance? And the way my uncle insisted that we include Teo, make him one of us. One of my cousins, I thought now. Season after season, my uncle would have carried this secret with him. All those years while he was telling his stories, another parallel story would have been developing and growing in the shape of a child he would rarely see and would eventually lose completely as a result of the same, impossible love that created that child.

"Have you always known?" I asked, though I could barely speak.

"I saw Stanley once with the boy and there was" – she was having difficulty – "there was something there I couldn't identify. I saw him touch the child's hair."

"That couldn't be all. He must have said something."

"No. That morning I told you about, that morning beside the tree, the boy held his hands up, fingers open, as he tried to get me to understand that it was all of the butterflies he was referring to. I had spent hours of my own childhood prying hands just like those from the rungs of ladders and the branches of trees, coaxing Stanley down." She was looking at her own similar hands, now decades older than my uncle's, and a half a century older than Teo's had been. "The hands," she said, "right down to the shape of the fingernails, were exactly the same."

So there was the crucial observation. But hypotheses always precede both observations and conclusions. I decided not to ask about that. Hypotheses, after all, can often manifest themselves as uncomfortably dark questions. She wouldn't want to remember her suspicions, to talk about them.

"Teo," I said.

"No, he didn't know. Certainly not." She shifted in her chair. "But why talk about that?"

I knew I was not expected to answer this question.

"Even after Stanley disappeared," my mother said, "Sadie believed that what she had discovered – the woman – could simply not have been important to him." She paused, then added, "But she was important. I heard him once call her Mariposa, and his tone and the way he looked at her when he used that name made me understand."

Listening to my mother, I remembered something from that wretched night, something I had caught for just a moment in my uncle's expression before he turned away and faced the wall. I now realized that what I had glimpsed was the remains of passion and the arrival of horror and weakness and fear. And all of this overlaid by shame. His knowledge of his own weakness, his inability to act in the presence of his son, had allowed that shame to own him. He was frozen in place as he had been on a ladder at twelve years of age with the apples and the leaves and his own father's anger all around him.

"No, it was as it should be," my mother was saying. "I'm sure of it. No one else knew." She looked at me for several moments. "Except Dolores, of course," she said, stating the obvious but, more important, naming my uncle's lover for the first time.

———

Dolores likely would have been the first to hear the sounds, the first to permit the faint noise of approaching footsteps to gain precedence over the surf sound of his hands in her hair or his whisper, their heartbeats. Being of a temperament more watchful, more careful than his, she would have stiffened slightly in his embrace. Would he have noticed this? Or had he entered too fully into pleasure. And the drinking would have put him at a remove. Not from her, never from her, but from the rest of the world, which was, of course, its function. It would be the rest of the world, the rest of his life that was approaching now, sensed by her, forgotten for the time being by him. The full brunt of this life, soon to come to the door, bringing anger and sorrow and everything he had tried to sidestep with it.

It was the end of summer. The butterflies were gathering. The cicadas had lifted up their nocturnal tambourines, had been heard, identified, and commented on, and then absorbed into a thrumming darkness that could be ignored and slept through. There were other sounds, of course, a breeze in the pines, a freight train in the distance, the soft beat of the waves against the shore. There was the sound of their limbs moving on the sheets as well, so subtle it was like a finger moving over paper. And there would have been the occasional random illumination, a quick glance of radiance from the lighthouse on the point, the moon between two banks of clouds. A single lamp might have been burning in the bunkhouse where someone who could not sleep was writing a letter destined to be read in a kitchen in a faraway country.

This grief, this anger had been pacing the paths of the farm for years, moving from room to room, field to field, looking for a spot to settle, something to name; somewhere to stop and take root and become a monstrous dark flower. And even as this blossom was seeded, would my uncle have been murmuring the secret name

Mariposa he sometimes called her, this woman who was now alert in his arms? Would she have been able to receive the endearment? It is one of the things I now think about: whether she was able to salvage one memory of tenderness, or whether what happened next removed all tenderness and even its memory from her life.

She would have known for some time that she had nothing more to give him – but she would have continued to give anyway while he gradually withdrew further and further into desperate garrulousness and eager social engagement with everyone else who was around him. During those last years, he might have half-committed to a meeting and then not appeared, and not have told her that he wouldn't be appearing. She would be left alone then, in the trailer beside the bunkhouse with the ghost of him and a bottle of wine, brushing her dark hair, because she knew he loved it.

On those nights she must have come to know herself as one who has been made solitary by longing. A person absent from both ongoing parties, the one that unfolded so naturally among her own people and the other enacted in the house she had no access to. Once or twice, from the trailer windows, she must have seen him walk out to the garden, talking softly to one woman or another, their cigarettes glowing in the dark, heard their quiet, relaxed laughter. And if he visited her after, she would have feared that he was bringing that woman with him to her bed.

Sometimes she would have wanted to break with him but would find herself unable to tear the love and compassion out of her heart. And then there would have been the warmth of him, for he was a caring man, the gentleness of his touch, the way their bodies had come over the years to know each other so that they would drift in and out of a kind of sleep even while fully aroused and in the midst of love.

Her brother, also a fruit picker, would not have understood the summer change in her and would likely tell her so. She would use the absence of her sisters, worry about their elderly father, anything at all to explain her sudden bouts of silent preoccupation. She was never going to betray him, her seasonal lover. Whether her son noticed, I will never come to know, but she must have wondered if he would some day sense the submission that was born in her each summer, her willingness to leave herself unprotected. "*Amor*," she had said that night. "Love," my mother said yesterday afternoon, remembering Teo.

———

When I thought of Teo and Mandy as I walked the stream today, and later when I stood near the lake where Mandy loved to swim, we were all still children and there was no darkness attached to us. Nothing had been ruined in any of us – not even in my uncle, my aunt. Then I thought of you, Vahil, how at the same time you would have been alone in your Ottawa childhood, your otherness made clear to you daily, how you would take the journey to the Middle East only to have your otherness made clear to you there as well. Those hopeful, informal sessions of prayers that you held, and still hold, and the comfort you receive from them. I thought of all this.

All the tough evolutions, the shedding of various skins,

followed by those difficult migrations, over great stretches of open water, and across vast tracts of land, to and from Mexico, or America, or Kandahar. That longing we have to bring it all together into one well-organized cellular structure, and then the heartbreaking suspicion that, with the best of intentions, we never really can. Remember, unlike their predecessors, who live only six weeks, mating and dying en route to the north, the fourth generation of monarchs is the strongest, lasting a full nine months so that they can return to the place where they started, overwinter, and mate, and begin the whole process again.

The games of summer are over. Soon it will be time for the routine of winter to enter life in the manner of such things, the way it always does. Time for schools and jobs. Time for adulthood and responsibilities. The field and the lab. The finches at my mother's winter feeder. Migrations to softer or harder places. Tours of duty.

Standing on those limestone platforms with the bright expanse of an inland sea my only horizon, I watched three lost children, one of them me, fold their paper boats one last time while the poets spoke in my mind: the dark arguing with the bright palette, neither of them wrong. It was Mandy who filled the atmosphere in the end, her recitation so clear it was almost as if she were standing beside me at the water's edge.

> Away down the river,
> A hundred miles or more,
> Other little children
> Shall bring my boats ashore.

ACKNOWLEDGEMENTS

Several individuals have given me help and advice during the writing of this novel. Chris Peters provided valuable information concerning the working conditions of Mexican migrant workers, while Sue Adamson shared her family's intimate knowledge of fruit farming in southern Ontario. The late Clifford Quinn's "Down on the Farm" was an excellent source of details concerning pioneer agricultural practices, and Andrew Trant spoke to me about science and orchardists. I am most grateful to them all.

I would also like to thank Dr. Michael Hurley and Lt. Col. Ian Hope, both of the Royal Military College of Canada in Kingston, Ontario, for clarifying some facts; Bonnie Mulligan for keeping a significant part of my life in order and for being such a devoted reader; and my brother John Carter for his attentive reading.

Thanks also to Emily Urquhart, Tony Urquhart, Mieke Bevelander, and Andrew Trant for being enthusiastic and insightful first readers of this novel, and to Rasha Mourtada, also a first reader and one with unique knowledge.

I am very thankful for Ellen Levine, my agent of many years, who has constantly provided the warmest of professional and personal support.

I am extremely grateful for Heather Sangster's meticulous

attention to my work in this book and in all the other books of mine she has worked on.

I sincerely appreciate all of McClelland & Stewart's efforts on my behalf, and would particularly like to thank Kendra Ward, Ashley Dunn, and Anita Chong.

Thanks also are due to Michael Levine for all the sound guidance he has given me on various occasions.

Finally, and as always, I would like to express my deepest affectionate gratitude to my publisher and editor, Ellen Seligman, for her brilliant work with the text and for her unwavering loyalty to its author.

———

The verses on pages 48–9 are from "The Playhouse Key" by Rachel Field.

The song lyrics quoted on page 78 are from the traditional folk song "Little Sadie."

The verse on page 99 is from Pablo Neruda's poem "La Canción Desesperada" ("The Song of Despair"), from *Twenty Love Poems and a Song of Despair* by Pablo Neruda, translated by W. S. Merwin (Penguin Classics).

The line by Carl Sandburg on page 146 is from the poem "Fog".

The Spanish lyrics and English-language translation for the traditional folk song "La Chamuscada" quoted on page 211 are from *The Mexican Corrido* by Maria Herrera-Sobek (Indiana University Press, 1993).

The verse quoted on page 235 is from the poem "Daddy" by Sylvia Plath, from *Ariel*.

The verses by Robert Louis Stevenson are taken from the following poems: on page 35, "Farewell to the Farm"; on page 189, "At the

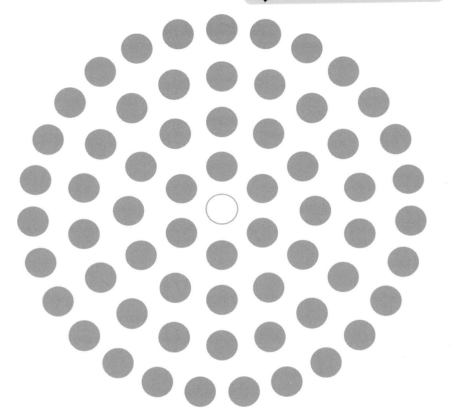

THE ART OF
CONTEMPLATION

Gentle path to wholeness and prosperity

Richard Rudd

GENE KEYS

This first edition published in Great Britain and USA 2018
by Gene Keys Publishing Ltd
Lytchett House, 13 Freeland Park
Wareham Road, Lytchett Matravers, Poole BH16 6FA

Richard Rudd

THE ART OF CONTEMPLATION

ISBN 978-0-9569750-9-6

GENEKEYS.COM

CONTENTS

ABOUT THE AUTHOR

Richard Rudd is an international teacher, writer and award-winning poet. His mystical journey began early in life when he experienced a life changing state of spiritual illumination over 3 days and nights in his twenties. This catalysed an extensive worldwide spiritual search. All his studies became synthesised in 2002 when he began to write and receive the Gene Keys – a vast synthesis exploring the miraculous possibilities inherent in human DNA. It took seven years to write the book as well as understand and embody its teachings. Today Richard continues to extend and embody the wisdom he received, sharing it with an ever-growing audience all around the world.

FOREWORD

A Gentle Path

From the moment we are born, our life begins to trace a mysterious arc against the blue sky of existence. Because of this, we each come into the world with a deep sense of anticipation that there is something special we are here to do in life.

The purpose of this book is to help you find, follow and fulfil the true curve of your life, and thus complete the circle you began to draw when you were born.

Whatever stage of life you are currently moving through, whether you are resting in a quiet eddy in the river or whether you feel immersed or even overwhelmed by the rushing cascade of life, this little book offers you a lifeline. As you imbibe the simple yet timeless teaching that lies inside, your life will gradually begin to evolve. At first it may hurt a little, as you come to see with crystal clarity that it is *you* who have stood for so long in your own way. But soon, as you follow the threads of understanding that dawn in you and as you begin to apply them to your life, many difficulties will drop away and you will find yourself living in a new way and inhabiting a new world.

Some of us read many books over the course of our lives. Some of us read only a few. It could be said that there are only three types of books in the world. There are books that entertain or inspire us. There are books that inform and educate us. Finally, there are books that touch our soul. Of these, some may also include either or both of the other two groups. However, such books are rare and come along infrequently into our lives.

The true power of a book is its ability to reach into our hearts and change us in a permanent way. The Art of Contemplation is intended to be such a book. It is the beginning of a journey that may stay with you for many years. The journey leads inwards although it will also affect your outer life in mysterious and beneficial ways. This is because our worldly life flows from the roots of our inner life – in how we think, in what we feel and in what we believe.

Before you begin this perennial journey into the internal landscape of your life, there is only one quality you will need. This is the quality of gentleness. As you will learn, the Art of Contemplation is a gentle path, and as you sow the seeds of this gentleness in the various corners of your life, soon all manner of good fortunes will begin to blossom and grow around you.

I wish you well on your journey.

Richard Rudd

INTRODUCTION

Contemplation as an Art

What *is* contemplation? Hopefully, by the time you have come to the end of this book, you will have a clear answer to this question. The answer however will not come through knowledge or reading alone. You might surmise that contemplation is a kind of deep thinking, which tends to be a more Western understanding of the word. However, the true nature of contemplation is a mystery. The very purpose of the contemplative way is to turn your energies inwards and make your life a centrifugal experiment in order to first discover and then embrace your true higher purpose in life.

The modern scientific mind doesn't always sit comfortably with the notion of a *mystery*. The purpose of science is to unlock life's many mysteries and attempt to understand the way things work. But there are subjects that may always be impenetrable to science. Consciousness itself is such a mystery. While we may one day understand how it works, its true depth lies beyond the domain of objective understanding. To know what we really are, we will have to go beyond the mind itself. This is the purpose of the Art of Contemplation.

Contemplation is an *art*, and because it is an art, it is something that we can learn. However, sometimes a sharp and powerful intellect can be a hindrance in learning this simple art.
Paradoxically, for many of us contemplation begins as a form of *unlearning*, as we let go of reliance on our intellect and open up new pathways of awareness inside ourselves.

In this book, you will be shown three simple techniques that will encourage the spirit of contemplation to grow in your life. It must be said however that these techniques are simply touchstones to help you get started. Once we find our true inner rhythm in life, we naturally become a contemplative person. We breathe more deeply, we take our time with things and we tap into a universal wisdom that can help us make sense of anything that comes our way.

One of the dilemmas in writing a book about contemplation is that you cannot access a mystery directly through techniques, and the modern world is somewhat obsessed with techniques. However, the good news is that contemplation can begin in our life as a simple practice, which we can over time turn into a habit. At the deepest level contemplation becomes a part of us, and when that happens, the techniques will naturally drop away and our whole life will be transformed.

The Difference between Contemplation, Meditation and Mindfulness

Many of us have heard about the practice of mindfulness, and we have all heard of meditation. You may even have practised either or both of these techniques. If you already have a practice such as meditation, it will not in any way conflict with the Art of Contemplation.

In fact, you could see contemplation as a very broad term that can contain other practices such as mindfulness. Thus, as you learn to contemplate, you will simultaneously deepen any other practices you are doing. If you happen to do yoga, for example, then contemplation will give you more inward focus and will help you integrate it even more into your daily life. If you do not do any other inward-focused practices, or have little or no experience of such things, this is also perfectly fine.

Contemplation is very generous and can pick up and put down anything it needs in order to achieve its primary aim, which is to bring you into a state of profound equilibrium.

The main difference between contemplation and either mindfulness or meditation is that contemplation also uses the mind in a proactive way. We make use of mindfulness by inwardly watching our mind, our emotions and body, but with contemplation we are also doing something active. Contemplation engages the power of mind, emotion and body. It fuses and uses their energy to bring about an increased state of self-awareness, freedom and general prosperity. Thus, the real power of contemplation is that it naturally turns into decisive action, and that action brings about fundamental changes in our life.

The other great advantage of contemplation is that it is a synthesising art. It brings together both left brain techniques and right brain leaps in awareness. For example, it makes use of the practice of mindfulness in the background while using the power of imaginative thinking in the foreground. In this sense, contemplation has many avenues of approach to suit different personality types. Whether you favour an intellectual, emotional or kinaesthetic approach, this is an art that can easily adapt itself to your needs.

A Breath of Freedom – *Spiro Ergo Prospero*

The Art of Contemplation leads us naturally into a state of prosperity. To be alive is to prosper. *Spiro ergo prospero,* I breathe therefore I prosper. This is not just a nice saying. It is the foundation stone of the contemplative way. As we grow from children into adults we gradually develop unconscious stress patterns in the body and mind that prevent us from breathing deeply. As you imbibe the secrets in this book, you will learn once again to breathe deeply. Breath is equivalent to freedom. The deeper we breathe, the freer we feel.

At some level we all seek the feeling of freedom. Whether we are trying to find freedom through having more money, or through new experiences or even through spiritual or health practices, we are unconsciously trying to return to the feeling we had as young children. The young child swims in the current of freedom. But this feeling we all seek cannot be brought about through any external set of 'perfect' conditions. It is directly linked to our breath patterns, so it can only be created from the inside. The main purpose of contemplation is therefore to unpick the false tapestry we have woven that promises us freedom while never delivering it.

One of the signs that you are on the path of contemplation is that your breathing becomes deeper and more rhythmic. However, this takes some time. You may be surprised to hear that there are no breathing exercises given in this book. This is because each person has their own natural breath pattern, and it must emerge naturally from inside you like a butterfly from a pupa.

As you learn the Art of Contemplation you will begin to experience the field of true prosperity. Prosperity is a living, vibrating field that unifies all areas of your life into a healthy, harmonic whole. And because prosperity is directly linked to freedom, as your breath deepens and you relax more, your mind will become more lucid and your decisions more certain. You will begin to swing into harmony with the spheres, engaging the power of synchronicity. Things may improve for you across the breadth of your life - relationships will become softer and more open, new creative currents will flow through you and fortunate circumstances may ripple through your life. It may seem as though a miracle has happened to you.

The miracle is that you are finding your original breath. You are finding that elusive feeling of freedom, and this transmits a sense of flow and ease into all areas of your life. Instead of your life feeling as if it is made up of separate compartments that are at odds with each other, now your life becomes a seamless whole. You feel whole and you feel prosperous. Your new creed becomes:

Spiro ergo prospero, I breathe therefore I prosper.

Being the Purpose of Life

We would all like to know what our true purpose in life is. Despite all the modern conveniences gifted through our technological age, the one thing that often eludes us is a deep sense of purpose and fulfilment.

Once again, we tend to believe that fulfilment may come from something that we create or do in our outer life. If we met the perfect partner, if we found the perfect home and if we had the perfect job, we believe that we might then know what it means to be fulfilled. This then becomes our mission in life - to try and create these perfect conditions.

The Art of Contemplation teaches us something different. It teaches us that the outer rests and relies upon the inner. We can have a perfect life on the outside but remain unhappy on the inside. And we can have very little on the outside but be joyous on the inside. The ultimate goal of contemplation is to bring both our inner and outer lives into balance. Then we can be inwardly fulfilled *and* outwardly content. Contemplation achieves this aim through teaching us how to cultivate a sense of presence. We will learn that the true purpose of life is not something we are here to *do,* rather it is something we are here to *be.* It is a quality or inner virtue that we bring to everything we do in life. To find our purpose is to find a nobility of spirit that pervades our entire life. When we have found this, what we *do* is of less importance because the *doing* may change. However, our being is the one thing that will never change. It alone makes us unshakeable, stable and radiant - we *become* the purpose of our life.

Contemplation throughout Time

The Art of Contemplation is as old as the hills. Many great and humble people have walked this path before you. The contemplative approach has long been the mainstay of all the great spiritual traditions from around the world. The first contemplators were the ancient shamans – those primal inner questers from pre-Neolithic times who sought to understand the connections between things. The shaman saw the link between the stars and the stones and was able for example to draw a clear, intuitive line connecting the patterns of birds in the sky with the events of our lives. This indeed is the purpose of contemplation – to find connections, to build bridges and to come to realise that everything in life is connected to everything else.

It has long been a strong and consistent intuition of humans that the things above are connected to the things below – that there is a deeper reason and purpose for everything that happens. Because this purpose is beyond the reach of our outer senses and our reasoning mind we have developed other ways of attuning to it. Contemplation is our tuning fork. All the major religions – Christianity, Hinduism, Buddhism, Judaism and Islam – all have strong contemplative elements. Myriad mystical techniques have sprung from this tradition – prayer, meditation, worship, singing, chanting and fasting are a few examples of contemplative practices.

Contemplation can either be done in solitude, as in the traditions of the lonely hermits and mystics, or it can be done together, as in the great monastic traditions. Sometimes contemplation also demands movement, as the contemplative sets off on long quests or pilgrimages. Other times, the contemplative remains in a single place and position for the duration of their entire life. The important thing to understand about the Art of Contemplation is the breadth of its generosity. It encompasses many practices, teachings and cultures, shaping itself to each human epoch. Thus, contemplation is as relevant and essential today as it has ever been and in many ways, as we shall see, it is even more so.

Contemporary Contemplation

The English word contemplation comes from the combining of the Latin root *templum* meaning a temple, and the prefix *con*, meaning with. One might therefore say that the inner meaning of the word is to go into one's own temple, one's own sacred inner space. The addition of the prefix *con* however adds an intriguing dimension to our understanding. When we go into our inner being, there is the notion that we are *with* someone or something. This is the essence of contemplation - that when we look inwards we begin to discover connections. We become merged *with* the mystery. This may sound mystical, and it is, but it is also something we all know already.

Most of us have already experienced contemplation. In fact, we already know how to do it. Sometimes when we are facing a problem or a challenge in life we find that an answer to our problem spontaneously emerges from within. Perhaps it comes in a dream, or as we lie in bed at night. Answers and insights come to us in many different ways, but we all know and recall these experiences. One purpose of this book is to increase the frequency of these spontaneous rushes of clarity in our lives. We have only to remember that the real answers to our questions and issues all stem from within us. It is that revelation that must saturate our lives.

In today's fast-paced world, you might worry that you simply won't be able to find the time to contemplate. The opposite is in fact the case. As you will learn, contemplation happens in the gaps of our lives. It goes on all the time in the background while we are busy, and then when we stop or rest or pause, suddenly something wells up in us as we realise a rare moment of pure being.

These magical moments may only last a few seconds, but when we look back on our busy day, you can be guaranteed that those few moments of calm and lucidity seem like an oasis amidst the noise and fury of our daily lives. The Art of Contemplation will widen out your life by shining a lens on these special moments until you find yourself hungry for more. As you learn the practice, you will also find that everything about your life becomes more efficient. Your body becomes lighter, your emotions come into balance and your mind becomes lucid and clear.

The Three Techniques – *Pausing, Pivoting, Merging*

The practical essence of this book is given over to three simple techniques that you can learn, refine and master over time. Each of these techniques relates to a potential transformation that contemplation can lead you through. The first technique is called Pausing and it relates to the mind. The second technique is called Pivoting and it relates to the emotions. The third technique is called Merging and it relates to the physical body. These techniques are easy to learn and ideally should be learned in the order they are given. In other words, it's better to properly grasp pausing before you move onto pivoting, since pivoting naturally evolves as you practise pausing. Likewise, merging is more advanced and will flow much more easily once you have fully grasped the first two techniques.

The Three Confirmations –
Insight, Breakthrough, Epiphany

As you learn to master the three techniques above, there are three indicators that will assure you that your contemplation practice is working. These are the three confirmations.

The first confirmation relates to pausing and is called *insight*, the second confirmation is called *breakthrough* and it relates to pivoting, while the third confirmation, *epiphany*, relates to the technique of merging.

Naturally, as with any new technique, you will need to be diligent and patient before you see the results. However, experience has shown that once you have mastered the first technique of pausing, then the other confirmations will follow naturally and easily in their own time.

Each of the three techniques as well as their confirmations, rewards and applications are described in the three main sections of this book. The epilogue consists of specific techniques and contemplations that can further enhance your practice and help bring the power of contemplation into your daily life.

The Great Reward of Contemplation –
Self Illumination

As you learn the Art of Contemplation there are many rewards that will come your way. You will feel calmer more of the time and your mind will settle and become clear. Decisions will flow more fluidly in your daily life and your body will remember what it means to relax, which may result in the healing of many old unhealthy patterns. You will be naturally more drawn to things and people that support and serve your evolution, rather than being pulled into difficult and challenging relationships and situations that drain your energy.

Above all, the greatest reward of contemplation is a process known as self-illumination. Self-illumination refers to a breakthrough or a series of breakthroughs that come about as our practice of contemplation deepens over time.

Self-illumination occurs as we let our contemplation wander freely through our life until it alights on something numinous, something that resonates very deeply inside us. When we discover such an image, idea or archetype, we can spend hours, weeks and months contemplating it. The simpler the idea, the deeper it will go in us until one day it simply detonates and we experience self-illumination - an unforgettable state of inner freedom and incandescence.

Using this Book

Despite its small size, this book has hidden depths. Each sentence contains a distilled shard of wisdom. As you piece these many fragments together, you will begin to inhabit the beautiful world of contemplation. Your life will continue on the surface just as it always has, but deep inside you something extraordinary will begin to grow. Perhaps in the beginning you simply need to read the words, and perhaps just a few of them will resonate inside your heart. This is a good beginning. Every time you read a sentence that opens a door inside you, pause for a moment and allow that to percolate. Contemplation, like a rare and fine tea, needs time to steep.

You might like to see your relationship to this little book as a journey. Perhaps you have found it during a period of your life when you really need a trusted guide. If so, this book can walk beside you for a time as you make the transition from one phase of your life to another. It can be a support and a comfort in that way. The book is designed to *remind* you how to contemplate. So even if you read it from cover to cover in a day or so, that is fine. But you will not easily be able to assimilate its depths in a short time. Contemplation is not a fast art. It is a wonderful, deep, lustrous, slow burn.

You are therefore invited to approach this book as you might approach a new friend. You cannot know someone new in a single, wild rush. You have to meet each other many times. You have to talk, listen, explore, travel together, perhaps argue and disagree at times, until one day you will simply find that you have found a trusted friend for life. So it is with the Art of Contemplation.

MENTAL CONTEMPLATION

Freeing the Mind

The human mind is an amazing instrument, and like a musical instrument it requires mastery in order for us to enjoy its full potential. You may have a beautiful violin but if all you can do is scrape a few harsh notes from it, it seems to be a wasted opportunity. Most people do not know how to get the most from their minds. Our modern education is akin to learning all the scales, but it doesn't extend much further, so we rarely learn to play the exquisite music that we were born to play.

The Art of Contemplation teaches us how to free our mind so that it can help us live a life of beauty and depth in which the mind is our ally rather than our enemy. For many people, the mind is something that causes us to worry and fret. It is useful for performing daily tasks and for helping us earn our daily bread, and it is fun to stimulate in all manner of ways, but we rarely treasure our mind for the sacred gift it truly is.

So, let us begin this journey by honouring the marvellous instrument we have at our disposal. Our ability to balance left brain logic with right brain intuition is a treasure that can take us wherever we wish to go in life. As you learn the subtle Art of Contemplation your mind will begin to realise its full effervescent potential. Once you have become your mind's master, you will begin to taste a sense of freedom and tranquility that you may never have dreamed possible.

Opening the Mind – *the Mental Plane*

If you truly wish to unlock the deep potential of your mind, you must approach contemplation with an open mind. Whenever we begin something new, we generally bring a great deal of learned mental baggage with us. When you enter a temple or a library or a museum, usually you are asked to leave your baggage at the door. This is a symbolic act as well as a practical necessity. Similarly, we enter the inner temple of our mind having taken our shoes off first. It's important to understand that you are not being asked to change your views or opinions or to discard any of your learning and education. You are simply asked to put it all down before you begin the process of contemplation.

Let's consider what you may have learned about your mind. Most probably you have been told that your mind is an extension of the working of your brain. Your brain provides the hardware and you decide which software you'd like to use and when and how to use it. This is more or less the standard common understanding of the human mind.

Here is an alternative way of looking at the mind. Imagine that your mind is a kind of radiant sheath that surrounds your physical body. It extends from every cell of your body and it permeates your body. Perhaps this 'mental body' extends far out into the room in which you are currently sitting. From this alternative view, you are living inside your mind instead of the other way around. Other people too are walking around with their mental bodies extending outwards into the environment. Collectively we are all inhabiting a world of thoughts and super-subtle vibrations that emanate from each of us.

Now imagine you sit down with a friend and these two mental bodies begin to overlap each other. You begin an animated conversation. Thoughts fly between you, carried by the vocal signatures of the words. Some thoughts remain unspoken but are perhaps still subtly felt by both of you. Your thoughts are mostly in resonance with each other, so you both feel comfortable.

Now imagine the opposite scenario. You stand opposite someone engaged in an argument. The subtle vibrations of your thoughts glance off each other, colliding and bouncing back and forth chaotically in a kind of swordplay. There is no resonance, so this feels uncomfortable and unpleasant.

The notion that thought exists on its own plane is not so hard to believe. It is a subtle vibration, and although we as yet have no definitive instrumentation for measuring such fine vibrations, that does not mean they do not exist. In this scenario, we might also extend our thinking even further. Through the universal law of affinity, we attract certain thought patterns through the mental dimension. A negative thought pattern such as 'I am not good enough' can attract a similar thought pattern through resonance. This would obviously lead to a challenging relationship, even though it began through resonance. Likewise, a positive thought pattern such as 'all human beings are essentially good at heart' can create and attract a very different set of relationships and life experiences.

Whether you choose to see the above as an eye-opening possibility or a colourful metaphor, the facts are self evident – the way we think determines the reality that coalesces around us. Our attitude moulds our thought forms. Like the world weather, a high-pressure system pushes the clouds away, whereas a low-pressure system attracts them. In the same way a clear mind repels confusion, doubt and negativity.

Contemplation creates Clarity

The easiest place to begin the journey of contemplation is through the mind. As you are reading these words you are already using your mind to contemplate. This is the first stage of contemplation.

You begin to think in depth about yourself and the purpose of your life. This is an ongoing process so you needn't feel in any way anxious about it. There is no right or wrong way. You don't need to sit down in a corner and close your eyes, and you needn't start any kind of special practice. Contemplation is a gentle path, and it begins right here, just with you thinking about your life. As you continue about your day, allow the contemplative stream of thought to simply emerge when it wants to, even if it's only for 5 minutes out of the whole day, or even if it's only when you open this book. The important thing to know is that you have now begun your journey.

As you move deeper into contemplation, and as it moves deeper into you, it has the wonderful effect of clearing your mind, as though you had just wiped a grubby windowpane with a warm soapy cloth. Such clarity is genuinely rare in our modern world. As it deepens you will become deeply respected by others, since a person who can see through the miasmas of the mind is someone who can help anyone in almost any situation imaginable.

What to Contemplate

There are many things we can use as a point of focus for contemplation, and there are two main approaches we can take. We can choose something that inspires us or we can choose something that challenges us.

If we choose something inspiring, like the action or life of a person whom we deeply admire, or perhaps a book, film or beautiful song, or something in nature, then our contemplation will begin to lift us up. It will raise our spirit, elevate our mood and suffuse us with a sense of peace and wonder. This is one major purpose of learning and mastering contemplation - to increase our capacity for joy and love.

The Art of Contemplation has universal appeal to all personality types. Whether you are visual, kinaesthetic or have a strong logical bent, you can adapt your favoured techniques to the subject of your contemplation. The main point is to use the moment to elevate your own thinking and feeling. If you are visual then you can use the wonderful power of your imagination to create an image of peace, love or beauty right inside your body and mind. If you are more physically oriented, you can use a physical practice such as running or yoga as a means to purify your thinking and bring focus and clarity to your inner state. As your practice becomes more advanced, you will realise that you can use anything as a subject for contemplation, so long as it inspires and uplifts your spirit.

The other purpose of contemplation is to create more clarity in our lives by helping us diffuse challenges. You can begin this process right now if you wish. You can think about the issue that you currently find most challenging in your life and make that the focus of your contemplation.

As you begin to wrap your head and heart around this challenge, and as long as you don't pressure yourself *in any way,* your contemplation will begin to reveal it in a new light. Your mind will stop tensing up whenever you think of this issue, which means you will more easily be able to come to an inner or outer resolution. This technique is really about holding the problem gently inside yourself and simply breathing into it. This second approach to contemplation leads to wisdom and clarity.

You can begin your journey into contemplation by choosing either or both of the two paths above. It is recommended that once you have chosen the subject you wish to focus on, whether inspiration, challenge or both, you stay with that subject until you experience some manner of opening occur inside you.

How to Contemplate

The actual process of contemplation is pure simplicity, although over time it reveals layer upon layer of depth and nuance. The three techniques in this book will take us into the process in some depth. Essentially, we begin our contemplation by focusing our awareness on something. If we are contemplating a challenge, then we focus on the resolution of the challenge. We hold that goal for as long as we can and when our awareness drifts away, we simply keep bringing it gently back again. There should be no tension in this process. If your life draws you away from the subject, that is fine. You can continue your contemplation later when you remember to. This unforced approach works extremely well over a period of time, because your awareness can follow its own inner rhythms.

Once begun, contemplation never ends. It goes on all the time even when we do not realise it. The more often we return to the subject of our contemplation, the deeper it enters into our unconscious mind. It even enters into our dream life. We simply contemplate whenever we feel like contemplating. That is the whole practice. If you are able to set aside a specific time each day for contemplation, that will greatly enhance the results.

In the beginning, you will probably find that your focus regularly drifts away from the subject, and at the end of the day you may have only spent a short time consciously contemplating. There are also certain times of the day that lend themselves more easily to the contemplative state. When we first wake up and before we go to sleep are examples of such times. We can take full advantage of these times when our awareness naturally turns inwards. Over time we will also find that we become more conscious of our inner state even during busy times of the day. This can really change the manner in which we approach the many tasks that each day brings us. We find that more and more breath enters into the fabric of our life, and even things we previously considered dull or monotonous begin to take on a new kind of shine.

The First Technique – *Pausing*

Once we have determined what kind of mystery we want to unlock, we need to create the right conditions for contemplation to occur. This requires that we cultivate a sense of spaciousness in our life. It is as though we have a pebble and we are going to drop that pebble into a large pool of water and examine the nature of its ripples. If the water is rough and disturbed, we won't have a clear view in which to see the ripples.

Pausing is the easiest of the three techniques in this book. The good news is that once you have mastered the art of pausing, the following techniques will come far more easily to you, so it is worth spending some time with it. It is also a wonderful technique in its own right. Done regularly, it can transform a person's whole life.

Think about the day you had yesterday. Try and recall some of the events that took place and then think about its overall feeling. When you came to the end of the day, how did you feel? Many of us get to the end of the day and just collapse onto the sofa or into bed without a sense of the day that we just had. As you learn the art of pausing, your days will begin to feel very different. They will expand as though you are somehow pumping more time and space into them.

Through pausing, you will also gain a wider sense of perspective on your life. Rather than simply hurtling through your day, you will see where it fits into a wider pattern, and this will give you an increased sense of patience and ease. You will begin to remember a fundamental life truth: If you push against the current, you will end up exhausted. Whereas if you find your own natural, harmonic rhythm, things will operate far more efficiently all around you.

The technique of pausing leads us to a wonderful paradox – the more we slow down, the more life appears to expand. In other words, the more frequently we learn to pause and take a breath, the more space we feel and the clearer our mind becomes. This lucid mind can then make clear and unhurried decisions throughout our day.

Harvesting Pauses

The technique of pausing involves nothing more than noticing life's natural pauses and then simply enjoying them. Everything in nature pauses. If you watch any bird, animal or insect, you will see it regularly pause for no apparent reason. Actually, there are many reasons for pausing. When you stop in your particular activity, you become more aware of your environment. You also become more aware of your *inner* environment. You may suddenly realise you are tired, or that your mind was spinning, or that your breathing has become shallow and laboured. Pauses like this often invite a physical sigh, as the body remembers to draw a deep breath and let go of some tension.

The first stage of the technique of pausing therefore involves finding and spotting the natural pauses that open up before you each day. Once you notice them, you can harvest them like fresh apples picked from the bough. Pauses are here to be enjoyed.

How long is a pause? A pause can be as short as a single breath or it can be much longer. You can begin this technique by finding as many short pauses in your day as you can. For example, when you are sitting looking at your screen, perhaps answering an email or a text, before you rush from one response to the next, try taking a few breaths between each one and perhaps look up and take in the environment around you. Another example might be when you are in your car and you get to the traffic lights just as they turn red. Instead of feeling frustrated or irritated, you could look at it another way. Life has just gifted you a pause. In that pause you can enter the field of contemplation.

These very simple techniques can have far-reaching effects in your life. A day filled with pauses is a calm and measured day. Nothing ever becomes overwhelming or causes you too much stress. What's more, when you get to the end of such a day, even though your body may be tired, your mind will still feel clear and uncluttered, leading to a deep sleep and a fine morning the following day.

Unexpected Pauses

When viewed in a certain way, life can be seen as very playful. We often find ourselves in the middle of an important task when all of a sudden something interrupts us. Although we may be irritated at having our rhythm broken or our plans thwarted, we may in time learn to see such disturbances as gifts. Every break in the flow is in fact a part of a wider flow, and this is sometimes how life offers us a pause that we *need*, even though we don't necessarily welcome it at the time. When we accept the interruption, and follow the energy that is calling us away, we often learn or experience something important that would otherwise not have occurred. Recognising pauses as *pauses* rather than annoying interruptions is an important part of the Art of Contemplation. Sometimes when we bat away a perceived disturbance, we are really closing the door to an unexpected moment of serendipity and good fortune. You may discover this for yourself the next time an unexpected pause surprises you.

The Magic in the Gap

Many great musicians, authors or artists have testified that the real magic of their art takes place in the silence between the notes or in the gaps between the words or images. This is more than simply a colourful metaphor. When we pause from a rush of outer activity, all the internal energy that we have cultivated through our contemplation suddenly pops up to the surface, like a basketball that we've been unconsciously holding underwater. At such times we suddenly remember ourselves once again, and we experience a moment of self awareness. Such moments are like glittering jewels in our day. We inwardly slow down for a short time, our breath deepens and perhaps we take a deep and luscious sigh.

Change takes place in the gaps. Gradually over time, as you learn to enjoy such pauses, your anxiety will diminish, your heart will soften and you will remember once again that your life can be filled with magic and mystery.

Creating Pauses

A major part of the Art of Contemplation is to engage your own spirit of creativity. It's up to you how you create more pauses in your day. Pausing is a form of self-discipline, and it takes some time to re-imprint the habit in your life. However, once we have begun the process, it can be both fun and very revealing.

There are many types of pauses. Pausing does not necessarily mean that you have to stop moving and remain still. This is only one aspect of pausing. Another type of pause is the transitionary pause between one event in our life and the next. For example, walking to work can be a pause. It all depends on how you walk. If you rush headlong down the street while at the same time gazing at your phone, this is not creating a pause. If, however, you saunter along the road at a leisurely pace, enjoying the fact that you are truly savouring this moment, then perhaps your lips will curl into a smile and for a few moments you will feel truly free and relaxed.

There are many such moving pauses in our lives. Walking is one of the great contemplative activities. Running can also be a wonderful way to contemplate, as can any aerobic activity that allows you a feeling of freedom. Your pauses can be silent or they can be punctuated with music. Anything that breaks the monotony of our ceaseless activity can be classified as a pause. The trick is to notice when pauses are happening and then to remember to enjoy them.

As we have already seen, sometimes when we are in a hurry life deliberately steps in and offers us a pause that we may feel is inconvenient. For example, we may be on the way somewhere and someone engages us in a conversation that we would rather avoid. These are moments to take note of. Instead of dropping our head and avoiding eye contact, we could try the opposite – being welcoming and warm. Most people love being listened to. Sometimes we may feel that such interactions are a waste of our precious time, but the truth is that they offer us a rare opportunity to be open-hearted and open-minded, sometimes with a stranger or a person we don't know so well. We never know what may come from such pauses until we engage with them. At the very least, we will have created a little more intimacy in the world.

Another gift you may like to give yourself is to learn the art of meandering, sauntering and lingering. This involves giving yourself more time than you need when you are going somewhere. Instead of rushing hurriedly from one place to the next, you might deliberately take a more circuitous route via a park or along a river, or even through a bustling marketplace. The trick is to be somewhere with no purpose other than pleasure and to take your time. We need to learn to saunter rather than stomp, and to meander rather than march.

Conscious lingering is another particular quality of the contemplative person. It is the ability to drink in an experience by pausing longer than appears to be necessary. Once again it is often when we give ourselves this extra spaciousness that unexpected gifts occur. For example, it is often after other people have left a meeting or a meal that a person lets their guard down, opening up a whole new level of dialogue or exchange.

Pausing really can be a beautifully simple and most enjoyable technique. As long as you are a little persistent and employ some creativity you will soon get the knack of it and begin to reap its many rewards.

The First Confirmation – *Insight*

You may recall that there are three confirmations that occur as a result of our contemplative practice. Each of the three contemplative techniques leads to some kind of transformation. The first of these is Insight. The more space and pauses you create in your daily life, the more relaxed and open your mind becomes. An open mind is a mind that can suddenly make a quantum leap in understanding. Insight is a spontaneous revelation about something that was previously hidden from our understanding.

There are many mysteries hidden within the human unconscious. For example, when we are young we learn various mental strategies for coping with unexpected painful situations, and these strategies are mostly lodged in our unconscious mind. Such patterns of thinking then follow us into our relationships, jobs and lives where they can undermine us when we feel threatened or overwhelmed. Our unconscious fears lie like twisted knots inside us that form into hardened opinions or judgments about ourselves, others and the world in general.

The Art of Contemplation gradually dissolves these hardened patterns, and the first stage is simply to create more inner space for them to be seen and released. This is the power of pausing. Pausing often leads directly to Insight, which is the spontaneous unravelling of one of these old knots inside our mind. As it splits open, and it can happen at any time, we suddenly feel a rush of understanding and release as we finally see and let go of an old pattern of thinking that has dogged us for years. The by-product of such an Insight is that a new light will go on somewhere deep in our mind, and this light will confirm and deepen our practice of contemplation.

As you practice the technique of pausing over a period of time, sooner or later you will experience a rush of such Insight. It may come suddenly, or it may well up gradually. When it does come, you will suddenly realise the power of contemplation as it impacts your mind, freeing you from limited ways of thinking and opening up a new way of seeing yourself in the world.

Silo-busting – *Applying Insight to Your Life*

One of the great advantages of having a free mind is that your thinking expands exponentially to encompass a huge diversity of fields. Genius is the ability to understand, both logically and intuitively, the central truth that unites all fields of knowledge and endeavour. Only a truly open mind has the ability to synthesise all this data.

Your contemplative practice over time will open up new neural pathways in your brain that bridge both left and right hemispheres. This means that whenever you experience an insight, you will see a vast web of interconnections, and you will sense the correct harmonic arrangement of those patterns. This new gift of understanding can then be applied to any field, from business to education to the arts. You will find that you can greatly increase the effectiveness of *any* system or method, from writing to doing the washing up, or from parenting to running a business.

The other unique application of a contemplative mind is its ability to break new ground. This is known as 'silo-busting'. Many of us develop a deep understanding in only one or perhaps two fields over the course of our lives. We often live within relatively tight confines, held back by the limits of our education, our culture and our conditioning. The contemplative mind is constantly breaking through these separate silos in which we unconsciously live. Through contemplation we begin applying our gift of insight to all manner of different areas of culture and thought, thus bringing into our life new ideas, new allies and friends, as well as a host of fresh opportunities.

The Reward of Pausing – *The Mind of Light*

Your new gift of insight can bring some extraordinary rewards into your life. Chief among these is lucidity of mind. After some time, you will find that your mind grasps the essence of any particular problem spontaneously and effortlessly. The main hallmark of a lucid mind is its ability to transform any challenge into a creative opportunity. As you learn the Art of Contemplation, you will even find that your thinking itself begins to pause as little spaces begin to open out between your thoughts. A clear mind repels both doubt and confusion. This new sense of inner spaciousness can give you a fresh confidence in the power of your own mind that you will transmit everywhere you go and in everything you do.

In Japan, where the art of contemplation has been perfected through the incisive practices of Zen Buddhism, one of the characters used for the word contemplation is:

参悟

The literal translation of these two characters is 'light flashed through the mind'.

Many human beings have intuited that the mind operating at its highest potential is connected to the notion of light. We speak of 'flashes of intuition', of illumination and enlightenment. All the great mystical traditions allude to this inner light that exists in a state somewhere just beyond our ordinary mind. The highest goal of the Art of Contemplation is ultimately to reveal this inner light.

Your mind's greatest spiritual potential is to see the same truth resonating within all things and all beings. This lofty goal comes as the result of many years of dedicated contemplative practice. However, despite being difficult to attain, such states have been shown to be real by many wise ones who have gone before us. Let this be a great encouragement for you as you sharpen and hone your mind's abilities through the Art of Contemplation. One day your reward will be to see through this universal mind and directly inhabit this magical state of unity known as the mind of light.

EMOTIONAL CONTEMPLATION

Cultivating your Higher Purpose

As your daily practice of the first contemplative technique deepens, you may begin to feel how all these pauses, both short and long, knit together to form a web of spacious calm. Now we may even find ourselves leading two kinds of lives – our old life, in which we are still like a spider blown around on the wind, and this new life flickering into form, in which we feel increasingly grounded and held by a new sense of stability and calmness. Our practice of contemplation invites us to continuously cultivate this feeling of core stability amidst the changing backdrop of our lives.

Without this sense of inner quietness and clarity, our true essence can never be felt or known. Many of us do not even realise that there is a transcendent force that lives within us. Like a seed that we are each gifted at birth, this mysterious essence requires gentle cultivation in order to reveal its true splendour within our lives. Through the practice and Art of Contemplation, this seed will rise up inside us as a powerful sense of higher purpose and vision.

Can you imagine the difference between a person who lives with a strong inner vision and a person who does not? Without a sense of vision, one simply drifts with no rudder on the currents of life, reacting and spinning from one event to the next. There can be little coherence in such a life, nor any real sense of purpose. Now imagine a person living with a strong inner vision. They may not know precisely where they are going, but there is a force, a commitment and a will running through the heart of their life. Their higher purpose wells up from a great pool of calm, manifesting in their life as a sense of virtue and noble activity. Such a life has a strong underlying sense of pattern that is deeply fulfilling. This is the contemplative life, and it is within your grasp.

It may be a useful image to see your contemplation as a garden that you are preparing. You are clearing spaces of weeds and turning over the soil. Every so often you carefully sow a new plant or a beautiful rosebush. Then you must be patient and wait, as all gardeners must. Before you know it, the new shoots will emerge and a new vision will begin growing before your very eyes.

Surfing the Emotional Wave

Rooted more deeply than our thoughts, our emotional patterns arguably have a greater impact on our quality of life than any other internal factor. Emotions are also inextricably connected with our thinking, which means that when we experience a change in our thinking life, we will also experience a change in our feeling life.

As our practice of contemplation continues, one of the first things we may notice is an increased awareness of our emotions. All emotions oscillate according to a wave pattern that takes us from happiness to pain and back again endlessly. Each person's emotional wave is unique and responds according to our constantly changing environment. Some waves are soft and undulating, others are sharp and spiky, others are relatively flat and subtle. When you get to know a person well, you also get to know the shape and cadence of their particular emotional wave.

Contemplation creates a sense of space around your emotions that allows you to stand clear of the impact of their powerful waves. This means that you no longer need be a victim of your changing emotional states or of the more extreme states of others. One of the greatest challenges we face is our identification with our emotions. When we feel irritated with someone for example, we don't realise that it is our identification with our emotional state that traps us. The inner space and awareness provided by contemplation chips away at this deep-seated process of identification, gradually dislodging our tendency to attach and blame external stimuli for our inner state.

Handling our emotional wave and the waves of others is akin to being out beyond the line of breakers with a surfboard. We have to attune ourselves to the rhythms of the different waves as they approach. If we get distracted by the rhythms and waves of others, we will mis-time our own alignment and get pulled under or overwhelmed by a wave. However, when we manage to hold our own equilibrium, even in a rough sea, we will hit that beautiful sweet spot that every surfer knows.

One of the hallmarks of a powerful contemplative practice is this ability to stay centred and stable amidst the many ups and downs of our emotional life. As we will see, this is the real core of this entire work.

Listening – *The Secret of Having a High EQ*

Many of us have probably heard of the concept of EQ - our *emotional intelligence.* As a counterbalance to our IQ (mental intelligence), EQ is a measure of our ability to discern the difference between our own emotional states and those of others, as well as our capacity to take responsibility for those emotional states. A high EQ therefore represents an ability to communicate your emotions clearly and respectfully with a high degree of empathy towards others. Having a high EQ improves all aspects of your relationships, enabling you to deal with challenging emotional situations with poise and courtesy. One of the great benefits of the Art of Contemplation is that it significantly raises your EQ by opening a wider space within your heart.

Once you have begun to breathe more space into your mind through the technique of pausing, this naturally opens up the wider orbit of your emotions. You will soon begin to realise how deeply interwoven your mind and emotions are. This enables you to listen more clearly to what is going on inside you at an emotional level. As your contemplation deepens, it is likely that you will enter into a period of emotional transformation as you identify and *root out* old emotional patterns that no longer serve you. This can be a powerful and exciting phase in your practice, and it can smooth out the emotional landscape of your relationships in fresh and dynamic ways.

The real secret of having a high EQ is however the secret of listening. Many modern people have forgotten how to listen to others because we have forgotten how to pause and be still. Only when you are still on the inside can you truly hear what is going on in another person. And when you can listen to the pain in another person's heart without rushing in to try and make them feel better, then you have learned to listen from your soul. When a person feels heard at this level it can be deeply healing, both for them and for you. This is another precious gift that you will learn from the contemplative way.

Your Amygdala – *Catching Shadows*

Deep within the recess of your brain stem lies a small almond-shaped neural chamber called the amygdala. Your amygdala is the processing centre for memory and emotions, particularly those which are rooted in fear. Difficult and challenging events in our early life are imprinted in this neural net where they can be triggered instantly whenever we feel unsafe or threatened. There is now growing scientific evidence that the painful memories of our ancestors are even passed on through our DNA and become a part of our own repertoire of emotional patterns and defence reflexes.

Your amygdala is like the detonator in a bomb. Operating at a level below our conscious awareness, it triggers learned reflexes that are relayed through our nervous system, which then manifest as emotional reactions. Psychologist Carl Jung named these patterns 'shadows', perhaps because they pursue us wherever we go. Emotional shadow reactions broadly come in two forms - extroverted and introverted. Extroverted reactions often manifest as anger or agitation whereas introverted patterns tend to manifest as numbness, anxiety or even despair.

If you contemplate the history of your relationships you will probably see that you favour one or other of these shadow reactions. Do you tend to turn inwards and compress your pain internally or do you lash out and express your pain in the form of anger or blame? Actually, if we dig a little deeper into this matter, we discover that beneath both shadow patterns lies a deeply embedded universal fear.

The deeper role of contemplation is to allow us to come face-to-face with this universal fear that all human beings experience. This is the role of pivoting, the second technique in this book. Pivoting shows you how to catch your shadows in action and thus disarm the neural detonator that propagates conflict. As you learn the technique of pivoting, you will over time reprogram the neurological patterns stored in your amygdala. This leads to a lessening of defensiveness, a letting-go of stress and a general softening and opening of your heart.

The Second Technique – *Pivoting*

Perhaps you already see and feel the benefits of the first technique of pausing. If such a simple technique can have such profound effects in our life, we may wonder what might happen if we go a bit deeper into those gaps and pauses? Let us contemplate the following sentence:

Every pause is a field of transformation.

This is the cornerstone of the second Technique, known as pivoting. The power of the pause is that it begins to create a circle of stillness inside us, like a calm lake on a crisp winter morning. When water is stirred up we cannot see through it, whereas when it is still, it becomes clear as crystal. The first phase is to create clarity, and the second is to drop something powerful into that space and observe its ripples throughout our being. The second technique of pivoting is about actively using our contemplation as a fulcrum to bring about a personal transformation. It's when our contemplation becomes action.

Pivoting is a practice derived from eastern tradition where it is seen as a means of transforming our desires or our *shadows* into a transcendent view of reality. In our contemporary version of contemplation, pivoting is an act of will that in the space of a single second, changes the direction of our energy from a downward arc to an upward spiral.

When you now enter into the space of a pause, imagine you are a car mechanic doing a quick engine check in the middle of a race. You scan the inside of your body for any discomfort, you observe your breath patterns, you check your emotional state and you do a general diagnostic of what thought patterns are running through your mind. You can do all of this within a matter of moments. This self-assessment trains you to work with your intuition. Your intuition will instantly pick up on a potential area or issue that needs deeper attention.

You might imagine you have three bands to diagnose – physical body, emotional wellbeing, mental state - and your intuition gives each one a score between 1 and 10. Another way might be to visualise a spectrum where green represents a peaceful condition, yellow represents a satisfactory condition and red represents an imbalanced condition. The trick here is not to over-analyse but to do the diagnostic quickly so that your intuition comes to the fore. This instantly gives your contemplation a focal point. You can do all this either quietly with your eyes closed or with your eyes open. With practise you can even do this exercise on the fly, moving, walking or even in a busy environment. The secret of contemplation is that you are one hundred percent with yourself, inside yourself.

Once you have ascertained which area or areas need the most attention, you can then bring your attention to this area and begin to look at it with honesty. It is this honesty that will bring about a breakthrough, as you engage in the powerful process of pivoting.

Below are 3 examples of how this might work in everyday life:

1. You are having a bad day. You are feeling stressed and anxious because of certain commitments that are putting you under pressure. This also makes you more irritable and touchy than usual. Your stressful state is therefore having the effect of propagating more stress around you. At a certain point, you remember to pause. For the space of a few minutes you discipline yourself to simply stop everything you are doing and let life catch up with you. During these precious minutes, you suddenly realise that you are caught in a self-destructive mindset. You breathe until you find a small pool of calm amidst the torrent of external pressures. From within this tiny

pool of quietness, you manage to change your attitude and thus the direction of your whole day. The sudden upsurge of your self awareness is powerful enough to become the pivot around which you can change from a victim mindset to a creative mindset.

2. You are feeling emotionally low. You have lost touch with any sense of joy or deeper purpose in life. You feel disconnected from others and you don't know how to get back to a brighter place. Instead of trying to distract yourself from the discomfort, you create a pause, a space inside yourself so that you can look at your inner state with honesty. On deeper self reflection you realise that the state you are in is a deep numbness. You remember that this is not unique to you but universal to all human beings. From this place of self compassion, you go further into yourself, into your heart, until you find the tiniest flame.

There is always a small flame in the midst of the numbness. You cradle this precious flame, like a tiny spark in a cold winter night. You gently fan the flame with patience until it grows inside you. This may take time, even several days. But over time, your awareness and courage help to bring this flame back to life. You begin to feel human again. You feel warmth and hope dawn inside you. You have made self-compassion and love the pivot for a total change in awareness, and having done it once, you draw strength from knowing you can do it again whenever you need. You have learned to bring your heart back to life.

3. You are feeling tension in your relationship. Whether you understand the reason for the tension or not, you can feel the pressure building and the probability of an argument breaking out. Instead of focusing on the other person, you take a pause and turn your attention inwards.

You take full ownership for your own discomfort, separating out your own issues from the those of the other person. This leaves you feeling clearer in your heart and mind. Now, instead of preparing for a defence or an attack, you are in a state where you can handle any emotions that come up from a place of empathy. Because of this, you decide not to speak to the other in a negative manner. You do not repress your feelings but you first listen to the other, acknowledging rather than defending. Then if appropriate, you speak openly and honestly, with an open heart and without blame. You have stopped the argument from your side. You have used a pause as the pivot for a total change in the direction of your emotional energy. Instead of an explosive and painful argument, you have created an atmosphere of acceptance and understanding.

In each of the examples above, the act of pivoting takes place within a pause. Obviously not every pause leads to pivoting, but by increasing the frequency of pauses in your life, you will also increase the possibility of these powerful transformations. Over time, using this simple technique of pausing and pivoting, you will find that you are breaking through many old negative patterns and you will feel a new sense of freedom and lightness flowing into each day of your life.

The beauty of pivoting is that it isn't something you consciously do. For the modern mind it can be difficult to comprehend that healing takes place without conscious action or effort on our part. The conscious aspect of the technique is taking the pause and then looking within to see what is occurring. The pivot itself, if and when it occurs, is unpredictable and mysterious. The pivot is something that happens on its own, simply by your being honest with yourself and by giving yourself the space for a shift to occur. We simply rest our attention on the nub of the problem, as a mother cradles her young child, and then we wait.

The Second Confirmation – *Breakthrough*

The second of the three confirmations that occurs as we practise contemplation is called breakthrough. Just as our first confirmation comes as a mental insight, the second is experienced as an emotional breakthrough. As the word signifies, this confirmation comes unexpectedly and powerfully as a transformation of some aspect of our emotional behaviour. Often the first stage of this breakthrough is simply to see our emotional shadow pattern objectively for the first time. This may come as a shock as we realise how much of a victim we have been of that particular emotional belief. Seeing the pattern clearly then leads to the gradual dissolution of the problem as our awareness continues to chip away at that pattern. Eventually our contemplative practise completely transforms the old negative shadow and it no longer haunts us or causes us the pain it used to.

Breakthrough can come either in the form of a sudden realisation or as a steady emotional expansion as we uproot an old paradigm that has dogged us and our relationships for years. In most cases, breakthrough lasts a considerable period of time since we are letting go of patterns that formed a long time ago when we were a child. If at any time you feel overwhelmed by such inner changes brought about by your practise of contemplation, you are advised to seek out a professional therapist or counsellor who will be able to assist you as you move through this transitional period.

Allow, Accept, Embrace – *the three stages of Breakthrough*

Breakthrough has three distinct stages that can help us surrender more deeply into the process. These stages can also help give us a solid sense of where we are in our own emotional terrain, as well as where we are heading.

The first stage is about *allowing* the painful feeling. Whether the feeling is anger, fear, numbness, resentment, grief or any other emotion, the first step is to simply allow yourself to feel it. You don't have to like it or accept it. You can even hate the feeling. To allow the feeling is to provide some space around it. Until you allow the feeling in, you are in denial of the pain and it will fester inside your psyche. The beauty of allowing is that it is so generous. It just opens the door a little, as much as we are comfortable. There is no pressure from allowing. We just take a peek at the pattern. We can even close the door again if it seems too painful. Allowing is a process in which we gradually open the door wider over a period of time.

The second stage occurs when we have done a certain amount of allowing. Acceptance occurs as we begin to get used to the discomfort. We realise that the emotional pain will not kill us. It can seem overwhelming, it can seem terrifying, it can make us feel irritated or deadened or filled with rage. As we come to accept a negative pattern, it is rather like taking in a stray dog or cat that has been abused. It takes time to rebuild trust. That hurt part of our psyche needs this acclimatisation period in which we gradually come to realise the depth of our pain. Whereas allowing makes space for all manner of feelings and extremes, acceptance brings us to a deeper and more mature place in which we are authentically facing our own pain or difficulty with love and understanding.

The final stage is *embracing* and it is the culmination of any breakthrough. Once an emotional shadow pattern has been fully accepted at the deepest level, it is effectively purged from our system. The painful memory that gave rise to the difficulty has been met with our deepest, most heartfelt compassion. It has been allowed to express itself without being projected onto another as blame. Neither have we in any way repressed the shadow as something shameful that we wish to forget. Over a period of time through our great courage, the pattern has been transformed, and in a beautiful twist it has become something remarkable – it has become grace. Grace can take many forms - it can come as forgiveness, self-empowerment, humility or any other profound sense of emotional resolution. The essence of the breakthrough is that our pain reveals its true higher purpose which is to bring us a profound sense of wholeness and love.

Applying Pivoting in our Relationships – *a Clean Slate*

As the power of pivoting spreads into your life, all your relationships will benefit. Personal relationships will become so much easier as you learn the art of empathy and patience that grows out of the technique of pivoting. Business relationships will also become clearer and more efficient as your increased sense of relaxation around others leads to open and honest communication. Enormous time is saved through simple honesty. It is as though you are beginning your life again with a completely clean slate in which negativity and dishonesty have been completely thrown out.

In Japan, there is a tradition known as *haragei* – it concerns the subtle communication that passes between people through chemistry, facial expression, body language and intuition. It has been proven that the greater percentage of all communication between humans takes place at this unconscious level. In *haragei*, the most important factor in communication is your honesty and your intent. If you are concealing something, then no matter how adept you think you are at hiding it, it will always be communicated at an unconscious level. Even if we override our own intuition, in the end the hidden factor will surface at some point in the relationship, usually leading to crisis.

The reason that the technique of pivoting creates such beneficial changes in our relationships is because it trains us to be inwardly honest. When you are honest with yourself and another, the relationship is clean. A clean relationship is like a well-tended garden in which the flowers and plants are given the optimum conditions for growth and prosperity.

The Role of Gentleness

As you can perhaps surmise, pivoting can be quite an intense inner process at times. We are confronting aspects of our selves that we may have unconsciously fled from for most of our lives. All our inner challenges are rooted in old fears. The emotional shadow reactions spoken of earlier are simply an understandable way in which we try to glaze over some form of deep-seated fear or trauma. Such tender areas in our psyche require the gentlest of touches. This gentleness is the quintessence of the Art of Contemplation. If you remember nothing else as you practise the Art of Contemplation, remember only this:

Above all, be gentle with yourself.

The core message that contemplation teaches us is that feeling fear is safe. That is, fear does not *feel* safe, but it is safe to *feel* it. Similarly, as we approach pain of any sort, instead of flinching, through contemplation we soften *into* it. When someone is physically wounded, our immediate instinct is to behave gently and calmly around them. Contemplation applies this same wisdom inwardly. We all carry tender emotional wounds of one sort or another. The touch of contemplation is the gentlest, most all-forgiving touch. When you feel any level of pain, this is the spirit in which you need to approach yourself.

Likewise, in your personal and professional relationships it's vital always to consider the feelings of the other. We must be honest, but we must also be gentle and considerate. The softer our touch, the greater the opening will be.

The Reward of Pivoting – *the Heart of Peace*

Pivoting is about dealing with the unknown, with change and with the unpredictable in life. It is also the knife-edge of contemplation. Like a scalpel, pivoting can be used to cut out dishonesty from our inner life. It takes courage to lean into our wounds, challenges and shadows in this way, but the rewards of the process are exponentially great compared to the difficulties. The technique of pivoting may do the surgery, but our ongoing contemplative practice will heal the wounds that are exposed. It is rare to find a human being without some imprint of trauma in their emotional life. The great antidote to trauma is love.

There is much hype in the modern world about the true meaning of love. Few are those who have truly discovered the source of love inside the human heart. Yet this is the reward of the Art of Contemplation. As our awareness continues to open deeper pools of calm, old patterns and pain come to the surface for healing, and out of these patterns emerges our higher purpose in the world.

The ancient Sufis of the Middle Eastern deserts gave the whole of their lives to the singular study of the subject of love. Over many generations they created an exquisite science of love that has never been surpassed. They distinguished many forms of love and gave them precise names. The name they gave to the highest form of human love is *Ishq* – pure love. Pure love is unconditional and arises in the heart when all wounds have been healed. This is the great love our poets have always sung of – the love that stitches together the very fabric of our world.

Although it may seem to many like a romantic dream, pure love is the only lasting legacy we humans have. There is nothing comparable to it in all of creation. All our knowledge and science and self importance falls away in the presence of such love. It is this love that we come from, and this love that we will return to. It is the fathomless mystery of the human heart. This pure love, though hard earned and seldom witnessed on our earth, is the ultimate reward of the deeper reaches of contemplation. Those few who have embodied this love throughout history have found few words to describe it. They speak of it as an indescribable peace that resides in the human heart. It is this heart of peace that lies buried like a glittering gem inside each of us. It awaits the day when we will gather the courage to pierce our fear and softly allow the petals of our hearts to once again open fully.

PHYSICAL CONTEMPLATION

Celebrating the Body

The great contemplative traditions throughout time have taken very mixed views towards the physical body. The more extreme renunciate paths attempt to transcend the body through intense discipline and even self-denial. Such paths can be harsh and unrealistic for the modern world. A more balanced approach is to use the body and its natural impulses as a means for gaining self knowledge and by celebrating our physical body on a daily basis.

Our body is like a beloved pet. The better we take care of it and love it, the happier and healthier it will be. If you neglect an animal, it will become increasingly unhappy and restless. If you feed it too much rich food, or not enough food, or if you neglect to exercise it, it will suffer. These are obvious but vital truths.

The deeper we enter into the Art of Contemplation the more we want to keep our body pure, because a pure body leads to a pure, calm inner state. This does not mean that we should be austere with our body or worry too much about it. Our body is our experimental mirror. If we put it under sustained stress it will either rebel or collapse. The body is therefore like a set of finely tuned scales. Over time we need to learn exactly what it needs in order to thrive and come into perfect harmony.

Thus far in our contemplative journey we have explored both the mind and the emotions. The physical body is the bedrock of both.

Our brain chemistry, our nervous and immune systems and all facets of our physicality are intricately interwoven. We are one pulsing, gleaming whole. In the body there lie many secrets. As we learn to treasure the body, it will gradually release these secrets. Our DNA is a labyrinth of undreamt of possibility. Only by bringing body, mind and emotion into perfect harmony can we unlock the higher possibilities latent in our DNA. Then we will celebrate a level of radiant health and heightened awareness that is currently dormant. The Art of Contemplation is the gentle path that can lead us to this state of wondrous wholeness.

The Body and the Seasons – *Attunement*

One of the strongest influences on our contemplation is the changing seasons. We can begin with the realisation that the body pulses according to natural planetary rhythms. Depending on where we live, the soft animal of our body quite naturally adjusts itself to the environmental cadences of the life around us. Our placement within a wider pattern that includes the position of the sun, moon and celestial spheres also lends a subtle shape to our personal contemplative practise. As we become more aware of these seasonal and local factors, we can fine-tune our own contemplation and harmonise with our environment.

Spring Contemplation

Every spring the earth awakens. As the buds begin to open and the creatures around us become busier and more externally focused, so our awareness naturally follows. With the Sun's return it is natural to wake earlier with the light. There is so much fuel for our contemplation! The sound of the birds, the sun bursting through the clouds after rainfall, the vigour of nature is apparent everywhere. In early spring, taking a pause from normal activity is highly recommended. In this pause, which can last a few days, you can extend your contemplation into your physical domain and clear out your life from top to bottom. This is also an excellent time to do cleansing contemplations – spring flushes that throw out old patterns, ideas and things that we no longer need or use. As spring moves into its fullness, you will have the wonderful sensation of beginning the year from a place of freshness and clarity. This also ensures that you are less likely to become overwhelmed later in the spring by your own busyness. Spring is also the perfect time to make a regular practice of the solar contemplation mentioned in the final part of this book.

Summer Contemplation

The summer months tend to be when we most need the practice of contemplation. We are often very busy and active which means we pause less. The less we pause, the less opportunities there are for pivotal moments, so summer often leads to a build-up of heat in our system. This can result in emotional overwhelm, exhaustion and other physical problems. In the summer one of the best contemplations is simply to regularly sit or lie and luxuriate in the sun or shade. You can model yourself on the cat, who is a master of this contemplative technique. If you work indoors a lot, then each break takes on vital importance as it attunes your body to its natural rhythm, rather than one imposed by air conditioning or unnatural lighting. In summer, the most natural contemplations take place when we are in motion. In this sense, a walk, run or swim can provide us with a welcome and healthy pause. You might like to try the active contemplations from the final part of this book.

Autumn Contemplation

Autumn is the contemplative's delight. It is the time of year most suited to the Art of Contemplation. In autumn, the earth's energies are naturally turning inwards, and so it is with our physical body. We must learn to gently let go of the fruits and memories of summer and embrace this inner turning. This is the time of year when conditions for contemplation are optimal. As the light recedes, moods change and our biorhythm slows. Now you can lengthen your pauses and allow your mind and heart to dive deeper and more frequently into the inner realms. For some people, autumn can be a time of sadness and sometimes depression. The Art of Contemplation can greatly help with these feelings and states because it actively and creatively harnesses our inward-looking tendencies. If you are affected by such states, you might like to practise the solar contemplation in the epilogue.

Winter Contemplation

Winter is the great feast-time of the contemplative life. The deeper and more refined your practise of contemplation becomes, the more you will appreciate and love this season. The body needs more sleep, rest and quiet in winter than any other time of year. Unfortunately, our modern lifestyle tends to make this one of the most stressful and busy times of the year. As a contemplative person, you may wish to tackle this challenge of culture versus chemistry head-on. If you do find yourself under increased pressure, you will need to increase the frequency of your pauses in order to retain a healthy inner state. Short regular pauses to take some deep breaths can literally reshape a whole day. As contemplation becomes more important to you, you may want to re-arrange your life to ensure your body gets the quiet inner space it needs during winter.

Equatorial and Other Rhythms

In many places on earth, the seasons are not as obvious as they are depicted above. Wherever you live on our blue-green globe, there are always subtle signatures and seasons of one kind or another. Around the equator and the poles for example, very different rhythms are found. In some climes, the rainy season offers an enforced pause that either comes in a single extended period or intermittently throughout a single day, as in the equatorial rainforest. Towards the poles or in the deserts, day and night play all manner of circadian tunes across the keyboard of our chemistry. At every place on the earth there is a natural rhythm of activity and pause, shaped by the atmospheric cycles and local geography. Your job is to heed this rhythm as it plays through the chemistry of your body and attune and adjust your practice of contemplation to these many subtle nuances.

Rhythm, Contemplation and the Body Clock

The Art of Contemplation is a profound practice whose roots will travel deep into our physical chemistry. In the beginning you may not realise this, as you begin to apply the techniques at a more surface level. You may also have noticed that the order of this book moves from mental to emotional to physical contemplation. This is because contemplation first begins in the mind. It then affects our emotional life and our relationships, where we may experience increasing clarity and calm. Finally, and after some time, your contemplation will also bring changes to your physical body.

Physical changes can come in many ways. You may find that your diet naturally changes to a healthier one which will impact your physical body. You will begin to make decisions rooted in self love, instead of decisions that are self destructive. The release of old emotional patterns through the technique of pivoting will also bring about a greater sense of freedom and vitality. Your entire view of yourself can change as your contemplation brings you greater self assurance and a deeper sense of self love.

All the above changes will have a gradual and subtle impact on the way your physical body operates. The prolonged effects of regular and rhythmic pausing will also bring you into a wonderful harmonic pulse with the heartbeat of life. Where others will sometimes rush past you in a flurry of activity and stress, you will feel more measured, more majestic and more independent than ever before. Another key area that changes as we become more centred in this way is our sleep. Each person has their own unique sleep patterns.

Many people in our modern lifestyle suffer from lack of sleep or disturbed sleep patterns. Contemplation can resolve such difficulties through attuning us to our own natural body clock. The physical body, being mostly liquid, has a natural tidal rhythm. Most people are unaware of it. Each time you pause, you give yourself an opportunity to settle into that deep inner pulse. The intracellular fluid that washes in and out of the cells of our body is endlessly pulsing and flowing. If you were able to listen inwardly to the sound of this process it might sound similar to the waves purling gently on a beach.

Contemplation aims to tune our whole body, emotions and mind to these softly soothing rhythms. Our sense of inner and outer timing changes. We find ourselves more often at the right place at the right time. It is fascinating to observe how our body clock changes as we refine our contemplative practise. Sometimes you may find yourself waking spontaneously in the night, enveloped by a beautiful state of peacefulness which you can deepen through conscious contemplation until you naturally fall back to sleep. Often when you awake the next day, the same feeling of serenity will follow you into your day. Many are the mysteries that come through the Art of Contemplation.

The Third Technique – *Merging*

In writing this book, an attempt has been made to describe and break down a process that is inherently mysterious and essentially intuitive. Contemplation is above all an art. As an art, it defies easy explanation. There are tangible stages and touchstones along the way, such as the technique of pausing. Anyone can create pauses in their day, but how will *you* take advantage of those pauses? To bring about the experience of pivoting, you will need to go much further than simply pausing. Pivoting is both a shift in awareness and a subtle act of will. You must have a profound wish to experience *more* of life. As pivoting flows from pausing, merging flows from pivoting. Pivoting is the field of transformation. Merging is the conscious application of that transformation into the many corners of our lives.

Merging involves moving deeper than ever into life, into the world, *towards* others. It is a state of flowering and an embracing of all facets of life. It is the threshold of our mastery. Merging is the heart of contemplation. Merging is an unflinching attitude we develop towards everything and everyone around us. No matter what happens, no matter what destiny brings us, we consciously move towards it, in a spirit of trust. *We move to merge with it.*

You cannot merge with something or someone unless you have already developed a vast open space within you. If you try and merge with a person without this inner space you will become entangled with them. This is a common story in human relationships. We become confused with the stories of others and they become confused with ours. This is also the narrative of many of our daily dramas. We fall into some form of experience or endeavour or crisis, then we unwittingly become entwined into its tapestry. Such experiences trap us and take energy away from us. This is not a healthy form of merging. This is codependent merging.

True merging happens as a conscious act of love. It is the result of many pauses and pivots. Merging is not a single event such as pivoting is – it is a new worldview that grows in us as our contemplation becomes deeper and more stabilised. Merging is a maturing of our soul - entering into everything we think, say and do. It is as though we have allowed our roots to spread into all the crevices of the world. There is nothing we try to escape from and no one whom we resent, envy or avoid. Because this kind of merging comes from spaciousness, nothing can stick to it. Thus, we do not lose our individual identity in true merging. In a wonderful paradox, our individuality becomes both more splendid and more humble. Life flows around us and polishes us as the green river polishes the golden stones. In this sense, merging is not really a technique. Rather it is the transcendence of technique.

How to Merge

Of course, we would like to know how to bring about the experience of merging. However, merging is a fruit of your contemplation. The seed of this fruit is the technique of pausing and the flower is the technique of pivoting. The fruit comes about of its own accord, falling from the tree only when we are ready. There are however three principles that you can practise that will greatly facilitate the experience of merging.

1. Generosity

Life constantly offers us the opportunity to be generous. We can be generous with our resources, with our time and above all, we can be generous with our spirit. To embrace the spirit of generosity in all that you do is to place yourself in service to the whole. To be generous is to become a conduit for all the rich currents of life. Like a great oak tree, you will draw all manner of creatures into your gentle embrace.

Generosity can be very subtle. The greatest form of generosity is that which is unseen. For example, a person may treat you with great injustice, they may wrong you, but instead of rushing to defend your own honour and engaging in a conflict with them, you might choose instead to bow to the experience and contemplate its deeper lesson, perhaps inviting you to let go of something. People usually expect a defence when they have launched an attack, but sometimes you can turn such situations around inside yourself, and your response can be courteous and generous, rather than reactive and proud.

For some, over-generosity can also be an escape from self-love. We can become trapped in patterns of over-commitment in which we allow ourselves to be taken advantage of by others. In this sense, the foundation of generosity is firm personal boundaries. Like a river with strong banks, we also need healthy boundaries to direct the current of our generosity in a way that serves both others and ourselves. Everything in life, especially our many small daily events and activities, can be openings for generosity. At the end of each day, do an inventory of your generosity, beginning with how generous you have been to yourself. See the ways in which you have been generous and the ways in which you could still have been more so. Generosity brings us closer to others, allowing us to begin to experience the joy and delight of merging.

2. Friendship

The great love poets of the Sufi tradition sing endlessly in their mystical rhapsodies of the wonder of merging. They refer to this condition as *the friend*. To these mystics, everything is seen as a friend. Every act or situation or object or person is embraced as an opportunity to experience the inherent unity of all beings. Seeing everything as your friend has the immediate effect of bringing the world closer to you. You enter into greater intimacy with people and things. Even if the other does not return your offer of friendship, it matters not. Friendship is an unconditional extension of your generous spirit.

When you next find yourself in a challenging life situation, see it as life offering you deeper friendship. As in the Japanese martial art of Aikido, when the challenge comes, move towards it instead of flinching away. Lean into it and offer it your friendly hand so that you can redirect its energy, rather than becoming a victim of its energy. Every time we pause and take something in at a deeper level, we open our hand to life in friendship and a part of us merges with another part of the world.

Finally, in the modern information age, we tend to have many connections but few true friends. Therefore, cultivate your true friendships with generosity. Give as much time as you can to those relationships in which you are able to experience the feeling of merging. Practise the profound art of *haragei* - the dialogue between friends that unfolds as much through silence as words. A true friend is a precious find. Spending time with a friend is like finding a beautiful old seat in a secret glade deep in the forest. What could be more important than taking the time to rest and enjoy such a special place?

3. Gentleness

We have already seen the importance of the role of gentleness when we explored the technique of pivoting. Here again, in merging, gentleness is paramount. In the ancient traditions of India there is a virtue known as *ahimsa*. Although often equated with compassion, *ahimsa* also conveys the notion of harmlessness and non-violence in all of life's activities. To embody this concept in your life is to attain a very high state of self-discipline. *Ahimsa* means we learn to be gentle not just externally but also towards ourselves. Though it may be labeled soft and weak, gentleness is one of the most powerful forces in the universe. True gentleness means that we learn to temper our words, thoughts and actions.

The technique of merging rests upon the rock of gentleness. When we are gentle towards others, it does not mean that we allow them to walk all over us. It simply means that when we decide to take a stand in anything, we do so with respect towards others. By adding a soft touch to our daily doings, we create curves where there are hard edges and we trigger smiles instead of frowns. Gentleness simply makes life easier.

The most challenging practice of gentleness is to apply it to oneself. Merging requires that we let go of our self-judgements and quit being so hard on ourselves. We can hold ourselves to the highest standards, yet we can still forgive ourselves for our fallibility. Gentleness is a quality natural to all forms of parenting. Sometimes when we are faced with violence or injustice, it helps to remember the wounded child that is always behind it. To experience merging we must become the compassionate parent, employing a balance of firmness and gentleness, of freedom tempered with natural boundaries.

The Paradoxical Strength of Merging

When you begin to contemplate and employ the three simple principles above, everything will begin to change in your life. If for example you begin using them in your business dealings, your entire strategy may have to change as you consider the implications of your activities on others and on the environment as a whole. There is no tougher discipline than gentleness. There is no harder task-master than generosity. There is nothing more clarifying than friendship. In the ancient Taoist teachings from China, the sages often spoke of the paradox of the softness of water. The very quality that makes water weak - its yielding - is the power that allows it to defeat all else, from the hardest rock to the most raging fire.

Merging conveys this same paradox. As we learn to merge, so we learn to trust everything that life delivers us. We give ourselves to it, allowing it to open us, even to shatter us if necessary. Sometimes our dreams are the wrong dreams. They may contain a grain of truth at their source, but sometimes our mind or ego also imposes its own agenda on our actions. It can be a shock to realise that sometimes we have been trying to force something to happen for years, only to realise that there is a much easier and more fulfilling path waiting for us somewhere else.

It takes great inner strength to be open, honest and vulnerable. We need not parade our vulnerability around, but neither do we need to hide it. When we can show our humanity, we immediately begin to engender trust from others. Merging brings people closer. It purposefully softens the boundaries between the illusion of the inner and the outer and between the self and others.

The Third Confirmation – *Epiphany*

Each of the three confirmations are signs that our practise of contemplation is unravelling smoothly. Insight begins in the mind, breakthrough tends to be more emotional, and finally epiphany is a powerful physical phenomenon that shakes our whole being. Epiphany is the most powerful of the three confirmations, and early on in one's practise it is relatively rare. Epiphany occurs at the crescendo of merging, when the walls around our heart spontaneously melt and life rushes into us. At such a time we may feel a kind of ecstasy surging through the cells of our body. Most of us have at some point experienced such an epiphany. One of the aims of contemplation is to increase the frequency of such experiences in our life.

Despite how it may sound, epiphany is not a high. It is rather a moment of profound merging as our soul remembers the higher purpose of existence. The English romantic poet

William Wordsworth called such moments of awe *spots of time* and he goes on to say how we can draw great strength from them. Epiphanies are in fact very natural events that do not take us up and away into flights of fancy, but draw us down and deeper into our body than ever before. Epiphanies arise outside of time, when our mind and heart are at rest and we have cultivated a deep love of pausing. They begin to occur at a more advanced stage of contemplation when pausing is no longer something we consciously *do* – it has become a part of us, like the moment of stillness between breaths.

Epiphany both fills us up and empties us out. It is a path of embodiment in which we finally refine our contemplation into an art. Art signifies that we have transcended all technique. Now we don't *do* the contemplation – it *does* us. Such is the mystery that lies at the end of the rainbow of our simple daily practice of pausing.

Applying Merging – *Perspective, Humour and Lightness*

The application of merging to our daily life has the delightful effect of lightening any load we are carrying through life. Merging gives us a sense of true perspective, casting a new light on all our so-called troubles. A vital ingredient of the contemplative life is a sense of humour. Humour begins with oneself, as we learn to laugh at our self and our over seriousness. When you touch the essential in life, all else falls into perspective, and contemplation brings you naturally to the essence of things. Things that used to seem important to you begin to fade. The need to be right, or the urge always to express one's opinion and be heard seems less important through the prism of contemplation. What does become important is to connect with people, to listen to their hearts and to enjoy their company as much as possible in the brief time we have on this earth.

Before and during the second world war, as the terrified victims of the Stalinist regime found themselves jammed into freight trains, hurtling towards the gulags, one character stood out above all others – the comedian. Among so many miserable people there would occasionally rise one who managed to crack jokes in spite of the terrible situation. Many jokes were at the expense of their captors, but they would generate unexpected chuckles and smiles. Above all they reminded all present that even in the darkest night there can be glints of light and communal warmth.

The Art of Contemplation teaches us to covet this precious but vital gift of lightness. Sometimes when the clouds gather and press in on us, or when our brows curl into furrows, the one thing we need above all is this sense of greater perspective. Contemplation reminds us that life has a way of resolving itself, in time often revealing a hidden higher purpose behind the events of our lives.

The Reward of Merging – *The Body of Being*

In the Christian mystical tradition there is a wonderful term called *kenosis*, which means literally to empty oneself out. Although similar to catharsis, kenosis offers us a far softer approach. While catharsis is associated with a dramatic and sometimes explosive releasing of emotional tension or anguish, kenosis is a gentler and subtler way of internal transformation.

The essence of kenosis is patience. You contemplate and you wait. You watch the ripples moving out and out – these are your thoughts, ideas, feelings, questions and confusions. One day you simply hit upon a place of wonderful emptiness. All those issues have simply resolved inside you on their own. Contemplation is kenotic in this way – it empties you. First thoughts exhaust themselves, then feelings, then even your will to understand leaves you, and you are left simply there, resting in your being.

At the end of his epic poetic quest for truth and peace, the great Austrian poet Rainer Maria Rilke experienced this sense of kenosis, which he caught in the immortal words:

Look, I am living. On what?
Neither childhood nor future grows any smaller . . .
Superabundant being wells up in my heart.

The reward for all the years you put into refining the Art of Contemplation is just this – to return to the purity of your true being – to realise your own wholeness and thus to be utterly at ease in your body and in the world. In all the great mystical traditions, the end of the journey always involves a return back to the world, whether that is carrying water and chopping wood, or living an integrated and peaceful life in modern society. The reward of merging is a life without fear, doubt or anxiety – a life of beauty, simplicity and prosperity.

TECHNIQUES FOR DAILY PRACTICE

Contemplation in Action -
The Road to Self Mastery

You now have in your hands the script of a new kind of life – a life teeming with potential and a clear road to follow towards self mastery. The only thing that remains to be done is for you to follow the script and bring it into your daily life. There are many ways to walk the path of contemplation. Working with this book is an obvious way. The concepts presented may seem simple but they contain hidden depths that will continue to emerge gently as you re-read the text and contemplate it over time.

The final section of this book lays out some additional ways and means of applying contemplation in your life. There are many specific techniques that you are invited to adapt, embellish or use as inspiration to find your own approach to contemplation – one that suits your particular lifestyle. You are also invited to be playful and imaginative in how you blend such techniques into your life. This is after all the purpose of this book – to bring the Art of Contemplation off the page, out of our minds and into action in the world.

Anything can be used as a means to enter the field of contemplation, and it can deepen or increase your focus in any endeavour or activity. Above all, the techniques below are designed to bring your life into a whole new dimension. They are portals into the deep mystery that lies just beneath the surface of our lives. As you experiment with the techniques and innovate your own, it's important to remember the core purpose of all contemplative paths, captured so beautifully in a line worth contemplating by Moinuddin Chisti, a revered early Islamic Saint:

> *To develop river-like generosity, Sun-like*
> *affection and Earth-like hospitality.*

Wu Wei – *Effortless Action*

As you can see, there are many rewards that spring from a dedicated practise of contemplation. The final reward concerns how we act in the world. Contemplation will create ripples in your external life. Although you will become more patient, you will also become more decisive. You will learn when and how to act appropriately according to your circumstances. In China there is an ancient Taoist wisdom known as *wu wei,* which refers to the notion of effortless action. Effortless action is a fusion of measured reason and intuitive insight.

Wu wei is the ultimate reward of contemplation, and far from being some arcane mystical concept, it is highly practical in nature.

Every day we are faced with thousands of decisions – physical decisions such as what to eat, emotional decisions such as how to handle your own or another's anger and mental decisions such as how to successfully complete a task at work. Imagine now that all these decisions are made for you by an inner master, a wise compassionate being with an uncanny skill at reading every situation that arises and responding accordingly. This is *wu wei.*

Contemplation also teaches us how to say an open-hearted 'no'. Sometimes our intuition leads us in a direction that may disappoint the expectations or wishes of others. At such times we need to be so certain of our decision that we do not fall prey to guilt. We can use courtesy and gratitude but our decision is clear and in tune with a greater harmony. We needn't apologise for ourselves or try and invent reasons to try and make the other feel better. It is best to simply be open hearted and honest. We cannot always see the results of such decisions until later, but we can feel their correctness inside us at the time. In the long run, such decisions will be better for everyone concerned.

Contemplation teaches us how to tread the fine balance between action and inaction, guiding us through the power of our pausing. All important decisions require pauses for consideration. On occasion however, an action also needs to be made immediately, without the luxury of a physical pause for consideration. To be harmonious, such actions must spring from a worldview rooted in kindness and altruism that we have nurtured over many years of contemplation and insight. This is the ultimate harvest of your contemplation – to act effortlessly, without anxiety, guilt or doubt – to let life choose through you, while you remain but a witness to the wheeling panoply of wonders that is your life.

Contemplation in Movement

There is a long tradition that connects all forms of movement with contemplation. Movement done from a contemplative state becomes ritualistic, turning the movement into a kind of sacred theatre. Anything you do – whether hobby or vocation – can be transformed into a contemplative dance. As we enter the contemplative state, our breath deepens and our mind begins to empty out. We learn to find subtler and subtler pauses – the pauses between breaths and the natural spaces and rests that arise within any activity. Above all, we can begin to see the activity itself as a pause and our minds can rest while our bodies remain in motion.

Contemplation taps into the spring of creativity that lies in each of us. When you are performing any moving task, try and do it as though it is the very last task you will perform before you die. When you do this, the task will become unique. Even though you may perform it a thousand times, it will never be the same task, but will always surprise and delight you in some way.

To perform your daily activities in the spirit of contemplation is more than simply being mindful. It is elevating that task to the status of an art. The secret of contemplation in movement lies in the intelligence of your hands. Instead of your mind, allow your hands to lead you through your day. Bring your full awareness into your hands, and watch the hands as you might watch two butterflies dancing. The more attention you give to your hands, the more graceful your movements will become. Imagine that you have no body but for two hands moving through your day.

Walking Contemplation

Few things in life are as healing to the human spirit as walking. Even though it is something most of us do every day without thinking about it, walking is an opportunity to come into deep rhythmic harmony in a short space of time. As you walk, feel the soft earth beneath your feet. Tune into your movements and allow your body to find a natural and easy rhythm. Rather than rushing from A to B, try and leave more time so that you can saunter and enjoy yourself. Use walking to feel your breath moving in and out and luxuriate in your own movement.

You can also use walking as a means to consciously contemplate a certain subject or challenge. Walks have a beginning and an end, so you can deliberately go for a walk and allow the rhythm of your movement to unlock the rhythm of your thinking and feeling. St Augustine once spoke the famous words *Solvitur Ambulando* – by walking it is solved. Sometimes by just going for a walk we return with an answer to something we have been mulling over. You can also apply this to a walk with a friend. If you feel the need for a deeper intimacy or connection with a certain person, invite them for a walk and let the contemplative space emerge between you. Two bodies and souls moving together create a space for pausing, pivoting or merging.

Running Contemplation

Running is a form of exercise that can be practised into quite advanced age, so long as you have a basic level of health and mobility. It is particularly suited to contemplation, although in a very different way from walking. Running involves considerable exertion, which pumps the blood through the heart and releases endorphins into the body. Along with the rhythm of our breath, these chemical changes create very good conditions for pivoting – seeing and feeling an old pattern in a new way. Running often involves pushing through various levels of discomfort, particularly if you are running in a hilly or rugged landscape. Sometimes the greatest effort is simply deciding to go for a run when you don't particularly feel like it. Offering us a physical mirror of our life, this willingness to push through our inertia can do wonders for our spirit, not to mention our physical and emotional health.

Another important aspect of running is connection to the landscape and the culture in which you live. Even in the city, you are urged not to wear headphones, which only isolates you from your environment. When running, we get to breathe in our environment with all its sounds and smells. It is perhaps the purest form of dynamic exercise we can do, although there are plenty of other types such as swimming and cycling, which afford similar contemplative opportunities. There is a great difference between one who runs solely for health and one who runs as a contemplation. The contemplative runner does not need to compete in any way. The contemplative runner runs because he or she loves to enter the field of transformation and freedom. Another benefit of this style of running is that it rarely leads to injury because it is rooted in listening to the rhythm of one's life, rather than imposing one's will over the body.

Contemplation in Sport

The overlap between sport and the Art of Contemplation lies in the twin areas of rhythm and focus. Every sport relies on our being aligned with the inner rhythm that comes from our core. Every sportsperson will at some point have had the experience of being in a zone of focus in which their movement arises effortlessly and perfectly. This is most likely the unconscious reason why we are drawn to sport – to experience this uplifting sense of a deeper harmony and perfection through movement and coordination. The very purpose of contemplation is to align us with this paradoxical inner state of focus and surrender. Whatever sport you are involved in, whether it involves individual participation or you are part of a team, contemplation will greatly increase your sense of timing, fluidity and focus.

Whenever you are engaged in your sport, bring attention as often as possible to the contemplative state. The more you cultivate contemplative stillness outside your sport, the more you will be able to tap into it when you are in the midst of movement. The results may well be astounding to you as you find yourself more and more in that magical zone of focus where everything comes together in perfect synchronicity.

Sitting Contemplation

Too lazy to be ambitious,
I let the world take care of itself.
Ten days' worth of rice in my bag;
A bundle of twigs by the fireplace.
Why chatter about delusion and enlightenment?
Listening to the night rain on my roof,
I sit comfortably, with both legs stretched out.

Ryokan

The above poem by the Zen Master Ryokan perfectly catches the spirit of sitting contemplation. Less formal than meditation with its focus on posture and technique, contemplation begins from right where we are in our life. When we do sitting contemplation, we should sit comfortably. Neither do we necessarily need a formal idea of what we are going to contemplate. If we have an idea, that is fine, and if we don't that is also fine. Sitting contemplation is about creating a space for our own inner guidance to emerge. Over time this practise can take many forms, but it should have no specific goal. As your contemplative practise naturally deepens, sitting contemplation will become more attractive to you, since it gives you the chance to experience many pleasurable and serene inner states of being. Many of the contemplations given in this book are well suited to sitting.

A Clean Space

One of the hallmarks of contemplation is simplicity. As you learn to contemplate, you will learn to gradually simplify your life. The less cluttered your external life is, the less cluttered your mind will feel. This contemplation is therefore about decluttering your life. Choose a space or room that you inhabit and discipline yourself to clean it, both literally and energetically. Pick up the various objects and ask yourself whether they are essential to your life. Imagine you are introducing someone to the Art of Contemplation for the first time and the first thing you show them is this room. Clean, dust and sweep everything until it shines with the spirit of simplicity. Recreate this room as a mirror of the internal space you wish to cultivate. Over time, you can perform this contemplation in many spaces and in many ways. It can also be a gift you offer to others, to help them clean out their spaces. This contemplation is both process and reward, and the reward is also found in the process. This contemplation is also a discipline you may need to maintain, especially if you share your space with others, particularly children. Clearing and cleaning a space can be transformed from a chore into a blessing when you see it as an integral part of your daily contemplation.

Serving Tea

In China, Taiwan and Japan there is an ancient tradition in which the serving of tea has become a symbol for the depth and beauty of the contemplative state. In some respects, the ceremony itself is a metaphor for how we may live our lives. Indeed, any activity in which you are serving others can be imbued with the same depth as the art of serving tea.

Today tea remains the most widely drunk liquid in the world after water. The beauty of tea is its simplicity, which makes it the true drink of the contemplative. Traditionally, tea is brewed in a small pot and drunk in small cups or bowls, which allows it to be brewed over and again in a single sitting. Each time the hot water is added, the leaves release another level of flavour and nuance. Those drinking the tea are therefore taken on a contemplative journey together that leads to subtler and more refined spaces. This whole process can be done formally in silence, or informally just enjoying each other's company. Wherever you live in the world this is a contemplative ritual you can learn and share at any time with anyone.

Urban Contemplation

It may be tempting to believe that it's harder to be contemplative in a noisy and busy environment like a town or city. This urban contemplation is somewhat unusual and perhaps even a little mischievous, but it can totally change your experience of being in busy places. It involves your putting aside a specific time to be in an urban or busy environment solely for the sake of contemplation. Deliberately go to a place where you often feel overwhelmed or stressed – this could be a bustling market, a supermarket, a shopping mall, a train station or even an airport. Be the only person who is there for no reason other than to deepen the contemplative state. Fill up a shopping trolley and then empty it again, stand in a queue for no reason or just sit and watch people going about their business. The point of this contemplation is to be in such spaces and be utterly calm, just breathing deeply and enjoying your own presence, like an actor on life's stage. Once you have done this and found peace within yourself, the next time you are in that place or a similar place, you will be able to go straight to the reference point you have created and tap into that same sense of peace and detachment.

Food Contemplation

Everything you eat or drink is harmonic in nature. Food alters our chemistry from the moment it enters our bloodstream. The food we choose to eat and the way we eat it therefore has a major effect on our contemplation. A good habit to develop around food is always to pause before selecting it and before eating it. Sometimes our hunger drives us to eat something which we later regret. When you look at food, contemplate the state it will leave you in once you have digested it. Eating the right food at the right time is like listening to the music that we love, and preparing food yourself is like playing a musical instrument.

The preparation of food is an ancient form of alchemy. Food prepared while in a contemplative frame of mind will be soothing both to the body and the soul. Another important thing around food is to be wary of eating when we are not hungry. Nowadays, when all manner of food is so readily available, our senses are bombarded by all the sights and smells of food. Many of us may be eating too much food too often. The Art of Contemplation helps to make you immune to the lure of excess while at the same time celebrating the wonder of taste and the feast of the senses.

Musical Contemplation

Like food, music is a kind of nourishment that feeds the soul. Contemplation can be enhanced by playing or listening to the right music at the right time. Sometimes the right piece of music can supply the perfect entry to the contemplative state. As with cooking, selecting the right music to harmonise with a specific mood and environment is a subtle art we can learn to master. Part of this mastery is also to know when to enjoy silence. Silence is the spring from which all contemplation flows, and the more you practise it, the more the music of silence will grow inside you.

Lingering

One of the insights you may have learned through reading this book is that the Art of Contemplation is not a fast art. Its gift is that it reminds us to slow down and appreciate every passing moment to the fullness of our potential. Lingering is an attitude of milking pleasant or uplifting experiences. Less a technique and more a habit to develop, the art of lingering can be applied to many situations. With lingering, we extend our pause just a little longer than our mind sometimes tells us. This is like being the last person to leave the cinema after a really good film.

Lingering is about attuning to the invitations that life offers us on a daily basis. Perhaps a dog approaches you and licks your feet. You pause and give him your attention for a few moments. Perhaps the sun comes out from behind a cloud while you are busy shopping. Instead of ignoring it, linger a little and feel its light dusting your body. Lingering does not need to make you late for commitments. A linger can be a few seconds long or it can be a few hours among friends. The important lesson of lingering is to learn to receive life at ever deepening levels. Finally, lingering also requires that you tune into the feelings of others - if you take your lingering too far, you may also overstay your welcome!

Laughter Contemplation

Although there are exercises that help prompt and provoke laughter, the experience of joy that accompanies a deep, spontaneous belly laugh cannot be set up or practiced. The very beauty of laughter lies in its unexpectedness. We can however contemplate the environment and occasions that made us laugh in the past. When you know what and who tends to make you laugh, you can create those conditions again. If for example you always laugh with a particular person, then consider spending more time with that person. In which environments do you tend to laugh the most? Make sure that you recreate those environments. This may sound like an obvious thing to do, but many of us forget to gift ourselves these simple pleasures. Part of our commitment on the path of contemplation is to make sure that our lives are as rich as possible.

The Avatar

This contemplation is an age-old tradition that engages the power of your imagination. An avatar is a great master or enlightened being, like Christ or Buddha. In this contemplation you imagine yourself in the presence of any great being of your choice. You contemplate their inner state and the light, love or wisdom that streams from them. You can focus on any particular quality you would like. You imagine yourself in their presence, walking with them, talking with them, imbibing their presence constantly. The deepest level of this contemplation is when you imagine that you actually are that being – that their perfected state of consciousness has been transferred into you. This is a very powerful and rewarding contemplation that is accessible and easy for anyone to do. At a certain point, the impression from your imagination triggers a spontaneous process of self illumination and you begin to experience a higher and more loving state of consciousness. When done over time, this contemplation takes on a life of its own and will afford you remarkable results.

Hui Gan

In our modern age we tend to be very future-focused. *Hui gan* is a beautiful contemplation that involves deliberately reflecting on the sweetness of a past event. You might bring back a memory of a time when you felt truly happy or at peace or deeply in love. If you are fortunate enough to have experienced a higher state of consciousness, then you may well choose this for your *hui gan*. Then all you do is you savour the memory, as though you are watering a precious plant. You let the memory flood through you and you draw upon its nourishment. Sometimes there is also a tinge of sadness that comes with such memories, which you can also embrace fully. *Hui gan* contemplation can be done over a period of time and can open you up to the sweet impermanence of life. The other dimension in this contemplation is that it brings the past into the present, encouraging us to embrace a state of timelessness. *Hui gan* can also be done as a dialogue with a friend or friends as you conjure up a time of joy and laughter together.

Contemplation and Illness

Illness is a natural part of life. There are many forms of illness, but all forms offer an opening into the contemplative state. Illness drives us deeper into the consciousness of our body, through the discomfort and pain that we are forced to confront. Illness tends to remind us of our mortality, so our contemplation might naturally swing in the direction of the subject of death. We do not generally know how we will die, but there is a chance that it may involve some physical pain and it will definitely involve the dissolution of our attachment to the body. Illness is therefore to be trusted at a very deep level. Whether we surrender to our illness or we fight it, it invites us to contemplate our own death and to open our heart to embrace the great mystery of life and death. Try to view illness as an opportunity to let go of some of the deep fears held in your body and trust that it will deliver you its own unique teaching. This is also the case when you are tending another who is ill. Taking care of another who is ill comes with all its own challenges and teachings. It is a great opportunity to demonstrate the endless patience and kindness of the contemplative state. Above all it is also a reminder to be kind and compassionate towards yourself.

Forgiveness Contemplation

In life, there are many emotional ups and downs. Sometimes we do things that hurt others, either consciously or unconsciously, and sometimes we are wronged or dishonoured in some way by others. You can only enter the full beauty of the contemplative state when you no longer harbour any resentments or hidden shame. Every pang of guilt or repressed blame muddies our still, inner lake. If you harbour such unresolved feelings from the past, part of your contemplative journey will be to let them go. This is usually a gentle process that may take considerable time. Depending on the depth of your wounds, you may also wish to consider professional help in this regard.

Forgiveness, whether of yourself or another, is about releasing yourself from a series of energetic hooks that link you to a certain person or past event. One contemplative approach is to close your eyes and locate these hooks inside yourself. Then using your breath, breathe into each one and let it go. If there was another person involved, you can also try and see them in a new light. Imagine them as a young child, and see the terrible sense of isolation they may have felt at some point. Even the most aggressive or heartless personality traits are rooted in certain tragic events in a child's life. The more you can come to understand others using the power of your imagination, the more compassion you will be able to feel for them. In time, this will help you to let them go.

As you refine the Art of Contemplation you will realise that there are no mistakes in life. Every event is a whetstone for you to further polish the blade of your worldly wisdom. We are here to learn from our mistakes and to find the inner forgiveness to move on and become a better person.

Nature Contemplation

Living close to nature ensures that you have the very best conditions for contemplative practise. Even if you live in an urban environment you can always find regular ways to keep connecting to nature. Nature connects us to the source of being, to the raw and pristine wilderness of the contemplative state. Anything in the natural world can be an invitation to contemplation. Sitting by a lake with no agenda, you will soon feel a natural calm coming over you. Gazing into a flowing river can smooth out all your thoughts and clarify your feelings. Swimming in or spending time by the ocean can expand your horizons and bring much needed perspective to your life. The higher we go in the mountains, the more rarified our thoughts become and the deeper we go into forests, the calmer and more grounded we feel. For every difficulty in life, there is a natural antidote, and it's usually right beneath our feet.

Other ways of accessing the field of contemplation through the natural world are gardening, handling natural materials or being with animals. Just spending time in the company of a blissful, purring cat, or playing with a delirious dog can be a physical, kinaesthetic reminder of the relaxed nature of the contemplative state.

Sometimes nature invites us into other levels of contemplation, as when she is very far from being calm but instead throws up storms and other extreme forms of weather. At such times you can either retreat indoors and take your contemplation deeper inwards, or you can defy logic and go out into the elements to experience them in their raw and wild state. Sometimes the latter approach can lead to a heightened state of exhilaration that falls into a blessed peace when you return indoors. Allow the elements to play upon your being in this way, rising and falling on the waves of change, and your contemplation will become like a musical symphony that adapts and delights in the weather and its many changing faces.

Tree Contemplation

We human beings live surrounded by trees. Although there are areas devoid of trees, it is often a great challenge to live for long in such places, since trees are bringers of life. Many of us develop a natural affinity for a particular tree, and there are few things more iconic of contemplation than a figure sitting under a tree. Wherever you live or travel in the world, let the trees around you be your contemplative allies. Every tree is a reminder for you to pause and breathe. Even if you cannot physically pause as you go past a tree, let it create a pause in your thinking. If you do have time, go and stand or sit beneath a living tree and you will find its soft umbrella a perfect invitation to contemplation. The power of the tree as a contemplative symbol is its perfect equilibrium. Every tree has roots that plunge deep into the earth balanced by branches that stretch like fingers towards the heavens. The tree's every branch, twig and root is part of an evolutionary impulse to maintain a state of dynamic equilibrium. Likewise, our contemplation is both grounding and uplifting.

Solar Contemplation

One of the most powerful forms to contemplate is the Sun. The Sun is a profound symbol of the perfected human being. The Sun is a pure expression of limitless giving, based on radiant health and balanced wholeness. The Sun also represents the eternal nature of consciousness that never sleeps or dies. The best times to contemplate the Sun are at dawn and dusk, when its rays are softest. However, you can contemplate the Sun at any time of day or even at night. As you move throughout your day, luxuriate in the Sun's rays, pause to feel its warmth on your face and breathe its light into your bones. The more often you do this exercise, the more radiant and positive you will feel. Imagine that every cell of your body is a tiny Sun and collectively they all form one giant Sun. Even when the Sun is hidden, during a grey day or at night, bring it back into your awareness and feel it burning within you, healing, softening and expanding.

If you are prone to melancholy or depression, or are moving through a difficult period in your life, there is no better contemplation than this. Over time as you contemplate the Sun, you will feel an inner light growing within you and it will begin to melt those dark feelings that we all carry. There is an entire inner yoga of the Sun, and when you commit to doing this contemplation, these teachings will naturally be revealed to you.

Nightfall

Certain contemplations are now necessary that once were simply part of ordinary life. Indeed, for those in less affluent and technologically developed cultures, these remain as natural patterns that most would not give a second thought to. One such contemplation concerns the passing of day into night and the way in which we go to sleep. If you have never simply sat and watched day turning into night, this in itself is a magical and powerful practise that is highly recommended. In the modern world, this is often a busy time, so you may need to specifically set aside that time.

The sliding of day into night is a mirror of the wonder of contemplation, as our thoughts and feelings gradually empty out into the purity of silence. Particularly if you can do this contemplation outdoors in nature, you will note the subtle change in your body as certain chemical pathways in your brain shut down in tune with the fading of the light. There is also a mood changeover in nature as the sounds and smells become more acute and the nocturnal creatures begin to flutter and rustle all around you.

For many of us, the beauty of the evening light is often lost to electrical lighting and our use of screens. The magic of candlelight, firelight, moonlight and starlight play upon our being, drawing out our more mystical nature and expanding our subtler extrasensory capacities. You can mark this time of day before bed as the best time for contemplation, and you can return to simpler times by honouring the time of nightfall.

Finally, you can imprint the power of contemplation deeply in your consciousness by making it the last thing you do before falling asleep. Sit there in the darkness for a few minutes and let the day and its concerns drop away from you. Open yourself to the great mystery of the unknown, and enter the quietness of night with a restful spirit. This will also ensure that when you wake the next morning, you will instantly remember the Art of Contemplation.

Eden

This contemplation is an imaginary journey that has a powerful truth embedded in it. When you allow your heart to lead you into it, you may discover yourself propelled into a timeless state of consciousness that suffuses your whole being.

Once, long ago, we humans inhabited a simpler world in which we were more merged with nature. Our brains functioned differently, our priorities were different and although the world may have been harsh at times, it was sparsely populated and more silent. Time moved differently, we shared a more tribal consciousness that afforded warmth, comfort and support as we moved and worked together to feed and care for ourselves and each other. In this contemplation, we bring alive this ancestral memory held in our DNA of a simpler age. You can use your imagination in any way to rekindle the songs, smells and sights of the early epoch of humanity. You can pay particular attention to the silence and stillness that sat upon the earth during that early time. This is one half of this contemplation.

The second aspect of this contemplation is to project your mind forwards in time, to a time of completion. Try to tune into the cellular certainty of our future as a time of harmony, peace and absolute fulfilment. We don't have to know how the miracle will occur, but it is stamped into our DNA. We come from Eden and we will return to Eden, just as all our stories and myths testify. Perhaps our technology will finally free us from the perils of war and fear. Perhaps we will break the limiting bonds of time and space and take our rightful place as a universal human. Allow yourself to dream of such a time, where all human awareness has evolved to know its own unity with all beings. Indeed, if you are bold enough, see yourself and humanity as inhabiting an eternal body, individual but interconnected, purified of all wounds and divides, once again whole.

Trace the mythic connection between our beginning and our completion, as we play out the greatest story ever told, from 'once upon a time', to 'and they all lived happily ever after'. Feel the joy and laughter rising within you and let its light fill your cells. You are part of an eternal spirit that can never die. Your life is but a sentence in this great storyline, so you will do your utmost to make yours a gracious narrative, filled with forgiveness, love and higher purpose.

17,000 Breaths

In a single day, you probably take a minimum of 17,000 breaths. You may take as many as 30,000 or more. How many of those breaths are you aware of? Generally speaking, the number of breaths you take are in relation to the state of your relaxedness and awareness. Longer, deeper breaths calm the mind, emotions and body. This contemplation is simply about bringing awareness to your breathing. The more frequently you pause and become aware of your breath, the more peaceful and balanced you will feel. See how often you can remember to pause. Note the relationship between pausing, breathing and your general state over the course of a day. Set yourself the goal of each day taking a few more longer, deeper breaths. Contemplate what a day might feel like if you were aware of every single breath you take.

The Contemplation of The Triple Flame

The Contemplation of the Triple Flame is a simple and very powerful pausing technique that involves pausing for three minutes every three hours. You can program your phone or other device to send you a reminder to pause and enter the field of contemplation at 3, 6, 9 and 12 o'clock each day during daylight hours. The gentle circadian rhythm of this process soon begins to saturate your daily life and after several weeks you may find you are attuning to this contemplation at a deeper, unconscious level. Whatever you may be doing at these times, the Triple Flame invites you to spend these three minutes in a contemplative frame of mind. If you are able to physically pause what you are doing, then you can do so. If, however, you cannot physically pause, then you can at least continue what you are doing with an increased sense of self awareness.

Although simple, the Contemplation of the Triple Flame has many dimensions to it. It actively brings the contemplative state into some of the busiest times of your day, which can be a transformative experience. Another element of this contemplation is to connect you to a growing global movement of people also learning the Art of Contemplation at the same time.

Philanthropy Contemplation

Although this is the last contemplation in this book, it has the capacity to transform your life in perhaps the most powerful way. Many of us live such busy lives that we do not often allow ourselves much time to consider the lives of others. In this contemplation, you are invited to imagine yourself at your own memorial service. Expand your own vision of what your life could be like at its absolute zenith. Listen to the things that people say about you and your life, both publicly and privately. Drift around and look into people's eyes, feel their hearts opening and see the magnificent influence you have had on them.

Imagine your life as an explosion of selfless giving from an overflowing heart. Now track backwards from your funeral to the events that led to this great celebration of one person's capacity for love. See the many courageous decisions you had to take along your life's journey - those pivotal moments when you took the road less travelled. See the countless other beings you have influenced for good without even knowing it. See how one person's life can become a beautiful flowering, no matter how simple or humble it may be.

The second aspect of this contemplation is to consider how you can begin or continue such a life from this moment on. What is the first decision you need to take? Take your time and contemplate deeply and carefully before you take any action. This contemplation may take you weeks or even months.

Philanthropy is about serving others from an overflowing heart. Even if you do not feel such a love now, even small acts of giving can be the trigger for a gentle expansion. As with all contemplation, begin gently and take care of yourself as you go along. This is not about you depleting your own resources. It takes great patience to learn to love and give in a balanced way, but the rewards of such a life are vast beyond our imagining. Dare to step a little outside your comfort zone and watch a smile spreading on another face somewhere in the world.

AFTERWORD

I believe that anyone can learn the Art of Contemplation.

I learned the Art of Contemplation out of necessity, to help cope with the many challenges of being a parent. One day I realised that I had lost all sense of calm. I had allowed myself to become overwhelmed by the sudden increase in my responsibilities. I felt I had lost all my youthful freedom and could see no clear way of finding it again. I felt trapped, isolated and lost.

Then one day while visiting a friend I became entranced by a painting on her wall. It was a simple image of a lone seagull in flight against a sea of blue. That painting stirred something deep inside my soul. I couldn't stop thinking about it. The bird seemed so silent, pure and free in that spotless sky. Every time I thought of the image, I began to feel like that bird. It was as though the painting had cast a magical spell over me. I only had to remember the image in my mind and almost immediately I was flooded by a feeling of deep calm and limitless freedom.

Over the months following this encounter, I returned over and over again to the image of the seagull in my mind. Whenever I thought of it my whole being paused, and for a short time I let go of the outer world and its distractions. I also learned to conjure up the image in my mind during difficult moments or conflicts, which gave amazing results. I experienced the power of pivoting, the ability to turn a difficult situation into a gift. In my relationships this changed everything – instead of contracting when faced with a conflict, I taught myself to stay soft and open-hearted. I continue to learn this lesson today.

In time I forgot all about the seagull. The memory of it only came back to me today, as I sat down to write these words. For me, that image was a doorway into contemplation, and once I knew how to find the door I no longer needed the image itself. Since then I have found countless other pathways into the contemplative state.

It has taken me many years to learn the Art of Contemplation, but it is the greatest and most useful art I have ever learned. I hope this small book may help you find your own doorways into the contemplative state. It is a state that our world needs more than ever to remember.

The Art of Contemplation is to a human being what air is to a bird – it is freedom, it is purpose and it is peace.

Richard Rudd

CONTEMPLATION AND THE GENE KEYS

an invitation from the author

If you have enjoyed this book and feel drawn to its central idea, you might also enjoy my other work 'The Gene Keys'. The Gene Keys is a grand synthesis of perennial wisdom that was compiled over several decades. Although it is mystical in origin, it is also a powerful psychological tool that is proven to have a transformational impact in one's life. The Gene Keys provide one with many pathways for deep contemplation, both through its rich language and its extraordinary depth of content.

www.genekeys.com